The Art of Vanishing

THE

Art of
Vanishing

A NOVEL

Morgan Pager

BALLANTINE BOOKS

NEW YORK

Published in the United States by Ballantine Books, an imprint of Random House, a division of Penguin Random House LLC, 1745 Broadway, New York, NY 10019.

BALLANTINE BOOKS & colophon are registered trademarks of Penguin Random House LLC.

Hardback ISBN 9780593875384
Ebook ISBN 9780593875391

Printed in the United States of America on acid-free paper

randomhousebooks.com

penguinrandomhouse.com

2 4 6 8 9 7 5 3 1

First Edition

Book design by Debbie Glasserman

The authorized representative in the EU for product safety and compliance is Penguin Random House Ireland, Morrison Chambers, 32 Nassau Street, Dublin D02 YH68, Ireland, https://eu-contact.penguin.ie.

For Grancy,
who taught me the magic of museums
and the power of my imagination

It is required
You do awake your faith.

—WILLIAM SHAKESPEARE, *The Winter's Tale*

The Art of Vanishing

1

JEAN

The final visitors of the day were ushered out of the gallery and I reached both arms above my head, stretching away the stiffness of eight hours spent sitting in one position. I put one hand on my chin, pushing it back in an effort to crack my neck. I heard a slight pop and felt that usual rush of relief, repeating the same on the other side. With another day of work in the books, I let myself bask in the sheer sense of achievement, even if I wasn't sure what, if anything, I'd accomplished today.

Nevertheless, I felt lucky to be here; I was sure there were many who would do just about anything for a job in the hallowed halls of an institution such as this one. Sure, we weren't as large or as prestigious as the massive museums of New York, Paris, London, Madrid, et cetera. But the art world was an exclusive one. I knew how hard it could be to get a foot in the door, or to have the means to try in the first place.

Some days I worried I'd become too accustomed to this space and would forget to take in how special it was. I challenged myself to take a real look today. I surveyed the room around me as I continued to stretch. It was unchanging in its day-to-day, mustard-colored fabric coating the walls that lay beneath multitudes of artwork. Every square inch of available hanging area was covered; these panels were heavy with paintings. In any blank space that remained, eccentric items were affixed: door hinges, sketches, coat hooks, rusting kitchen utensils. Wide wooden baseboards connected the overstuffed walls to the floor, which was scuffed from the constant steps of that day's patrons, trying to get a closer look.

I peeled my eyes from a particularly curious hinge hanging on the wall opposite where I sat and looked back out into the gallery. I saw her, standing directly in front of me. I wondered if she could see me too, the real me. She was staring straight at me like she knew what I was thinking. But that was impossible, wasn't it?

I quickly lowered my arms to my sides, but she maintained eye contact. She asked me a question with her eyes, and I was tempted to speak aloud to answer it.

Our mutual reverie was interrupted by the sound of plastic wheels clattering against the wood floor. Linda, a fixture of the museum, pushed a bucket into the room, steering its trundling mass by the handle of a mop. Linda was dressed in her typical uniform: a navy blue jumpsuit with her name embroidered in white script just beneath her left shoulder and a pair of graying athletic sneakers.

"Come on, Claire—it's Claire, right? We'll get started in my rooms today. Once we've got that down, we'll move on to your assignment. I know they call it training, but you better be prepared to work tonight because if we don't get my portion done in half the hours it normally takes me, we'll have no time for yours."

She, Claire presumably, was dressed in a matching navy jumpsuit. It was the wrong size, the fabric bunching around her calves. She had cuffed it as well as she could at her ankles, but her pant legs still skimmed the ground behind the heels of her sneakers. Claire said nothing in response, just nodded and followed Linda out of the room. I craned my neck, rising out of my seat to attempt to watch them for as long as I could, but the canvas held me back and I lost track of where they had gone. I sank back into my chair and heard my older sister, Marguerite, snort as she passed behind me, heading out into the garden. Alone now, I strained my ears to listen to any sounds of their progress. The sun set through the grand windows, and I waited in the darkness.

I was used to it, the waiting. I am the foremost expert in a single page of an unremarkable French novel from 1917. Time and repetition have dissolved the words from a segment of story into an indiscernible pattern of lines and curves. Within a small margin of error, I can confidently say I could re-create this page so precisely, you wouldn't be able to tell it from the original. After all, I've been staring at it for more than a century.

It wasn't always just me and the page. For decades, I whiled away my days watching the passersby for the fraction of their lives that they shared with me. Until one day I stopped. To be completely straight with you, I was bored. The constant progression of people, all similar in their inherent differences, felt so incredibly predictable. Which is how I came to waste my time looking at the same piece of paper, hearing my younger brother plunk out the same melody on the piano under my sister's perennially patient stare. Now it is only at night, when we are freed from the duties of the day and can stretch out within the relative comfort of our own home, that I peel my gaze from the page and take in life as it stands in front of me.

What felt like an eternity later, Claire and Linda reentered our room, the lights snapping on as they registered the women's movement.

"Dear lord, it's like you're doing all of this for the first time," Linda moaned as she sank the mop's sopping tentacles back into the dingy water.

"I am," Claire responded. The sound of her voice struck a chord dangerously close to my soul. Now that she'd returned, I was eager to have the chance to study her. She was beautiful; there was no other way to put it. But it was more complex than that. After one hundred and two years of life like this, I had seen an inestimable number of people, so many of them beautiful. She was enchanting. It was as if something magical emanated from her fingertips, dripping off her in each enthralling motion.

I wondered if I was already in love with her, laughing at myself as the thought entered and exited my mind.

She was small in stature, but then again, so was I. Her eyes were a rich brown, not the kind that seemed flecked with light but a much darker brown, one that seemed to go on forever, nearly blending in with her pupils. Her hair was piled on her head in a towering loose construction of a bun; it was nearly the size of her small head. As she watched Linda demonstrate the proper technique, she nervously scratched behind her ear.

"You have no cleaning experience?" Linda asked. Claire shook her head. "Literally none? How the heck did you get this job? Your dad work at the agency or something?"

"I didn't go to the agency. I just came to the museum and asked if there was something I could do and they gave me a number to call. I thought I was coming in to interview or something, but when I got here yesterday, they just handed me a uniform and told me to come back tonight. I think they got confused and thought I'd already been hired."

"Well, aren't you a lucky one." Linda passed Claire the handle of the mop. "Come on, you've got this room. This doesn't have to take all night."

As Claire pushed the mop along the floor by our frame, she breathed in so deeply, it was like she could smell our garden through the open window. Linda, already tired of waiting, sat on a bench and pulled out her cellphone.

"You play *Candy Crush*?"

"No, never got into it."

"Oh. Well, I'm, like, really good at it," Linda said.

Uninterested in and unable to understand what it was they were talking about, I simply watched Claire push the mop around the room. Linda was right, she worked incredibly slowly, unhurriedly looping back to reach the sections she'd missed while she'd been staring up at the pieces on the wall. In Claire's defense, there was a lot to look at. The walls were brimming with art of all sizes and styles. I had grown accustomed to the congestion over the years, but I did remember that not all museums were so full.

"Do you have a favorite?" Claire asked.

"A favorite what?"

"The paintings and stuff—do you have a favorite?"

"I don't really look at 'em. Since the mop is on the ground, and everything," Linda said with a pointed glance at the floor. "I just try to get done as fast as possible."

"Oh, yeah, makes sense, I just thought, since you'd been here for a while, you know—"

"I only took this gig because you don't have to talk to people. I was at a hotel before this, and there are *always* people around and they always feel like they can always ask you for something even if it isn't your job to help them with whatever BS they need."

"That totally makes sense," Claire said, mopping a bit more furiously.

"Nope, don't care about the paintings. It's all the same to me. Just, like, random colors and people and stuff on a wall."

"Yeah, I don't really know anything about art either," Claire claimed, but the glint in her eyes as she scanned the room said otherwise.

I've always felt people expect too much from the experience of looking at a painting. They think if the meaning of life doesn't leap off the canvas and into their minds, they're not doing it right or, worse, the art has failed them and the whole thing's been a waste. Who says a painting is supposed to do all that work for you? You look at it and you see what you see and you feel what you feel, and it might be transcendent or it might be just another moment in your life and all those things are okay.

I can say this with confidence because I've spent my whole life around art, my father being who he is and all. My father, Henri Matisse, has art hanging on nearly every wall of this museum. If you were to count the paintings in this building, he's the creator of fifty-nine of them, but that's just scratching the surface of that calculation. If you go a layer deeper, you'll find that so many of his paintings contain allusions to or even direct copies of other work he's made. Even within my own frame, the painting in the corner above the head of my brother, Pierre, is a rendition of another of his own paintings. They say copying is the sincerest form of flattery and my father loved nothing more than to be flattered.

Claire returned the mop to the bucket and Linda reluctantly dropped her cellphone into her pocket. She picked up a small cloth and showed Claire how to run it along the tables and the sturdier frames. Claire hesitated before coming close enough to the paintings to touch us. She held her breath as she gently dusted our edges. The intensity of her eye contact intimidated me.

Linda looked at her phone again. "Shit, it's nearly midnight. We're good here; let's go back downstairs. Tomorrow we can do the windows."

When she reached the doorway, Claire turned all the way back and gazed around the room one last time.

"*Claire!* Come *on . . .*" Linda's voice trailed off as she bustled away from our gallery.

Claire walked backward out of the room. I sat there long after the automatic lights turned off again, thinking of the sound of her footsteps.

Marguerite startled me when she returned to the piano bench. In my fluster, I dropped my book. I snatched it up off the ground.

"What's got you all in a tizzy?" Marguerite asked with a grin that was greedy for gossip.

"I never said I was in a tizzy."

"You didn't have to; it's painted all over your face." I waved her off, hoping she'd drop it but knowing better than to expect that. She lit a cigarette, taking her time with the first drag. "Not this again," she said as she exhaled.

"Not what?"

"Not you falling for someone out there. I thought you'd given that up after last time."

"I had. I have."

"Life inside here is great. Everyone else gets that, apart from you. You can't see it because you're too busy living with one eye on them, as always. You would give up our whole world for one room."

"Marguerite, give me a break. It's been one night."

"I'm not being cruel. I'm only saying this for your own good. You could be happier."

"I'm plenty happy."

Pierre's return sealed Marguerite's lips, trapping whatever snide retort she'd had planned against her vocal cords. He climbed up onto the bench next to her. He was the youngest of us, and they had that bond that is so common between the eldest and the youngest siblings, leaving me, the middle child, out.

"What did I miss?" Pierre asked. His question was greeted with silence. "That's fine; don't tell me." As the sun's rays began to creep in, I could see my mother returning to her seat in the garden.

The gallery filled once again with a stream of patrons, young and old. Unable to focus, I watched them all day. I didn't even realize that, in my haste to regain my composure, I'd opened my book to a different page.

2

CLAIRE

This was without a doubt the most magical place I had ever been, and, dear lord, was I exhausted.

I flopped onto the bench in the break room, torn between which needed my attention more: the back of my neck or the bottoms of my feet. Those wood floors had been tough on my heels, standing for hours on end without a break, but my neck was putting up a fight from the odd angle at which I'd been forced to bend it over the mop all night. I understood now why Linda sat down so much—it was going to take some time to get my body used to this. I decided to rub my feet; they were having the worse go of it. I didn't want Linda to catch me like this; I was afraid to give her any reason to tell them I wasn't up to the job. I listened closely to hear any sign of her coming back from the bathroom.

One night of work done. I'd never worked nights before. I thought I might get tired since we normally were asleep by nine in our house, but the adrenaline pumping in my body had made it easier than I had expected to power through.

It was the art; I knew it. Being close to so many paintings made my heart beat so quickly, I thought it might even be unhealthy. They'd all looked incredibly real up there in their frames, as if they were breathing and blinking just like I was.

I'd been here once before, when I was just a kid—well, not *here* here, but to this collection in its old building—and I remembered something our guide said to us that day. She said she liked to pick a favorite painting in every gallery, like we might know who our closest friend was in every class. And just like we might have more than one best friend, she might have more than one favorite. But she said it made them familiar, as though they were there waiting for her each day. She felt comfortable seeing their never-changing faces every time she got to visit them.

It was too early to pick a favorite; I couldn't make that call after just one night. I needed to give them time to speak to me and to give myself time to notice all of them. But there was something immediately attention-grabbing about that huge canvas with the piano. It was enormous, of course it would catch anyone's eye. Was it just me or was that guy in the corner kind of cute? I sounded silly now. That painting was probably like a hundred years old at this point. If he was a real person, he was probably dead.

Morbid. I was getting tired; I could feel it in my muscles. I needed to drive home before I hit true exhaustion; I didn't want to fall asleep at the wheel, and they weren't going to let me stow away here overnight. I still couldn't believe I'd get to come back tomorrow, to do it all over again. And that someday, Linda would leave and it would be just me and the art.

There was a life out there waiting for me, whether I was ready for it or not. I peeled off the way-too-big jumpsuit they'd issued me today; I had been assured they'd order one in my size once I'd made it through the probationary period.

I was so excited about every little thing—a jumpsuit in my size was so silly but it made me feel a little bit more like I belonged here. This was just a job, a way to pay the bills. Why did it feel like something more?

3

JEAN

The room burbled to life as it always did; every day here was the same in that no two days were ever completely alike. Tourists wound their way through gaggles of local school groups; museum members popped back in to check on their old favorites. Children tugged at their parents' hands, eager to show them a secret treasure they'd discovered in one of the paintings, something best viewed at their eye level.

Afternoon turned to evening and the gallery emptied of its patrons. I could hardly believe my ears when they caught Linda's distinct bellow and the rumble of her bucket heading in my direction. Claire was coming back. I shifted in my seat, struggling to find a position that didn't make me appear *too* eager. I leaned forward, forearms on my knees, trying to balance my chin in one palm, crossing and uncrossing my right leg over my left, before giving up and settling back into the way I always sat. My spine curved in a way that would make a chiropractor shudder. Butterflies hammered against the inner walls of my stomach.

I worried I might pass out. I was making myself nauseous over a girl I hardly knew, and one I would certainly never be able to speak to. I was practicing what I would say in impossible future conversations, inventing questions she'd undoubtedly be eager to ask me, imagining the compliments I'd give. This was ridiculous. I was losing my grip on reality. I'd seen her for a mere hour the night before, had heard her speak a hundred words, and none of them to me. My self-chastising had shifted into high gear by the time she reentered the room. The result of my anxious fidgeting had ironically left me in exactly the position I'd inhabited all day.

Linda, of course, was with her. The awkward cobwebs of last night's conversation were nowhere to be found; Linda was orating with the stamina of a waterfall. Linda was quick to turn strangers into friends. Claire soaked it in silently, nodding where appropriate, laughing without making a sound.

"I didn't even wait to hear his side of the story. I put the baby, Didi, she was just a baby at the time, in her stroller and packed a single bag with enough diapers and food to get us through a week and put us both right through the door. I actually forgot my coat and had to go back to get it. I was literally burning with rage. I didn't even feel the cold when I was out in it."

"There wasn't anything else you wanted to take?"

"There wasn't anything else I needed."

"And how old was Didi then?" Claire asked.

"She couldn't have been any more than two. She was so cute then, all baby babble and curly hair. All I really wanted was for her to be safe. I didn't know how I was going to do that, but I knew I'd make it true, no matter what." Linda plopped down onto the bench. "When you have kids, you'll get it."

Claire laughed shyly. "What did you do then?"

"So, we walked to the nearest bus stop and we took it all the way to the depot at the center of town and we got on the first bus that was heading as far away as we could go. It took us to Philly. I'd never been to Philly, never even thought about going to Philly, but it seemed like as good an option as any. We went to the cheapest hotel I could find within spitting distance of where the bus had dropped us off, and I paid in cash for two nights. The next day, I went down and asked for the manager and he said, 'What can I do for you?' And I told him it wasn't about that; it was about what I could do for him. I bet him that I could clean a room better than anyone else he had on his staff at the time and that he should let me show him. He agreed, slow day, and I ran circles around his staff."

"Well, you've got a gift. One I don't seem to have," Claire said as she accidentally sloshed the water from her bucket all over the floor.

"You just gotta think about it as a big picture," Linda said as she pushed herself to her feet, walking over to take the mop out of Claire's hand. "It's not about this one spot, it's about seeing the whole space and knowing how what you're doing here affects how it's going to look over there."

"Sounds like painting," Claire said.

"I knew it! You are an artist." Linda snapped her fingers at Claire.

"No, no." Claire gently pushed Linda's hand away. "No, I've never done any art. I just admire it from afar."

Linda studied Claire. "You're a tough one to crack, aren't you? But I'll get there. I always figure people out."

"I'm nothing special," Claire replied. "Nothing to figure out here."

I begged to differ, and I could tell Linda agreed with me. There was something about Claire that was prepossessing, something that left you wanting more.

"Okay, we're still at your first gig—the shitty hotel," Claire prompted.

"Right, well," Linda continued, "that's how I got my start—in hotels. I stayed in that dump probably longer than I needed to because they let me keep Didi with me all day long. I'd stick her on top of the cart and push her from room to room and she loved it. But I knew I could make more if I went somewhere swankier. I kept moving up but the better the pay and the tips got, the more disgusting the people got too.

"By that point, I had friends in the business. A few of them had taken more private jobs—cleaning houses for just one family or whatever, but I was ready to be as far away from the whole people-thing as possible. So, this place was the perfect fit. I never take the day shifts anymore; I'm the best they got and they let me have my pick. So I stick to the night shift. You get used to the weird sleep schedule. And it's so much better in here with no people."

"It's magical, having this whole place to just us," Claire said.

"I guess," Linda said, "but mostly, I like how fast I can work when no one else is around. No people one step behind you, mucking up your clean floors. Total control."

"Do you train everyone?"

"Yup, all the newbies go to me first. I'm the only one who can handle it without any change to my normal load. Plus, I think they trust me to tell them if someone is a dud."

Linda said that last sentence without any specific weight to her voice, but Claire picked up the pace. What Claire lacked in grace with a mop, she made up for in gusto.

Linda concentrated on her phone screen for a while as Claire looped and swirled her way across the gallery floor.

"Got any siblings?" Linda called out.

"Nope," Claire said.

"Any other gigs?"

"Just this one, right now."

"And you live with your man?"

Claire stopped in her tracks. It was then that I noticed, for the first time, the ring on her left hand. The ring itself had a classic look. It was not particularly large, but it was a legitimate-seeming gem. Something about its place on her small hand made her look even younger. She spun it around her finger by the stone; the band was a bit loose on her and moved easily in a circle again and again.

"Oh, I'm sorry." Linda's hand flew over her mouth. "I shouldn't have assumed it was a man. Partner?"

"I live with my grandma," Claire said. Her jaw was set tightly now.

"She gave you that rock?"

Claire looked down at the ring, her mouth twisting to the side. She opened her lips, but no words came out. Linda shrugged and Claire turned back to her mop.

With Claire's concentration glued to the ground beneath her, I took another chance to study her. It was a difficult game, dressed as she was in the museum's janitorial uniform, which betrayed nothing about the world she came from outside these walls. Her nails were painted but the skin around them was raw; she picked at them. She had woven her hair on top of her head in a new bun, this one so large it threatened to pull her whole neck to one side. Her shoes were scuffed white sneakers, little to remark on except that everything about her felt remarkable to me.

She was young, maybe a few years older than me. But she had an intensity about her that said even though she appeared quiet, she would be a worthy opponent if threatened.

Why did I feel somewhat comforted by Claire's complex relationship with the piece of jewelry on her hand? Styles may have changed, but I remembered what a ring on a woman's finger had meant in the outside world. I'd never gotten to that stage myself out there, placed into this world as I was before

I'd even turned twenty. But I'd seen my fair share of proposals in the gallery—lovesick people getting down on one knee, asking their partners to spend the rest of their lives with them. I felt foolish for caring. Whatever Claire thought about the someone who had given her that ring should be none of my concern.

They wiped away the tension. Linda taught Claire to dust the chairs, sanitize the benches, and spray the windows with a toxic-looking blue liquid. "They hire real window cleaners to keep these things clear; we're just here to remove thumbprints and forehead marks and whatever other nonsense from people touching the glass; who knows why."

Each night for the rest of the week, they repeated this routine. They entered in a tandem trundle; Linda plopped down mere moments later. Claire grew more comfortable managing the cleaning process on her own each day. And every night, Linda was back, determined to get more than Claire had been previously willing to give.

"So, you're from around here?" Linda asked, swiping at the rainbow fruit that combined and combusted across her screen.

"Sort of," Claire answered.

"Ever tried anywhere else?"

"I've actually never left the state," Claire said casually.

"Seriously?" Linda's hand holding her phone dropped to her side. "Why not?"

"We didn't have the means, growing up."

"What about now?"

"Now . . ." Claire considered. "Now it's just too complicated."

Incredibly cryptic, as always. Claire was like a puzzle to be put together, little pieces scattered, meaning very little until they were assembled, and I longed to be the one who assembled them.

It didn't bother Linda. "I'm going to miss you, kid," Linda said, "when you start taking this room on solo. I don't mind your company. Even though we've been doing this for days, and it still feels like I don't know a single thing about you."

"There's not much to know."

"That's what people with really interesting lives say."

Claire laughed lightly, like she hadn't really committed to the laugh. "Not me. I think I'm still trying to figure out what my life is supposed to be."

"Said like a true young person." Linda smirked. "You can't wait around for life to reveal what it's supposed to be. It just is what it is. And if you want something else, you have to take it."

"Well, I'll always be just a gallery away," Claire said. "You can come find me when you need a little chatter. And you know I'll probably still have questions for you after tonight."

"Yeah, I know you will."

"Thank you for teaching me all this stuff. I know you don't normally have to start with the basics like this."

"Someone taught me once too. Plus, I realized you were going to need all the help I could give you to actually keep this gig."

"I'd have been lost without you."

"I know."

The women made and held eye contact for a moment longer than what I'd expect of two erstwhile strangers. "Come on, let's go have a cup of shitty break room coffee. My treat."

"I thought it was free?"

"Shhhh, don't ruin the moment." Linda wrapped her arm around Claire's delicate shoulders; standing almost nine inches taller, Linda was quite literally taking Claire under her wing. Claire awkwardly hobbled along next to her as the two made their way out of the gallery.

4

JEAN

The sun came up on another day, the room springing to life with the tour groups who were often the first to enter the museum. Susie, one of the most unique tour guides, was in today, with a group of women all dressed exactly alike.

"Now, before I let you go today, I want to introduce you to one of my personal favorite paintings in the entire museum. Any guesses who is in this painting?"

"A family," a bold member of the group jumped in immediately.

"Absolutely," Susie commended. "Does anyone have any idea whose family this is?"

The crowd was silent but pensive, the looks of consternation on their faces showing they were actually trying to figure it out. Unwilling to put forth a wrong answer, the woman who had responded earlier kept her lips sealed. Finally, another brave soul toward the back of the pack guessed: "The artist's?"

The group turned around to acknowledge this good guess. "Exactly right," Susie cheered. "This is a painting of Matisse's family. In the foreground, we have his children: Jean, sitting here with a book—"

"It looks like he's got a Kindle in his hands!" cried an enthusiastic member of the crowd.

"All the kids' groups always ask why he's got an iPhone," Susie joked. "The French publishers of the early twentieth century occasionally took to wrapping books in paper to hide salacious titles or covers." She winked at the group. Susie always made it sound like I was reading something erotic while sitting next to my brother and sister. As the decades dragged on, sometimes I wished I could trade this novel in for such entertainment.

"Over here, at the piano, are his older sister, Marguerite, and his younger brother, Pierre. Pierre, of course, is the one who would go on to be a famous art collector. Marguerite was a child born out of wedlock, the daughter of the artist and one of his models, before he was married. Matisse and Marguerite had a complex relationship; there is some great scholarship on it if you have the time to check it out. I think he was a hard man to have as a father. Even though this scene evokes sound: music, instruction, chatter, it's known that Matisse made his family sit in silence as they posed for him. And of course, in the backyard, the artist's wife. Her distance here from the rest of the family shows how her relationship with the artist was strained by 1917, when this work was painted."

I held my breath so I wouldn't scoff. Of course, the guides and docents took liberties with their descriptions of all the paintings. But it always felt so personal when it came to us. We were the family; everything had to be an indication of strife or love or fear, didn't it? I was sure the Renoirs got the same treatment when guides came to their family portrait in the next room.

"Otherwise, why would she be sitting so far away? We all know that feeling of needing an escape from our 'loved ones,' don't we, ladies?" Susie's words felt like someone pushing their elbow into your side. The ladies tittered in agreement. "In 1917, France was in the throes of the First World War. Actually, Jean"—Susie gestured to me—"had just been drafted so this painting is a fictive imagining of a family reunion." Susie was ready to bring it home. "Now, the artist included a bit of himself in this painting too, even if he doesn't actually appear here. It is his family, after all; he had to carve out a bit of space. Any idea where in this painting we see the artist represented?"

"It's certainly not the sculpture in the back," one of the women said with a laugh.

"No, it is not," Susie agreed. "Though, if you'll pardon the slight digression, that brings up an interesting facet of Matisse's work. He loved to include representations of his own work within new paintings. This painted sculpture is based on a real Matisse piece, *Reclining Nude I,* sometimes called *Aurora.* We see this woman's figure appear a number of times in the artist's work, including in *Studio with Goldfish,* the blue painting across the room." The group turned to look and let out a synchronous *ooh.* "But back to our game—can you spot the artist?"

"Is it the violin?" the woman in the back guessed.

"Yes, ma'am, that is it exactly. The artist was a casual violin player, and maybe a fan of Haydn, we can infer from the sheet music on the top of the piano. From where the instrument is placed, in the very front of the image, you could imagine he might be able to reach right in and pick it up." A chill dripped down my spine. I shivered.

"Well, that's all the time we have for today. I so hope you

enjoyed the tour." Susie bowed her head and a cacophony of voices chimed in.

"Enjoyed? We are *obsessed*."

"There is truly no other way to see the museum!"

"It would not be the same without you, Susie."

"I wish we didn't have to leave you, Susie!"

The women swarmed Susie, an adoring crowd greeting their fearless leader. They said their thank-yous and vowed to come back soon, and Susie gave recommendations for the rest of their day in the city. The throng finally splintered off, revealing one last member of the tour group I hadn't seen before, a tall woman with a head of boisterous red curls. She was dressed casually in a thick sweater and a pair of jeans that somehow accentuated her height. She wore glasses with chunky black frames. They covered so much of her face that it took me a minute of studying her to realize she wasn't as old as her clothes and eyewear made her seem. She stepped forward to have her moment with Susie.

"I wanted to introduce myself," she said, offering Susie her right hand. "I'm—"

"Jamie Leigh, the new museum president, I know." Susie cut her off, enthusiastically shaking Jamie's hand in hers. Susie studied her. "You're so much younger than I thought you'd be."

"I hope you don't mind that I tagged along for the last few rooms of the tour today. I've been studying the art for weeks, but there's nothing quite like getting to know it in person with a trusty guide."

"Of course I don't mind! I'm flattered you joined us."

"Have you been doing this for a long time? The patrons obviously adore you."

"Oh yes," Susie said. "I've lost count of the years. I do all the museums in the area, but the foundation is my favorite. Is this your first official day on the job?"

"I don't technically start until Monday; I just wanted to have some time under the radar to get familiar with it all."

Susie breathed in deeply, closing her eyes for a few seconds as she did. "Be warned"—she reopened her eyes and they twinkled—"this place is nothing short of magical. You're going to get addicted to it."

"I can tell," Jamie agreed. "There's something, dare I say, hypnotic in the air here."

Three people bustled into the doorway, stopping for a moment to collect themselves. I recognized them as having some affiliation with the team that governed the museum; the three of them popped up in here from time to time, always distinguishable from the regular visitors by their somewhat more formal way of dressing. They spotted Jamie and hurried over in her direction.

"*There* you are," one of the women exclaimed. "We heard you were here! We've been looking all over for you."

"I'm Henry Wallingham." Henry took Jamie's hand and gave it a single firm shake.

"Lisa Meyer," Lisa said as she leaned forward to give Jamie a kiss on each cheek.

"And I'm Christie Hall," Christie said with a brief nod. "We're on the board and have been just dying to meet you."

"Of course," Jamie said. "I've been looking forward to it as well."

"We were planning to be here to greet you on Monday, when you were scheduled to arrive. We rushed down when we heard you were here early," Lisa said.

"Could we take you for a cup of coffee at the café? We were so disappointed not to be on your interview committee; we'd love to get to know you better," Christie said.

"Absolutely," Jamie said, clapping her hands together. "I'm free as a bird, not on the clock until next week, of course."

"So much for incognito," Susie said quietly with a little wink.

"Best-laid plans," Jamie said. "It was nice to meet you. Thank you for the tour."

The group ushered Jamie out of the gallery. Jamie turned back to wave to Susie, whom none of the board members had even acknowledged. Susie smiled at them, waiting until they had a few minutes' head start to follow them through the exit.

The evening arrived and so did Claire, on her own for the first time, pausing in the doorway, illuminated by the light of the gallery behind her, not yet far enough into our room to have triggered the overheads. She glowed like something supernatural, like she didn't belong to the world she was standing in. I couldn't look away.

She inhaled with confidence and took a step into the gallery. The lights flipped on, and she and they warmed the space around them. She pushed her mop and bucket to the center of the room and abandoned them. She crossed to the wall next to ours that held three paintings of three sisters each—nine sisters, in total, on one wall—and took her time, gazing up into each one. She inched along the floor, not daring to miss a square foot of what was on the walls in front of her.

Everyone remaining in this gallery's frames froze in their steps. The rules were unspoken, but we knew what was expected of us. We were supposed to appear permanent. During the day, we remained in place as our painters, sculptors, creators had staged us. At night, we took liberties. If we were in the same room as someone on the night shift, we were supposed to pause, to move with caution, to fade into the background, but at each person's own discretion, of course. Some of my peers were looser with this than others but, to their credit, the night staff rarely looked at us.

We were only open five days a week, Wednesday through Sunday, but the museum was rarely empty on Monday and Tuesday. It was quieter, but you'd still catch the occasional VIP group or museum employees using those days to update archival photographs or descriptive text or to take photos or videos for the museum's promotional platforms. We were free at night.

Claire continued her lap and by the time her measured pace had carried her around to me, I was far too nervous to make eye contact. I hid my face in my book and felt her eyes crawl all over my body. I felt hot; a fire had begun inside my stomach that was burning its way along my skin. I was terrified that this feeling would end and my nerve endings would go back to the temperature they were before.

My sense of time remained completely distorted. It might have been three minutes, it might have been an hour that she stood there with her gaze on me, setting me aflame. When she took her first step away, my insides began to cool and I shuddered at the sudden change in temperature. She slowly continued her circle, completing one full turn about the room like a woman in an Austen novel. She was Elizabeth Bennet in a janitorial uniform and I, Fitzwilliam Darcy in oil on canvas.

Was it just my delusional brain, or had she lingered in front of me longer than in front of anyone else?

She still had responsibilities to attend to. She reluctantly pulled the mop from its soapy swamp. I counted how many seconds would pass before she looked back up at the artwork. I rarely got past twelve. She relished dusting our frames; the proximity was entrancing. It was with reluctance that she left the room at the end of the night, forcing herself back to the world she had come from.

A few nights later, Claire entered and crossed straight to me, bucket and all. After she'd moved on, Marguerite, who had chosen to loiter at the piano tonight, much to my chagrin, dropped her jaw in shock.

"Does she always do that?"

"She always comes to stand with me at some point. She normally warms up with a circle around the gallery first."

Marguerite's cigarette dangled in her left hand and she tapped her ash off mindlessly. "Do you think she knows something? Have you given us away?"

I was annoyed, unwilling to share this new part of my life with my cynical sister. "What is there to know, Marguerite? I think she likes art and I think she likes us."

"You think she likes *you*."

I was afraid to put those words into the air.

"Some of us are going to hang out in *Le Bonheur de vivre* tonight. I assume you're not coming?" She didn't even wait for my response. "That's your loss," she said as she swept out of the room. I could hear her greeting my mother as she walked into the garden.

I looked back into the gallery and was shocked to see that Claire was standing in front of me again, her eyes trailing along the painting as if she had just watched our spat and Marguerite's departure. I froze, unsure of how much she had just seen. She smiled slyly and returned to her work. I didn't move for the rest of the night.

A week in, Claire started talking to herself during her shifts. "I've never really been one to just talk, like, out loud when there's no one else around," she confessed as she chattered on. "Except for you all, of course." My heart thundered at her acknowledgment of us, even if it was in a joke. "But I also never was the kind of person who felt welcome in places like this." She giggled shakily. "This is so weird, just talking into the air. I guess Gracie does it all the time, but she's kind of batty, God love her." She anxiously spun her ring around her finger.

She continued her work, exchanging her mop for a spray bottle and a cloth and moving toward the window. I waited for her to come back in my direction.

After she had finished spraying down the windows, she sat on the bench directly opposite me. She leaned backward, sinking lower. She sighed. "This schedule is brutal." She rubbed the heels of her hands against her eyes. "Something's going to have to change if I'm going to keep this up. Now I really understand that phrase 'burning the candle at both ends.'"

She looked right up at me and continued. "It was so impulsive of me to come work here. I don't even know what got into me; I'm sure I could have found a day shift somewhere if I tried. That would probably make more sense. Maybe I can ask them if I can switch to the opening shift." She shook her head. "No, but then I wouldn't have this whole place to myself.

"I just can't believe I get to be here. Me. Every day, like it's no biggie. I wish little me could see me now." She looked down at herself, running her hand over her jumpsuit-clad stomach. "I guess she'd be pretty shocked to see me in this janitor's uniform. But I always thought growing up would mean big parties and going to museums whenever I wanted. I guess I got part of that right. Why am I talking so much? Am I losing it?"

I once heard someone say that people in solitary confinement often lose their voice in the first few days because of how much they talk to themselves—telling stories, singing songs whose lyrics are trapped in the recesses of their memory. The night shift had some kind of similar effect on Claire; as she worked in solitude, she got chattier and chattier.

More of her life slipped out each night—she thought her grandmother Gracie was a saint whom she didn't deserve. Gracie was teaching Claire to play poker and Claire sometimes reviewed the rules aloud, describing potential hands and announcing herself the winner.

As I got to know her through these nocturnal monologues, I became even more endeared by her. I understood at first that it might just have been the novelty of our situation; I had spent decades in the same place with the same cast of characters and here was someone new. But it couldn't be that simple. There was something special about Claire. She was serious, logical, thoughtful, and a committed employee. Even so, there was something bubbling under the surface that being in this place was unlocking in her, a childlike curiosity about the art and its home that couldn't help but spill over. She spent untold minutes just staring at a single painting. We captivated her the same way she captivated me.

I thought and hoped it was more than just an appreciation for art. I was pretty sure Claire was flirting with me. What began with furtive glances grew into sustained eye contact. She even referred to me once as "a handsome guy like you," and then quickly turned bright red with embarrassment. As she dusted our frame, I could practically feel the heat radiating off her blushing cheeks. When she had finished for the night, she hurried out of the gallery without a backward glance.

5

CLAIRE

I had just told my imaginary friend I thought he was hand-some and I was humiliated, even though I was only talking to myself. He wasn't even real! I mean, he was real in the sense that he was in a painting sitting there in front of me. But he wasn't a living, breathing, talking person. Except . . .

I'd been in the museum for about a month now, five days a week, sometimes more frequently when they needed additional coverage after special events. I'd gotten better at my job and more comfortable marching through these halls on my own. And I'd soaked in as much of the art as I possibly could, studying the hundreds of paintings I was surrounded by in every free moment I could grab. The walls were so heavy with art that there was always something new catching my eye, something I hadn't taken in the day before.

As I looked at these paintings night after night, something unbelievable crossed my mind. Was it just me or were they maybe moving? Shifting around in their frames? It was hard to tell when I was looking directly at them; it felt like we were playing a game of Red Light, Green Light and they froze every time I turned around. I could have sworn I'd seen subjects in one frame on a Thursday night and in another painting, in another gallery completely, on Friday.

Was I imagining things? Quite possibly. Or I could just be wrong. There must be thousands of paintings in this place; there was no way I was correctly remembering who was supposed to be in which frame. But I couldn't stop thinking about it, couldn't stop my brain from going back there, from watching the walls. I could have sworn they were thinking, maybe even whispering, though I couldn't hear what they were saying. And that one guy, the guy in *my* gallery, the one I'd taken to talking to when things were a little boring—he looked at me like he knew I knew he was looking.

It was silly. It was just art, I kept telling myself. I was still getting used to seeing so much of it. I checked the time on my phone; it was definitely time to call it a night. It must be the adrenaline, the adjustment to the night shift, the thrill of finally getting to do something all my own. A little more sleep and I was sure I'd regain my senses, though I doubted the magic of walking those halls at night would ever fade.

But if I was right, if they were alive in some way—what if he'd heard me tonight? Oh god.

6

JEAN

Claire had greatly improved her mastery of the mop, no longer having to double back to cover spots she'd missed. If Linda could've seen her, I knew she'd be proud. But Linda never came by. I didn't mind. It meant I had Claire all to myself. Well, myself and anyone else who stuck around in the paintings of our gallery at night, but they tended to pay Claire no mind.

At the end of each night, Claire came right up next to me, dusting the frame that ran just under my toes. Having her this close made me feel like something magnetic was running its way along my skin, charging up something that had me ready to shoot off through the ceiling. Even as I maintained my relaxed posture, every muscle in my body clenched. My forearms were on fire. She had this look on her face, as if she might be wondering what it would be like to be held by me. Or, at least, I was hoping that's what the look meant.

Nothing about Claire implied an education in art; she lacked the pretension of the curators, assistants, and guides who marched through these hallways like they ran the place, which they did to a certain extent. I could always tell when someone had studied art or art history. They projected a confidence that said "even if I don't understand something yet, I will before anyone notices." Claire had no preconceived notions about anything that hung before her. She was looking at us sheerly for what we were. It was reminiscent of the way the collector saw us as well, for our shape, our colors, and our light.

Unlike in other museums that I was familiar with, we were never moved around at a curator's whim. We were on the walls in specific places, based on four principles drawn up by the man who had put us here: light, color, line, and space. And as none of those things were ever changing about us, we never went anywhere.

After he died, people tried to challenge that. A claim has been made for everything: for rearranging us, for sending us out on tour, for moving us miles away to a brand-new building identical in its layout to the original space—that one actually happened. You name a change; someone has thought of it. But for the most part, we stay where we are and I like it that way.

At least we roam somewhat freely at night. Marguerite would not have been satisfied if we were housebound. We were so different, she and I. Born to a different mother, she was brazen and bossy where I was quiet and contemplative. Five years my senior, she acted as if she was another maternal figure to me. A very intense one at that; she was opinionated and critical of every decision I made, whether she spoke her thoughts aloud or just allowed them to register in the way she looked at me. If I was completely honest, I was incredibly intimidated by her.

If we'd been hung in a different museum, one with a more

flexible collection, we might have been sent out on tour. Marguerite would have relished the constant change, shifting from gallery to gallery or museum to museum. She would have thrived in rooms we didn't recognize, displayed for patrons speaking languages we didn't understand. I'm sure she found our reality dull, but she didn't let that hold her back. She'd carved out the life she wanted here. She'd been the first of us to learn English, desperate to understand every passing conversation between patrons and to befriend as many of the other painting subjects as she could. Pierre was quick on her tail; my language skills took somewhat longer to develop but I became fluent eventually. I wasn't sure my mother had ever learned; she certainly never spoke anything but French to me.

I admired that piece of Marguerite, her ability to make life a thing she wanted to live. I was paralyzed, waiting for my purpose to come and find me. She sought hers without needing anyone's permission.

As the leaves through the windows changed from their vibrant green to the reds, yellows, and oranges of autumn, so too changed my level of satisfaction with our situation, mine and Claire's. I could happily listen to Claire talk all night long, but I yearned to be able to show her I was listening.

I became increasingly interested in demonstrating to Claire what I had come to feel for her, or at least in being able to communicate with her in some way. Out of sheer desperation, I turned to Marguerite for advice.

The galleries had just emptied out for the day. Marguerite stood up almost immediately, her back cracking twice as she relieved it of the stress of perching on a wooden piano bench for an entire shift. She checked in with Pierre, who smiled as he zipped out of the room. She made to follow him.

"Marguerite—" My voice cracked with anticipation. She turned wordlessly in my direction. "I was hoping I could—err—that I could ask for your consultation."

"On what, younger brother?" Her tone sparkled with authority; this was Marguerite's favorite version of herself.

"As you've probably seen and heard, Claire has become somewhat attached to me." Marguerite impressed upon me with her gaze how obvious this statement was. "As I have to her."

"There's no denying you two both are holding on to some confusing infatuation. Everyone has been talking about it."

Until this moment, it hadn't really crossed my mind that my contemporaries in other canvases would care what I'd been up to but, of course, everyone in our gallery had been able to hear her clear as day. Naturally they must have gossiped about it. To their credit, there'd been little to talk about in the past few years, and now they had star-crossed lovers in their very own home. Or maybe it was just me, lover, singular.

"Right, well, right you all are, I guess. Anyway, I think I need to show her that I am listening, that I can hear what she says."

"Jean," she said, a sharpness creeping into her tone. "Are you sure you want to go down that path?"

"I know, I know this could go all wrong. You think I'm insane for asking and I think I'm insane too, but I believe I'll go truly out of my mind if I don't at least try."

"And what do you need from me?" Marguerite said as she exhaled a delicate cloud of smoke, its airy quality the opposite of her stone-cold demeanor.

"I don't know." I was growing wary of her stony expression. "I thought maybe you might have heard of something like this before?"

"I don't know what magical information you expect me to know, Jean, or why I'd be the one to know it."

"Of course not. I'm sure you wouldn't have waited this long to tell me if you knew." I caught a glint of something cross Marguerite's face, something that told me if she *had* heard, I wouldn't have been the first one she told. I waited, hoping that twinge of guilt might work to my advantage.

"I know you know that you won't be able to get out there," she said. Her tone felt like an eye roll. By "there," she meant into the museum, out of our frame, into their world. I did know that; it was the first anecdote I can remember hearing once we'd entered into this painted state, of poor souls who had grown bored of the world on the walls or were desperate to reach someone from their past life. They'd tried to escape, but it was impossible.

"I am aware of that," I replied bitterly. "I was thinking more of some way to communicate with her, to pass her a message."

"They talk about her in the other rooms too. Not all of them, but the other galleries she cleans can tell there is something different about her."

"What do they say?"

"They think she can see us."

"See us how?" I knew Marguerite did not simply mean that Claire could see us hanging in front of her, as paintings in gilded frames. Of course she could see us like that. She meant something with more nuance, something I thought I understood as well, but I needed to hear Marguerite say it. Because there was a small part of me that hoped, but hardly dared to admit it, that Claire saw us for all that we were and that's why she was looking extra-long at me.

"Andromeda has been testing her. She noticed Claire standing directly in front of her the other night, mimicking her posture. Andromeda started moving ever so slowly into a slightly different pose. A few moments later, Claire followed suit."

I exhaled, my breath coming out as a shudder.

"But, Jean." She eyed me warily. "I don't tell you this lightly. I'll never keep a secret from you. But I'm afraid you'll take this too far."

"Marguerite, I'm a grown man. I don't need you to be my mother."

"I'm just saying I've seen you hurt before. I wish you'd never have to feel that again."

Silence hung heavy in the air, like a cloud of fog neither of us would wave away.

"Are we in any danger? If I try—" I hesitated, not knowing what I was even about to attempt. "If I try something, could I put us or our world at risk?"

"I don't know. But if I were you . . ." I held my breath as I waited for what she had to say. "I wouldn't risk it. I can't say if there might be some hidden consequence lurking for us. But I am anxious it might put her in danger. You of all people should know that." She offered me a cigarette and we finished them, together, smoking in silence. She knew what I'd gone through before. She didn't need to say it out loud.

The last thing I wanted was to endanger Claire. Something about her was special; I could just tell. But I had to know for sure. I set about to make a plan to get Claire's attention, even though it was obvious I did not have Marguerite's approval, and probably never would. I was on my own in this.

7

JEAN

If Marguerite was the confident one, Pierre the smart one, and my mother the welcoming one, I was the reserved one. Day in and day out, I sat in the corner of our parlor with my head in a book. Even before Claire, I had not explored much after the sun had set. I was comfortable in my chair with my words and my thoughts. I had rarely wished for anything larger. But now I did. I wanted to communicate with Claire, and suddenly no chair could possibly be comfortable enough for me to stay seated.

The only thing to interrupt my internal strife was the consistent influx of patrons in the galleries. We saw everyone from locals to tourists, school groups to private tours, art students to amateurs. There were two large benches directly in front of our painting, a novelty in these galleries, so we were frequently joined by those who were reaching the weary side of their museum day. They would take a load off, check their cellphones, close their eyes and ears to the chatter of those they'd come with.

My favorites, of course, were the tour guides. Full of knowledge, some of it accurate, some of it invented; we almost never heard the same exact thing twice. There were only a handful of them who worked with the museum or led private tours in the area, so we saw a few dozen guides on a loop, Susie being one of them. I had come to be familiar with all of them, pinning down which guides knew a lot about art and whose analysis took more artistic liberties.

Today, it was a young woman I'd seen a few times before; she was relatively new to this gig, with a group of students who were around Pierre's age. Judging by the voices echoing throughout the halls, I guessed they were part of a larger crew, divided up for ease of moving through the museum.

This group clustered around one of the benches and the guide came to stand directly next to my right-hand side. If we weren't locked in our bifurcated worlds, she would have been close enough for me to reach out and brush her shoulder.

"Okay, here we are! Now, remember Picasso? We talked about him downstairs." A handful of the kids nodded, enough for the guide to forge ahead. "Great, well, he and this artist were bitter rivals. They were constantly pushing each other to try new things, new styles, to not get stuck in the past. What do you all notice about the style of this one?" She gestured to us. The kids were silent. "Anyone?"

"They kind of look like cartoons. Like, it's a cartoony style," one kid offered up.

"Okay!" The guide grasped at this. "Cartoony. Cool. What do you mean by that? What about the painting makes you think that?"

"They're not super detailed."

"Great! Thank you. Anyone notice anything else?"

"There's instruments there," another student said.

"Yes! There are! What instruments do you see?"

"Um, those two are playing a piano. And that's a violin just there."

"Yes, absolutely, these two characters are engaged in some kind of piano lesson. Can you guess who all these characters are?"

Ah, I thought. *Here it comes.* The children had no guesses.

"It's the artist's family!" the guide squealed. "This is a family portrait." She rubbed her hands together. "Now, let's make a personal connection here. Imagine you're going to paint your own family portrait—tell us about it. Who's in it? What kind of objects are there? Musical instruments? Something else?"

As expected, the children were silent. The guide chose a victim and called on him. "What about you? Who is in your portrait?"

After some consideration, he said, "Just me."

"Just you, that's great!" Her forced enthusiasm said otherwise. "What are you doing in your portrait?"

"Um, I'd be eating."

"Amazing, probably eating one of your favorite foods?"

"Yeah, like a sandwich or something."

"A sandwich! That's great! Thank you!" She was practically squeaking now, her voice hitting a higher pitch with each sentence. "Anyone else want to share?"

"Mine would be me and my cousin," someone else said.

"Cool," the guide encouraged. "Very cool."

The adult man tagging along with the group, conceivably the teacher, joined in now. Gesturing to me, he said, "Mine would be me, just like that guy. Wearing a three-piece suit but chilling out."

This made the guide laugh. "I could be into that." Was she flirting with him? She checked her watch to find that time was up and she was officially off the hook. "Well, thank you all so much for coming along with me today. I hope you found a way to see yourselves in the art here."

The group muttered their somewhat enthusiastic thanks as the teacher shepherded them out the way they'd come in to meet up with the other groups for a boxed lunch. He looked back at the guide, tipping an invisible hat in her direction. She giggled. I wondered if I'd just witnessed the start of a relationship.

The sound of our gallery faded back down to its usual din. The rest of the day passed unremarkably, or at least that's how I remembered it. Everything about this day was unremarkable in comparison to what was about to happen.

Since my last conversation with Marguerite on the topic of Claire, my family was careful to leave our frame every night as soon as they were able. They usually left me to my devices, but someone might linger or decide to remain in our living room for the evening. Not any longer. Where they went, I was not entirely sure, but whether I liked it or not, they would not be witnesses. I fretted over how best to make my next move and in the wealth of options with no clear direction, I was paralyzed by the potential choice.

I decided to start small—I planned to bring my chair closer to the edge of the frame, just a few inches at a time. I thought I'd do it as soon as she got there the next evening, in the time she normally spent looking at each painting, saying hello, before she jumped into that evening's work. But when she showed up that night, I panicked, frozen in my spot like a human icicle. It wasn't until hours had passed and she was fully immersed in the mop that I convinced myself to scoot forward a few inches. The sound of my chair grating along the wood floor was the loudest noise I had ever heard. Claire did not look up. Twenty minutes later, when she was spraying down the windows, her back to me, I tried again, scooching even closer to the edge. Still no reaction.

She left that night and nothing had changed. I'd need to go

bigger if I wanted her attention. The night following, after the gallery had emptied out, I immediately stood up from my seat. I did a few push-ups to get out the nervous energy, a habit I'd picked up in my brief bit of army training, having been drafted only weeks before I was pulled out of that world and into this painting. I crossed to the other side of the room. Still afraid to move too much in her presence, I had decided to stand on the opposite side of the frame, to see if that elicited any new response.

I was embarrassed to do any of this in front of my peers, those who were spending the evening in the frames on the walls beside and across from me. It was funny to develop this self-consciousness now when I'd been on public display every day for a century. I pushed what they might be thinking from my head and committed to my plan.

Claire was different that night. Her head was elsewhere; she cleaned the way she had when she had first started training. It took her too much time and she had to hurry away to what I now understood to be her other assignments. She'd never even looked at me.

The third night, I was ready for a grand gesture. I took up my father's violin, which rested on the end of the piano. No one had touched it since he had left it there; it felt like it was reserved for him were he ever to come and join us. I had played as a young boy, though not as well as Pierre did, and hoped a bit of that skill would come back to me in some way.

In a humbling attempt to practice, I tucked the body under my chin and began an initial drag of the bow across a single string. It let out a terrible whine, like a cat being slowly lowered into a tub of water. I startled myself, nearly dropping the violin to the ground. It occurred to me that a violin that had gone unplayed for just over a century probably needed to be tuned. After taking a moment to do so, I wound myself up to give it another go.

This time, with a more confident hand, I was able to extract a sound that vaguely resembled a musical note. I'd take it. I moved slowly into the first song that came to mind, a simple minuet from my days in lessons, one Pierre played on the piano frequently. Right on cue, Claire came into the gallery.

I begged my hands to keep playing, despite the sledgehammer in my chest that had replaced my heart, and they did just that. I lost myself in the music. I cycled through any song I'd memorized in my childhood, abruptly moving on to the next if my memory failed and I could play one no further.

Claire propelled herself across the room to me, leaving her mop and broom in her wake. She stood directly in front of me, about a foot away from the frame that separated her world from mine. She waited as I played, watching me carefully and admiringly.

When I'd finally finished a tune that I could remember in almost its entirety, I lowered my bow and my violin and I looked down at her.

"I can't hear what you've played, but I bet it was beautiful."

I was speechless—not that she would have been able to hear me even if I had been able to find the words. She gave me a wry smile. We were both in on her secret. The door to the way we were before closed behind us.

"I'd love to watch you play another. If you'd like to, of course. No pressure."

No pressure, a turn of phrase that felt so Claire. I pushed the violin back in the space between my shoulder and my chin and combed through the options my memory provided. I knew she couldn't hear me, but I wanted something that suited the moment.

I settled on a waltz, a rhythm that had always felt romantic and heightened to me. I threw my body into it, knowing now that she might not hear my playing but I wanted her to see it and feel it. I nodded to the left and the right as the beat came in familiar patterns of threes. She danced a bit, following my lead, and it was not at all a match to what I was playing but it was perfect.

After I finished, she rewarded me with an enthusiastic round of applause and I took a modest bow, which earned me an extra cheer. I was filled to the brim with joy. She knew I was here for her. I'd been right—she was somehow, some way, special.

We might have passed a whole night like that; I could have been satisfied with an entire lifetime of accompanying her clumsy jig in her janitorial uniform, but something in me called for more. I dropped the bow to the ground; it fell with a loud clatter that I knew meant nothing but silence on her end. The noise hardly even registered to me; my body was moving faster than my brain. My hand was reaching forward, as if of its own accord, extending rapidly toward Claire, toward a world I'd never before touched.

At the edge of where my reality collided with hers, my hand stopped. A force I could not see held me in place. I looked at her and saw in her eyes her shyness, her uncertainty. I waited for her.

She took one step in my direction, and then another, and then another, until she was as close as she could get. I stood a few feet taller than her, as I was naturally so, and the floor beneath my feet was higher than hers. I lowered my hand as she stood on her tiptoes and soon it was within her reach. Slowly, as if the air was as thick as molasses, she pushed her hand up toward mine, through the glossy boundary between my world and hers.

Our palms connected. Her hand was real and warm as our fingers intertwined. Without a second thought, I tightened my grip and pulled her in.

8

JEAN

We crashed to the floor. My upper and lower jaws collided and sent reverberations throughout my skull. Once I had come back to my senses, I whipped my head around, desperate to make sure that Claire was okay. She was a few feet away from me, pushing herself onto her feet. I rushed over to offer her a hand.

"Claire . . ." I began, unsure of where to go next. I was suddenly aware of my bizarre pronunciation, my English sticky with my accent, and of the croak in my voice that betrayed how many hours it had been since I'd last spoken aloud. My throat had gone groggy since Marguerite and Pierre had left for the night. No need to continue on, for she interrupted me.

"You know my name?" she questioned as she looked around, trying to comprehend if this could possibly be real. Or, more likely, knowing it couldn't possibly be so, and trying to figure out what had just happened. She rubbed at the back of her head like she had just hit it on something.

I nodded. "I can hear you, you know, out there." I gestured to the gallery she had just stood in.

"You can?"

"I can. I listen to everything you tell me." She smiled at that, but I could tell she was attempting to mentally catalog all her ramblings of the past few months.

"Oh" was all she responded. She shuffled her feet a bit. "Sorry for all my, my blabbering. And my singing, oh god . . ."

"No, no, please don't apologize. I love to listen. It's the best part of my day, every day, when you get here, no matter what you say. Or sing. I don't mind. I like it."

Claire looked startled, but I wasn't sure if it was because of my compliment or because of the startling amount of intimacy I had with her already. I looked at her again, hardly able to believe my eyes that she was here. Her awestruck face betrayed the same feelings. "That's really nice of you. To say. You don't have to say that."

"But I mean it."

"I can't believe this—like, really, I can't even wrap my mind around this. So, it's, like, old-fashioned in here?" She ran her hand along the edge of the piano, just above its surface, as if she was afraid to actually touch it. "I feel like if I press down on it, I'm going to smudge the paint even though I'm sure it's been dry after . . . how many years?"

"More than a hundred," I said.

"Oh my god, I don't think you're supposed to touch a hundred-year-old painting, much less stomp around inside it. What if I hurt something? Did I hurt you?" she asked, suddenly assessing the state of my hand.

I held it up and wiggled my fingers, the paint not at all smudged. "All is well over here."

"Thank god." She exhaled a sigh of relief. "I couldn't stand to be that girl who ruined a masterpiece. If I got caught. Oh my god, could I get caught?" She rushed back to the edge of the painting, but the gallery was deserted. She stopped when she saw the watery texture of the translucent divide between my world and hers.

"So, this is what it looks like when you look out into the room? A little wavy, like looking through an old window?" I joined her and nodded. She looked down at her skin, which was as smooth as it always was. I pulled up my shirtsleeve, revealing my forearm and allowing us to compare. They both took up the same three dimensions, but my skin looked like someone had covered me lightly with oil paint. "How freaking cool is that," Claire said.

She was looking around for something to do and saw my bow on the ground. "I think you dropped this." She picked it up and returned it to me.

"Look," I said, gesturing to where she'd gripped the bow. "The paint is fine. I don't think you have to be worried about what you touch." She nodded but continued with a delicate hand. I found the violin that had fallen from my hand when I'd reached to pull her in. I placed it with the bow in their usual spots on the piano.

"This is so insane. Where do we even begin? I guess I don't know your name, but you know mine? Do you even have a name? Wow, okay, saying that out loud it sounds so rude. I didn't mean it in any kind of bad way." Claire was speaking quickly, the words tumbling out.

I laughed, wishing I could put us both somewhat more at ease. "I have a name. It's Jean."

"Jean," she repeated, mimicking my pronunciation. It rolled off her tongue like an inside joke. I wanted to do whatever I needed to so she'd say it again. "So, um, have you done this with many women?"

I snorted before reminding myself of the validity of her question. We'd broken almost every rule of time and space that I'd understood up until this point, but she didn't know I'd never tried anything like this in the past century. "No, never. I don't know that anyone has ever done this before."

If we could have better comprehended the weight of our situation, I'm sure it would have sunk down upon us. But it was too big to be believed. Instead, all I could focus on was how badly I wanted to hold her hand again. I kept that to myself. I got the sense that she was uncomfortable in these surroundings and I could understand why. Everything had a slight crust on it and a bit of an oily sheen; that was just the texture of the paint. You got used to it. I hoped she would have the chance to learn that herself.

"Would you like to go for a walk with me?"

"Out there?" She looked through our open window, and I nodded. "Can I? I mean, will I even be able to? God, I can't wrap my mind around what is happening right now. This all feels like some kind of a dream."

She might have felt out of place, but she was not fearful. Or maybe she didn't know if she'd ever be back and was eschewing all fear for the time being. She eventually answered my question with a nod, and I led her out into the garden. We walked past the chair my mother inhabited all day, which she had thankfully vacated for the night. We wandered down the path and made our way toward Aurora, the statue in our garden, who had chosen to stick around tonight, lounging in her usual spot beside the pond. Aurora was a mix of mediums, a painting of a statue, posed by day with one arm draped in the air, her hand behind her head. She'd relaxed her stance for the evening, resting on her elbows. She turned her head toward us as we passed and the silhouette of her jaw dropped.

Of course Claire noticed. "So, you're all alive in here?"

Alive. I didn't know how to answer that. I said, "When the museum is open, we must remain where we're supposed to. But at night, we're free to move about as we please."

"It's like *Night at the Museum*. Does that make me Ben Stiller? Or like that scene in *Mary Poppins* where they jump in through the chalk drawing." She was laughing now; she had completely lost me, but I just stood there, soaking her in.

"Where are the others? You're not always alone in your painting."

"Yes, that's my family. My mother and brother are probably at a friend's home or resting or reading. I'm not quite sure what they do to pass the nights. It's been a while since I asked. My sister, she's the social one. She's probably at a party in one of the nearby galleries."

"You can move from room to room?"

"We can move between paintings."

"Wow. That's so freaking cool."

"Others seem to think so. I tend to stay in our room, in our frame. I don't really see a reason to move around. To spend every night making small talk with the same people. Our museum never changes, no new paintings ever come in. Every night is just the same."

She nodded. I wondered if Claire was more like Marguerite or like me. Would she dance her way from scene to scene? Would she have cultivated a network of friends, never to be left alone with an empty evening?

"But you, you can see us. You've been watching," I said.

"Yeah. I mean, yes," she answered. "At first, I thought I must be imagining things. I'm newly afraid all the time that I'm losing my mind. To be totally honest, I'm not so sure I'm not losing it at this very minute."

"If you're losing yours, surely I'm losing mine too." Whatever this was, we were in it together. I wanted her to know that.

"I started to notice that there were small changes from night to night—sometimes you'd be alone, sometimes your— you said she's your sister?"

"She is."

"Sometimes your sister would be there with you. Some of the other paintings had the same thing happening. And then there was this woman in the gallery just before yours who I think maybe was playing, like, Simon Says with me."

"'Simon says'? Who is Simon?"

"There is no Simon. It's this game we play out there as children. Where you, like, imitate what someone else is doing. Like this woman with these flowers draped across her body." She gestured to where the flowers hung. I nodded to indicate that I knew whom she was talking about. "She would move her body into a certain position and then I'd copy her and then she'd move it another way."

"Flowers draped across her body, that must be Andromeda," I reasoned.

"Andromeda, what a name."

"Did you ever tell anyone about any of this?" I was incredibly nervous to hear her answer. As excited as I was that she could see us, I knew where the danger in all of this could be hiding.

She shook her head. "No—partly because I worried people would seriously think something was wrong with me. But also because I figured no one in my life outside here would care or believe me. And I didn't want to tell anyone here because I really, really don't want to lose this job." She looked around, suddenly remembering she had work to do. She hurried through the rest of her thoughts. "I don't know if I'm the only one who can see or if no one else is looking."

"I'm happy you looked. And kept looking."

"Yeah," she said. "Me too." We walked in silence for a handful of minutes before Claire began the conversation again. "I'm not normally like this, you know."

"Like what?" I asked.

"Like, whimsical in any way. I'm so logical it's scary. Life keeps you in line, you know. I don't try things like this. I don't even really daydream anymore."

"Well," I said slyly. "Good thing it's nighttime."

We had made a natural loop around the path that ran alongside the pond and through the gardens. It had taken us back up to the house. From where we stood, you could see through the open living room window and into the gallery, blurry from this vantage point.

"I think I probably have to get back out there and do my job. I have no idea how long it's been since I came in here, but I probably need to speed-clean if I don't want to make anyone suspicious about . . . this."

"Right, yes, needless to say," I said, even though I was obviously hesitant to let her go.

"Would it be okay if . . ." She hesitated but pushed forward. "Would you be down if I came back tomorrow? Would you help me back in?"

"Yes, dear god, yes. Please come back. I'll be here. Of course." We slowly progressed into the living room and arrived back at the frame.

She smiled. "And you can hear me? When I'm out there?"

"Yes, I can. But please, don't stop singing on my account."

"Maybe . . . no promises." I held her hand as she lowered herself to sit on the frame's edge. "Bye, Jean," she said before she swung her legs around and out into the gallery. She hopped to her feet and turned to face me. I raised a hand to wave goodbye, and she raised one in return.

I didn't want to leave my living room; I didn't know where I would go or whom I might bump into and I wasn't ready to talk about this, so I sat down in my chair and I picked up my book. I had no intention of reading it, but I needed something to hold to keep me tethered to the moment. I didn't trust my body not to combust into a million pieces, as it felt like it might do.

Claire hustled over to her mop and bucket and began whirling her way across the room. When she was done, she hurried to the exit, but she didn't leave before she'd turned around and given me a little nod of goodbye.

"How was your evening?" a familiar voice asked me as the

sun rose through the gallery windows. I turned to find my sister peeling her way into the room, pinning her hair up as she took her usual seat at the piano bench.

I mumbled a sound that implied it had been fine and didn't ask how hers was in return. I couldn't tell if she somehow already knew. And I didn't know how I would tell Marguerite. I had no desire to share this night with anyone. I wanted to keep Claire's magic all to myself, for now.

I was saved by Pierre rushing into the room; he hopped up next to Marguerite and her attention was instantly distracted. She didn't press me for more. I was sure in that moment that she must not know, for she couldn't possibly have left it there if she did. Aurora had let this secret stay mine for a bit longer. I needed to thank her the next time I got the chance.

9

CLAIRE

My feet hit the ground beneath the frame harder than I anticipated, like I was quite literally crashing back to reality. I was still reeling from the past hour. Had I fallen, slipped on a puddle of soapy water, and slammed my head on the bench? Was this a hallucination, the early symptoms of a concussion? At least I had real health insurance for the first time in forever.

I took a chance and looked back over my shoulder and there he was, Jean, standing up, out of his chair, looking back at me. My new friend, I guessed you could call him. He was smiling and lifted his hand into a small wave. I returned it, feeling a wave of shyness rush over me. I couldn't remember a time when someone had ever just watched me the way he was doing now. Not waiting for anything, not expecting anything, just watching me because he could. It was sweet but activated my self-consciousness and suddenly, I needed to get out of there. But first, I had to do my job.

When I was done cleaning, I rushed over to my cart and rolled out of the room, giving Jean another little nod goodbye. As soon as I cleared the doorway, I hurried to the nearest corner I could find and sank down into a crouch. I just needed a moment, just a moment to figure out what the heck just happened and how I felt about it. If it had actually happened.

My fingers roamed the fabric of the sleeves of my uniform, my arms crossed over my chest. A few days ago, I'd been upgraded to the proper size; they had to order it specially for me and I guessed I had lasted long enough for them to go ahead and do so. I was small, notably so. I had been my entire life. I had never fit into anything that fit anyone else. Pinnies they handed out in gym class hung on me like a dress. Most of the time, I had hated it. It was hard to feel like I'd ever measure up.

But I could fit *into* just about any space. It came in handy—reaching my hand behind a piece of furniture to grab dropped keys, slipping under the bed to find a rogue sock, or in that moment, sliding my body in between the cart and the wall, creating a place where I could be alone. Except, as I looked up at the wall above me, heavy with art, I realized I'd never truly be alone in this place.

The people in the paintings overhead paid me no mind; they continued on about their evenings as if I wasn't having a mental breakdown and questioning my own sanity in their midst. The painting to my right was on a much smaller scale than Jean's living room but, if I was looking for it, I could still see the movements of their tiny arms, the clinking of their miniature wineglasses, the shaking of their heads. I stared at them, a little lost in the wonder of it all, until I remembered why I was sitting there.

The way I saw it, there were two options. The first was that something was very, very wrong with my brain because this wasn't just a moment of hallucination, a daydream gone absolutely rampant, in which I had convinced myself I'd been inside a painting and gone for a walk with its subject. Maybe it was some kind of imbalance. Too much coffee today, not enough sleep, I'd been too close to the cleaning chemicals.

No, it wasn't as simple as that, because as I sat there on the floor, I was sure that I was still noticing changes and movement in all the art around me. And if I was honest, I'd been seeing it for weeks.

So that led me to option two: that I was right. That everything I had just experienced was real, that these paintings were alive in their own way and that I had a—seemingly—unique ability to visit them. I only said *unique* because if there were other people who could do this, wouldn't we know? Wouldn't everyone be talking about it? Wouldn't art take on a whole new place in society, not just as something quarantined on the walls of museums but as narrators of history? Watchers of time? Did I have to tell someone about my discovery?

"Holy shit," I whispered as my mind spun with the possibilities. And just as quickly as that window of thought opened, I shut it again. Just as I'd said to Jean, I knew I could never tell anyone about this. They would only see the first option, that I was unstable and potentially insane. And what if they thought I'd be a danger to the art? They'd never let me back in here.

That could be the end of everything. What if I could only do this here, in this museum? Was there something special about this place? Before I'd started working here, I'd come to visit just once before, as a kid on that field trip. Did this have to do with that? No, I could never tell anyone who had anything to do with this museum. And would anyone in my life outside the museum even care? I thought about what it would be like to try to convince them, of their reactions, of the way they could make me feel small.

I cleared that train of thought from my head. I needed this job too much. Our landlord had let us know earlier in the week that the rent would be going up again, the third year in a row. I'd spent the last three days doing the math and we could afford it, barely, but we couldn't handle another gap in my employment. Not right now, before I'd had a chance to set anything aside.

This would be my little secret, I decided. Well, mine and Jean's, of course. I felt something when I thought about him, a hint of embarrassment, maybe. A flush in my cheeks, a slight racing of my heart. He had been so warm, so easy to be with. And so different from anyone I'd ever met. We shared none of the same worries of the world. For the hour we'd spent together, I'd forgotten about all the things that usually fog my brain. I'd just been happy to be there, talking to someone new, learning little bits and pieces about him, looking into his steady brown eyes.

"Oh my god," I said aloud. "Do I actually have a . . . *crush?*" The woman in the painting above me looked down at me, a little twinkle in her eye. She raised her glass. I forgot they could hear me. I groaned and checked my watch. It was just past midnight and there was still work that had to get done.

10

JEAN

kept a closer eye on the patrons the next day, but I didn't even know what I was looking for. I thought about testing a few of the guests who lingered in front of us, wondering what would happen if I stood or moved about, but I knew I was frozen in place for the duration of the day. Whether it was magic or my own sense of decorum, I couldn't say. But the insatiable desire to crawl out of my frame that had gripped me for the past few weeks was subdued today. For once, I knew, or hoped I knew, the outside world would be coming to me.

That night, Claire rushed into the gallery and walked right up to me. I was waiting for her, sitting on the floor with my legs crossed at the ankles like a young boy. From this position, we were just about at eye level.

"Hi," she said with a smile. I waved and mouthed "hello" in return. "Tonight, I'm going to get my work out here done first so I don't have to worry about it once I come in, okay?" I nodded; anything she wanted was fine with me. "Okay." She gave me a thumbs-up. "Be back in a bit."

She returned to her supplies and pulled a tangle of thin white cords out of her pocket, inserting them into her cellphone and pushing play. At first, she was silent as she began her cleaning of the gallery, but I soon heard her softly singing, not full songs but brief snippets. I thought she might be singing along to something I couldn't hear. I felt weird watching her; now that she knew I was here, it felt like an invasion of her privacy. I got up and sat at the piano bench for a bit, flipping through the sheet music Marguerite and Pierre kept on the music stand. Maybe I could learn something new to play on the violin. I began feeling out the rhythm and despite myself, got a bit lost in the moment.

As I played, I grew anxious. What if we couldn't repeat the magic that we'd performed the night before? What if it was a onetime occurrence? Or if it had all been a dream of some kind? I shuddered at the thought and looked back out into the room. Claire was standing in front of the frame.

"Okay," she announced. "I'm ready."

I crossed to her immediately, kneeling down to offer my hand. She grasped it and I pulled her in, holding my breath the entire time. This time, she gave herself a bit of a push. The whole maneuver was much more graceful than what we'd done the night before.

"Hi," she said once she had found her footing.

"Bonsoir," I replied, delighted that all my fears had been for naught.

"Bonsoir, how fancy." We brushed our clothes back into place, both of us in uniform, in a way, now that I thought about it: Claire in what the job required, me in my only option.

"How was your day?" I asked, as if this was the start of any normal conversation.

"It was good. Fine. Actually, I don't really remember. All I could really think about was getting back here."

"I'm familiar with that feeling myself."

"I'm not," Claire confessed. "It was incredibly distracting. Should we go for another walk?" she asked. This time, she led me to the open garden door. "I feel like I've got to do something with my legs."

I liked her proactivity. I responded, "Yes, let's do that," and followed her lead. I pulled my cigarette case from my inner jacket pocket and offered her one.

"Oh, god no. Ew," she said with a wrinkle of her nose.

"What?" I asked, pulling the case back toward myself. I was a bit embarrassed by her reaction.

"Smoking is, like, not a thing anymore. Well, I guess it still is in some places. My grandmother still smokes, even though I've been trying to help her quit for years. She thinks she hides it from me, but I know."

"Well, where I come from, smoking is very much a thing," I said as I pulled a cigarette out and lit it.

"And where is that?" Claire asked.

"France."

"What part of France are you from?"

"Are you familiar with the country?"

"No, god no. I mean, I wish. It just seemed like a proper thing to ask."

"It's been a very long time since I was there, in Paris. I can't imagine what it's like now. I wouldn't say I'm familiar with it either, at this point."

"Where are we now?" She gestured to the garden around us.

"The neighborhood just to the south of Paris where my family's house is. It's called Issy-les-Moulineaux."

She repeated it back to me, butchering the French with a smile and I was overwhelmingly charmed. I complimented her on her attempt. "If only you saw how it was spelled."

"And what year is it?" she asked.

"In here? I think it's 1917."

"1917, wow," Claire said as she took in her surroundings. "What was life like in 1917?"

"Dark," I said. "We were in the midst of a war and every day brought some kind of danger."

"I've never experienced a war at home like that, but I can imagine how scary that would have been." She said it with such care, I felt her empathy wrap around me like an embrace.

Night after night, we walked and we talked. I became obsessed by chatting with Claire. There was something about getting to talk to her that was better than I could have ever anticipated in those imaginary conversations I used to dream of. She was a real person, intense and questioning and funny.

"It's so awesome," Claire mused one night. "Even when I thought I could see you all moving in the paintings, I still thought of you as art, like it was an effect of some kind. I never imagined what the sound of your voice would be like or that we'd even be able to converse."

"Maybe that's better," I joked. "Then you're not over there thinking, 'Wow, his voice is so much more grating than I expected.'"

"Never," she said sincerely. "You have a perfect voice." Her compliment dangled in the atmosphere between us like a swing just abandoned by a child.

Conversation flowed easily between us. We were both hungry to learn more about each other, but she preferred to answer my questions with ones of her own, putting the spotlight back on me. But I stumped her when I asked if she'd ever considered herself an artist. I told her I'd noticed the care she took to see each of us here on the walls.

She dropped her jaw at the suggestion. "You'd put me in the same sentence as the works in this room? That makes me laugh out loud," she said, but I heard no such laughter. "No," she continued, "I've really never been very good at any kind of art, not even doodling in class and stuff. I just like to look at it. Where I come from, there aren't a lot of places to even do that. Not like this, at least."

"Where is it that you come from?"

"A little town just a few hours away from here, if you just drive, like, straight west into the state. I remember hearing someone say one time that it was one of the poorest towns in the country. Not sure if that's actually true, but it sure as hell felt that way sometimes. We never really went anywhere else for my whole life, had no way to get there, so art-wise, we got what we had.

"I'd never been to a museum until I was eleven," she went on. "My school held a contest and anyone who wrote an essay about art would be included in a field trip to come here. Well, not here, this was before they'd moved all of the art to the city. We went to the old location, but you know, same art. You remember that old place better than me, I'm sure," she said. I nodded; a single curl had come loose from her bun. I tucked it behind her ear and she blushed. She continued.

"I didn't really know anything about art. Or anything about anything. But my mom had this one print that hung in our kitchen, no frame, just thumbtacks in the corners. She probably found it on the street; she was always bringing stuff back other people thought was trash. It drove everyone else up the wall. But this print was bright and sunny, and I used to stare at it every day. I literally couldn't help myself; I couldn't keep my eyes off it.

"It was of a kitchen, but that kitchen was nothing like the one I sat in while I ate my cereal or my noodles or whatever had made its way to the table that night. I'd stare up at it and imagine I was there—it was warm and yellow and had flowers on the table and a window that looked out on these green hills, and it's in that style where all the lines are a little wobbly, and it felt like something from that moment right before you wake up where your dream starts to shake back into your reality.

"I was a super short kid; I was always the smallest in the class, and I always felt like if that picture had been just a little closer to the ground, a little closer to me, maybe I'd know it even better.

"So anyway, there's this essay contest and you just had to write about art, any art, so I wrote a story about a little girl who loved a painting and she stood and looked at it every single day, but it was just a little too high up on the wall. One day, she stood so tall on her tiptoes, peering down into the painting, that she lost her balance. She fell forward and her nose hit the canvas, except it didn't hit the canvas, she just kept going. She toppled end over end and when she landed on her butt, she realized she was smack-dab in the kitchen of the painting. And it was real to her. She could sit at the table and feel the sun on her face and smell the grass on the hills through the window. It felt like a dream, but she never had to wake up.

"And I submitted the story and I won. I think even my mom was proud of me. Actually, that might have been the last time I ever felt that she was. The school brought the whole class here. And we wound our way through all the rooms and there was art everywhere, not just one painting on each wall but five or seven or ten paintings all together, and they were in frames and it was overwhelming.

"Because I'd won the contest, they printed my story and gave a copy of it to all the other students on the trip. People laughed at me because no one else had written a story, they had all written some boring essays just listing the things they could see in a random piece of art because they'd wanted to go on the field trip so they could skip class for the day. Except for my one friend, Brianna, who told me she thought what I'd written was so cool and that we should try it ourselves. So, at one point, when the teachers weren't watching us, we crept over to a painting that was so big, the bottom of the frame was below our knees, and we started to get up on our tiptoes, when a guard came running over. He scared the crap out of us and yelled at us for standing too close to the art. We backed off and ran to rejoin our group.

"I never thought to try it again. I had no idea it would actually work." She smiled a little bit. "I wonder if Brianna's been doing it this whole time," she said.

Part of me thought about telling her right then and there that I was in love with her, but my fear of coming off as the heartsick lonely man in the painting, desperate to fall for the first girl he had touched in decades, kept me quiet for the moment. The intensity of my feelings shocked me; nevertheless, I was certain that there were no other words to describe the way I'd come to feel about Claire.

And of course this wasn't the first opportunity I'd had. People fell in and out of love all of the time in our network of interconnected art. I knew Marguerite had her fair share of past dalliances. I think my mother had even had a suitor or two try to catch her eye, though she was a tough woman to please, but I'd never had the same luck within our world. Time had shown me that it was me, not them, who could never make it fit. I had only myself to blame for my self-imposed solitude.

"Does she know that her kitchen painting started it all, your mom?" I asked.

"No," Claire said. "I don't speak to her anymore." She offered no further explanation and I certainly was not going to press. I allowed silence to fill the holes of the conversation.

Claire took her hair down and screwed it back up. When she had finished and relaxed her hands at her sides, I reached to hold one of them in mine. While we clasped palms each night as I pulled her into my world, this was something hitherto unexplored. A little squeeze from her let me know she was feeling it too.

CLAIRE

I stumbled away from Jean's gallery that night, giving him a small wave from the doorway before I disappeared down the hall. My legs were wobbling and my heart was racing; once I was safely out of his sight, I stopped to catch my breath.

It had all started when he brushed one of my perpetually out-of-place curls away from my face, his fingers warm against my forehead. Sparks had followed his touch, and I wanted the curl to fall back out of place so he would do it again.

I'd covered for my obnoxious heart, beating so loudly I was sure he could hear it, by plowing on through that story about my first visit to this museum. I'd even snapped at him when he asked about my mom, my brain putting up all its usual walls to keep us protected. But then he went and took my hand in his, not to shake or to help me get somewhere, just to hold, and my body went on the fritz all over again.

There was just something about him. Even though I hardly

knew him, with him I felt like a whole new version of myself. I could show him all the pieces of my brain, even the ones I hadn't fully figured out. He seemed to understand all of it. He was so much more alive than I ever could have dreamed during all those weeks I'd spent staring at his painting, wishing he could talk back. I couldn't wait to see him again.

I needed to get back to work, but as I surveyed my next assignment, curiosity got the better of me. Of course Jean's living room had been the right place to start. I would never have worked up the confidence to try to cross through without his obvious invitation. I would have been too embarrassed to try and fail, even if it was just in front of the other paintings. But now that I was alone and aware of what I was capable of, I wondered if my abilities were confined just to that gallery or to that frame. Did I need Jean's help to make it through? Would my magic work in other paintings? Would it work in other museums, or was there something special about this place?

I picked a warm landscape, a few trees on the beach leading to the bluest ocean I had ever seen. It was tranquil, empty of any inhabitants except for some sailboats in the distance. The shady sand looked like a soft place to land if I stumbled on my entrance.

The bottom of the frame came right up to my waist. I placed both of my hands on it, preparing to kick off the ground, when I heard a voice call across the room.

"Claire!" Linda bellowed. I lost my balance, cutting my jump short and stumbling backward. I landed on my butt and she walked over, offering me her hand. "What in god's name are you doing? Trying to lick the paintings?"

"Just got a little excited trying to dust the frames is all." I laughed it off. "How have you been?"

"Can't complain, can't complain. You done in here? I was just heading out, if you want to walk out with me."

"Yup, all set!" I answered before she could get a good look at the place and realize I'd only just begun. "Let's get our stuff and I'll walk you to your car. How's Didi?"

That was a close call, closer than I ever needed to be again. I needed to be smart about this. I'd be more wary of where Linda was in the museum before I next dared to try something like that.

Jean and I picked up the next night right where we'd left off.

"What about you?" I asked. "Are you an artist?"

"I don't know," he confided. "I loved to create things as a kid, but I wasn't even twenty when I was frozen in this version of myself. I'd just left for the war a few weeks before and had kind of put making plans on hold until I learned more about what life had in store for me. Maybe I would have been a great soldier and would have traveled up through those ranks. Or maybe I would have died young. Or maybe I would have survived and done something else entirely. I loved art, but that always seemed like my father's calling. I don't know if it was mine too."

I wanted to know more about Jean—I'd offered up bits and pieces of myself the last few nights, but I couldn't help but ask him more questions every chance I got. I wanted to know everything.

"He painted you and your family, your father did?"

"He did," Jean confirmed. "He painted us from memory, placing us where he wanted to see us in this domestic scene. I was gone, training for the army."

"But he didn't paint himself into the painting?"

"No, just the rest of us. He's the uncaptured viewer. It's honest, truth be told, to how we operated as a family unit. It would have been a bit bizarre to have him in here with us forever."

"So, you are . . . were?" I slowed down for a moment. I didn't want to offend him, but I was desperate to understand how this all worked. "You're a real person? Or you were at some point before you were made in this world? Not that you're not a real person now—clearly you are—" Somehow, we were holding hands again. I tapped the back of his hand with my thumb as if to prove my own point. "But in my world? There exists—or existed—another version of you?"

"Yes, I guess that's kind of how I see it," he replied. "But I realize now that I just assume that's how it works. I don't have any real way of knowing."

"And you don't know what happened to other-world you?" I asked.

"I mean . . ." He was being surprisingly sheepish. I waited, giving him time to fill in the silence. "Part of me hopes that the me out there became an artist. But I was so young, it embarrasses me a little now. I don't know if I really was on the precipice of having some kind of talent or if I was just saying what I thought my father wanted to hear. I did hear a guide say something about it once."

"What did they say?"

"They called Pierre a collector—the guides talk about that occasionally. He must have been a big deal. But this guide, he also described me, calling me a sculptor, I think," Jean admitted. "For months, I was desperate to know more, but it was never mentioned again. It was so brief; I wasn't even sure I'd heard them correctly."

"I could google it, if you wanted me to," I said. I wasn't sure why I hadn't thought to do so before, but I could answer this question. I could help Jean fill in this puzzle piece.

"What does that mean—'google'?" he asked.

"That I could look it up on the internet," I explained, not sure how deep I needed to go into my explanation of search engines and the World Wide Web.

"Could I ask you for a favor?"

"Of course," I said, wondering where he was going with this.

"Could you not look it up? I don't know what access you have to newspaper records or whatever sources might give you the answer, but I'm a different man from the man I was out there. I've spent many, many years as this version of myself. And while I don't know what happened to the former me out there, I don't want more versions of me to live in your head. I want it, this, to just be us. Does that make any sense?"

"Sure," I said. I was surprised by his question. I hadn't really assumed he had anything in common with the man he was more than a century ago in a different world. I tried to explain why this request didn't bother me. "I mean, the many versions part gets a little screwy in my head when I try to think about it too deeply, but I get what you're asking. This is just about us. But—" I knew this was my moment to get all that I wanted, all that I craved, which was just knowing Jean. "You have to give me a little more. Who is *this* Jean? Who are you in here?"

So, he let me in. He gave me so many little pieces of himself. He confided in me that he was a little afraid of his older sister, Marguerite, that their relationship had always been somewhat fraught. Marguerite and Jean's dad had a complex relationship and the trauma from that still haunted her. But she was also like another mother to Jean. I loved hearing him talk about his siblings and his mother, what their relationships were like, how Marguerite and Pierre had gotten closer out of sheer proximity in the painting.

"Do you have relationships with other people in here?" I asked on another night as we circled the garden path yet again.

"What, like friendships? Or like love?" he asked.

"Oh, I meant friendships," I said, taken aback by his reply. "But now I obviously need to know about the love part." Was that jealousy that was heating the back of my neck? I told that voice inside my head to stop being ridiculous.

"Well, yes, relationships pop up in here all the time. Some are short-lived, some people have been together for decades."

"You didn't really answer my question," I pointed out. "I was asking about you."

"I've had a few—um—dalliances before." He coughed and I gave him one of those looks. "But nothing really of note. And nothing for a long time."

"What about people like me? Has anyone ever knocked on your frame before?" I asked mostly as a joke, but the look on Jean's face told me I had struck a chord. "Wait, really, though? Who was she? What happened?" He looked so stricken. "It's okay, Jean. You can tell me."

"It was a long time ago, multiple decades at this point."

"And there was someone else who could see you?"

"A new curator, just out of school, probably only two or three years older than me. She had just joined the team. Well, she had joined in the sense that she had technically been hired as staff at the museum. But the men in charge of the foundation at that time, they basically refused to acknowledge her presence. They would walk through the halls and leave her trailing ten steps behind them. I watched them turn away whenever she dared to raise an idea, carrying on as if their ears couldn't hear the sound of her voice. You could just see it on her face—she'd fought hard for this position and the reality of it was a bitter one."

"That sucks," I said.

"It did; it sucked. Did I use that right?" he asked. I nodded. "The foundation has come so far in its leadership. But not fast enough. This woman, Ellen, she started wandering the museum by herself instead of following the pack as they moved through the galleries. She visited us often. And she started to feel like a friend. She'd come by after the museum had closed with a notebook or a sketch pad and just hang out. She was brilliant with a pencil. She'd draw these little comics of her interactions at the museum. And when she was done, she would turn her pad around and show them to me."

"Oh," I gasped. "So she knew you could see?"

"I think so," Jean said. "At first, I thought I was just her imaginary friend." I smiled, knowing I'd called him exactly that before I'd met him. "But after some time, I could tell she was really watching me, watching us. And while I could never speak back to her, she kept talking to me, showing her drawings to me."

"What happened to her? Did she get a new job? Somewhere they respected her?"

Jean shuddered. "The horrible part is I'll never truly know. The knowledge of our secret world, she couldn't keep it in for very long. I get it; she had dedicated her life to art and here she was with this discovery that could change everything."

"But they didn't believe her." I guessed the ending to this story.

"Not even for a second, they didn't even try. They mocked her mercilessly when she tried to explain."

"And then they fired her?"

"If they didn't, they made her so uncomfortable that she was forced to find another position. I haven't seen her in a very, very long time."

"That's heartbreaking. And she never came back."

"No, it's been dozens of years, but I do think I'd still recognize her."

"That must have been hard for you, losing a friend." I could see the lingering hurt in his eyes.

"It was," Jean said. "It wasn't just how lonely I felt when she was gone. It was also that I felt complicit in her dismissal, in the way they'd tortured her. Like I'd shown her too much, gotten her in trouble. I took it really personally."

"But you didn't do anything," I assured him. "That world was stacked against her. It's not your fault that she could see more than those men ever could."

"I put her in danger. I could tell she could see the real me and I didn't follow any of our usual rules of decorum. I didn't stay frozen for her. You have to keep this a secret, Claire," Jean begged. "I mean, you don't have to do anything, of course. But I can't imagine what I would do if the same thing happened to you."

I felt my heart flutter; I loved how much he cared. Goodbye always came before we were ready, but it was time and I had to get back out to my real world.

"Don't worry about that," I said. "I'm not going anywhere." I made to leave for my world but changed my mind and turned back to Jean. I stood on my tiptoes, just for a moment, and placed a whisper of a kiss on his cheek.

JEAN

Monday and Tuesday, Claire's two nights off, nearly killed me, but Wednesday finally arrived, as it always did. We were reunited like nothing significant had happened the previous weekend. Claire cleaned and clambered through the frame. We ignored the fact that everything had changed when she'd kissed me on the cheek. It was all I'd been able to think about for three days, but from the moment she arrived, I could tell she didn't want to discuss it so I followed her lead. I lit a cigarette and we strolled along the usual path through the garden. As we headed in the direction of Aurora, Claire interrupted the silence to ask a question.

"Why does she—I'm sorry, does she have a name?" We'd walked past Aurora a handful of times, but Aurora hadn't yet spoken directly to Claire.

Now Aurora answered for herself. "I'm Aurora."

"It's a pleasure to meet you," Claire said with an awkward

demi-curtsy. "I've been trying to figure this out and have come up totally empty. Why does Aurora look so much larger from farther away?" She was right; if a viewer of the painting assumed that perspective was working the way we understood it in the natural world, Aurora should be two or three meters tall. But when we walked up to her, she was tiny.

"It has something to do with my father and the way he was able to weave humor into his work. *Aurora* is a real statue out in your world as well, and that statue is the size you see here, about half a meter long. My father loved to paint his own work into new paintings, so when he included her again here, he kept her original size."

"I'm not the only one here too," Aurora chimed in. "He was kind of obsessed with this pose of a woman leaning on her side, propped up on one elbow, the other hand reaching behind her just so—" Aurora demonstrated, folding herself naturally back into the posture she held all day long. "I think the first one of our kind was in *Le Bonheur de vivre*."

"Le what de what?" Claire asked.

"Another one of his paintings that's also in this museum," I said.

"You haven't taken her over there yet?" Aurora asked with false astonishment. She'd been around often enough to know that we'd not yet moved beyond the well-worn paths of the garden. "You have to make him take you. That place is the most fun, no competition."

"Take me there? You think I can move between paintings, like you?"

"It seems to me there's no harm in trying," Aurora said. "Don't you want to see where Marguerite and the others go when you two are flirting it up all around our backyard?"

I felt hot with embarrassment, too afraid to look at Claire for her reaction. "Well," Aurora continued. "You two have so much to explore. You best get started." She raised her stone eyebrows at me. It hadn't been purposeful, keeping Claire all to myself. We just had so much about each other to get to know. And I wasn't much in the habit of leaving our landscape. And I was somewhat afraid of running into Marguerite. But I hadn't considered that I was keeping Claire from experiencing even more.

"Would you like to go see what it's like over there?" I asked her.

"Absolutely."

"Well, then." I took her hand in mine. "Let's get on our way."

"Have fun!" Aurora said. "Don't do anything I wouldn't do."

"And then some . . ." I muttered to myself as Claire called out her goodbyes to Aurora. We headed back into the trees, climbing the hill at the end of our garden. Claire's silence was comfortable, mine was anxious. I hadn't spent much time thinking about the possibility of having to share Claire with the others. I was unsure of what to expect. I wondered where Marguerite was tonight.

As we crested the hill, the world around us changed, the colors shifting from the cool, natural colors of my world to the fiery oranges, reds, and yellows of *Le Bonheur de vivre*.

"Wow," Claire exhaled, looking up at the pink sky peeking through the orange trees. "This is magic."

I chuckled. "I thought we knew that already."

"We absolutely did but this is a whole new level. I can't believe this is your life." The tone of her voice betrayed her jealousy.

"Just wait until you meet this cast of characters. They're . . . hard to describe. Maybe 'spirited' is the right word?"

"I hope they're okay with my being here," she said. I hoped the same. Not knowing what to say but wanting to seem, and feel, confident, I squeezed her hand in mine.

We walked through the trees into the central clearing and Claire uttered an involuntary "Oh my god" under her breath.

Around us, the ensemble of *Le Bonheur de vivre* mingled with the subjects of other paintings who had made their way here tonight as well, naked and clothed bodies alike laughing and drinking and dancing and embracing. I had forgotten how much more sound there was here; conversation rang across the field, a small band had formed off to the side, and the sounds of flutes swelled in accompaniment. Claire rocked back and forth on her feet, clearly eager to be a part of this joy but unsure if she'd be welcome.

We weren't alone for long. Quickly, a woman approached us, the red outlines of her body highlighting all the curves of her figure, flowers draped across her chest.

"Jean!" she exclaimed and kissed me on both cheeks.

"Andromeda," I greeted her in return. "It's nice to see you."

"Of course it is. You wouldn't have to be reminded of that if you came around more." She smiled to let me know this was all said with affection. "And you." She turned her attention to Claire. "You must be the young woman I've been hearing so much about."

"You're the one! The one who has been playing with me, trying to get me to copy you. But what do you mean you've heard of me?" Claire was dumbstruck by both this revelation and the kisses Andromeda was placing on each of Claire's cheeks as she said it.

"Just a bit of teasing, that's all," Andromeda defended herself to me. "And heard of you? Chérie, you're the talk of the town. Isn't she?" Andromeda asked, as she raised her glass in the air. The crowd across the field let out a large cheer in response to her toast, even if they hadn't heard a single word she'd said. Claire couldn't help but smile.

"Everyone is wondering how you do what you do. How do you get in here, on that note?"

"I don't really understand it myself," Claire confessed. "I just felt like I could, if I got close enough, and one day it worked."

"There's certainly more to dissect there, but it's hardly the time. It's a party, after all! Can we get you a drink?" Andromeda gestured with the stone goblet in her hand and something that resembled wine splashed up against the edge.

"I think yes. Please. Thank you," Claire said enthusiastically. Andromeda took Claire's hand in hers and led her across the field, introducing Claire to each group of people we passed. I trailed behind them, listening to Andromeda as she took charge of introductions.

"This is Claire! Yes, of course, *that* Claire." Andromeda's statement was met by yet another chorus of cheers. We approached the group of dancers and were quickly saddled with our own glasses of the deep red liquid. "Santé!" Andromeda called as she tapped her glass against ours. Claire took a sip and grinned. "Do you like it?" Andromeda asked.

"It's delicious. Sweet but not too sweet? I love it," Claire said as she took another sip and Andromeda raised her eyebrows at me. "What are you celebrating?" Claire asked her.

"Celebrating?"

"The party?"

"Oh." Andromeda laughed. "This is just what we do. Every night is a party!" A third cheer in response among the revelers confirmed this. "I guess tonight we might be celebrating your joining us, even though we got started before we knew you'd be coming." This last comment was pointed at me.

"Aurora recommended we stop by," I said.

"I should have known," Andromeda answered. "Well, I'll leave you two to explore. Claire, you are welcome anytime and every time. I hope to see you again, and soon."

"Me too. Thank you," Claire said earnestly. Andromeda frolicked back to join another group. We set up camp in a shady spot, resting our backs against a large tree trunk and taking it all in.

"What do you think?" I asked.

"I love it, it's amazing. Everyone here is so . . ." She searched for the words as her eyes found a couple locked in an embrace so intense that it would not be acceptable in most public spaces. "Free."

"Have you looked at this one much from the other side?"

"Not as carefully. Not yet at least. I don't have a lot of time in that gallery."

"Well, now's our chance. What do you want to do?"

"Everything. I want another glass of whatever this is." She shook her empty goblet at me. "And I want to dance and I want to see those little goats over there and lie in the grass and try it all."

I obliged. We refilled our glasses and crouched down next to the goats, who were happy to receive our scratches on their heads as they snacked. We joined hands with the others and danced in a circle, spinning around and around until we clutched at our heads, laughing off the dizziness. We lay in the grass, eyes on the pink sky, and let the sounds of the flutes wrap around us like a light blanket. We ate sweet sugary confections that matched the rainbow colors of the landscape. My jacket and tie were cast aside, crumpled in a pile somewhere twenty meters away, and Claire's hair was freed from its usual place on the top of her head, curls tumbling down around her shoulders.

"I haven't felt like this in forever," she said. "This is what I always thought growing up was going to feel like—one big party. I couldn't have been more wrong."

"I don't think I've ever felt like this," I said as I rolled onto my side to face her. Her expression was one big smile, which got even wider when she saw that I was looking at her. We held that eye contact long past the moment when it might have ended. I needed to kiss her. Instead, I asked a question. "What has growing up felt like?"

"Like one long string of responsibilities." She let out a sigh as she took a big swig of her drink. "Like there's always something I'm falling short on, always something I'm behind on, always something I didn't do well enough. I know I'm too young to feel this way, but it seems like life is already passing me by." Claire chewed on her bottom lip. "But it's not all bad, of course; sometimes life is beautiful and awe-inspiring in ways I never could have expected. I just have to remember to take the time to see it."

"I think we all feel that way sometimes," I said. "Even in a place like this, where it feels like there's nothing but time."

"Do you ever wish you could leave this world?" she asked. Her question took me by surprise.

"Of course I have. I spend all day watching strangers for a fraction of time before they hustle back to their lives, wondering what it would be like if I could just follow them out through those doors, if that would give my life any sense of purpose. It feels like all there is to do in here is waste time, except time goes on forever. But, aside from its being physically impossible, it's been so long and so much must have changed; I can't even picture life out there. Your being here, my learning little things about your version of reality, it's bracing. The world out there is so much larger than I've been imagining it."

"But it used to be like that for you too, that large. Before, you know, you were in here."

"Yes, I guess you're right. One hundred years is a long time. I don't remember that as my reality anymore. It feels more like a dream."

"I can't even imagine."

"And I have barely a frame of reference for what your life is like. I can't even conjure up a mental image of what it looks like when you step out onto the street, just outside the museum walls."

"You've moved, though, right? Didn't the museum used to be outside the city?"

"Oh," I said, nodding. "Technically yes, we moved a handful

of years ago. It was a whole to-do; the collector had been so particular about what he acquired and how we were hung and who was allowed to come in and see us. He would deny access to some of the most elite members of the art society, back in the day, just because he could. He'd been so exacting about his specifications for the foundation that after he passed away, it took them years to get the approval to move us here. And even then, they did not want to change anything about the way we were displayed. That was one of the special components of the experience, after all, so they rebuilt the interior here exactly as it existed—"

Claire gasped and sat straight up. "No, no way."

". . . exactly as it existed in the old gallery."

"So to you all"—she gestured to the revelers who surrounded us on the lawn—"it looks exactly the same. You're staring at all the same things. All day long."

"Yes, precisely."

"That's . . ."

"Monotonous, certainly."

"I was going to say hella boring, but yeah, monotonous too." I laughed at how sincere her concern was. "Well"—she reclined against the yellow grass, her body casting an indigo shadow behind her—"there are worse places to be stuck."

"This is certainly true." *Especially now that you're here*—the words remained unspoken. I wanted to tell her how much these past few weeks had meant to me, how they had changed everything. Instead, I said, "Have you ever wished you could just stay here?"

"I am so entirely different in here," she said. I noticed that was not an answer to my question. "Like, outside this world, I'm all business. I don't even know how it happened, that wasn't what I was like when I was younger. But all of a sudden, bam. I'm an adult and all I can do is worry about everyone at home making it through to the next day."

"You're hardly a full-blown adult—how old are you?"

"Twenty-one. Technically, I guess. But I feel like I'm forty. I had to grow up pretty fast."

"I think I get what you mean," I said. The thoughts were coming to me as I said them. Normally, I waited to speak until I had time to process everything, sure that I meant what was coming out. But now I didn't want to wait. "I was still a teenager when I was dropped into this life. So I feel like I was just starting that part of my life. And I guess it exists here too, but it's different." What was different was her. If she hadn't walked right into my world, I would never have had the chance to meet anyone like her.

"Yeah," she agreed. "It's different but the same. It's not that I wouldn't want to stay here with you." She had returned to answer my question. "It just doesn't seem real. And this version of me, this person who asks every question that crosses her mind and jumps headfirst into someone else's home and drinks wine in the middle of a lawn, this just isn't the real me. But if all of that didn't exist, sure, I think I could be very happy here. I feel safe in here, with you."

"I'd be happy to have you. Any and all versions of you." We smiled at each other; I could feel the corners of my eyes crinkling as my smile stretched all the way up my face. She leaned forward and I thought, for a brief second, that she was going to kiss me. Instead, she grabbed her glass, draining it as she reclined.

I wanted to kiss her. This wasn't the first time the thought had crossed my mind, but if there was ever a moment, it felt like it was right now. I didn't, of course. I couldn't. I was frozen in place, an embarrassingly earnest grin on my face. I felt as restricted as I did during the day.

"I hate to be this person, in this moment," she groaned, "but I should probably get going. I've lost literally all sense of how long I've been here." She pulled her cellphone out of her pocket. It was the first time I had ever seen one up close. She brought the screen to life with the nearly indiscernible tap of her finger against a button I hadn't noticed. "Oh, how bizarre," she said, staring at the colorful piece of glass in her hands.

"What is it?" I asked.

"I don't have any service. It's like this world is a total dead zone."

"No service? What does that mean?"

"It means I don't have any reception. This thing"—she clutched the device in her hand—"won't work in here."

"It looks like it's working to me?"

"No, not working like that," she said. "It will physically turn on and, like, keep the time, but it won't be able to do any of its technological things that connect it to the outside world. Of course there's no cell reception in—what year is it in this painting?"

"1905 or 1906, I think."

"Oh my god, I have to get going," she said as she double-checked the numbers on the screen. "I shouldn't stay too long—what if I missed a call . . ."

I could tell she was getting panicky, though I couldn't imagine who would be calling at this hour. "Right, right, let's get you back," I assured her. I always regretted any chance that I could put her job in jeopardy. I stood and offered my hand to help her to her feet, a gesture we were now intimately familiar with. She rose and we made our way back, giving Andromeda our best.

"Come back and see us sometime! Please, do not be a stranger."

"Thank you! I promise I will," Claire said as Andromeda wrapped her arms around Claire, pulling her in tight for a hug. We headed back to the forest, the atmosphere around us turning bright orange and red as we made our way into the tree cover. I was moving hastily, worried about how much time had passed and who might notice how long Claire had been gone, so it took me by complete surprise when Claire stopped walking. Her hand was in mine and her halting was like an anchor; our arms were taut and I stopped, turning back to make sure everything was okay. As I turned, she pulled a bit, bringing my body in line with hers and suddenly, I was right in front of her and she was reaching her hands up to my face and bringing me closer for a kiss.

A firework went off somewhere around my kidneys and robbed my body of its breath. I stepped back, stunned, and saw worry clouding her face.

"I'm so sorry," she began, "I went too far. I just thought—" I'd regained my wits and I was back, wrapping my arms around her waist, her hands in my hair and our lips moving greedily against each other. I wanted to hold her so tightly that there'd be no air left between our bodies, but I also needed to run my hands over as much of her as I could possibly touch. After what somehow felt both like a lifetime and a few seconds, she pulled back; we were breathing heavily and she held my elbows in her hands, as if she'd lose her balance if we disconnected.

"I have to go," she said. "We shouldn't have done that." I opened my mouth to apologize, but she cut me off. "What I mean is, I really, really wanted that. But this feels so absurd. Is this even real life? Don't answer that." We slowly stumbled down the hill, back toward my house. As we approached the frame, she said, "I'll be back. The day after tomorrow." And even though I'd known she would be, it brought a swell of relief through my lungs to hear her say it. "I've got some things to figure out."

"I'll be here," I said, meaning it as a joke, but neither of us laughed. It felt more like a promise, one I wanted to double down on. "I'll wait; I can wait for as long as we need." I didn't know what exactly I was referring to, but it felt like what we both needed to hear right now.

"Okay," she said.

"Okay," I replied. She lifted up onto her toes to kiss me once more, before she crouched down and hopped back onto the gallery floor. She pushed her cart with her mop and bucket out of the room.

CLAIRE

I gripped the counter in the break room, leaning in with my full body weight, trying to force the contact of the linoleum against the palms of my hands to bring me back to reality. Not that I even knew what reality was anymore. Clearly my understanding of that word was at an all-time low.

Did I just kiss him? I tried to remember the last time I had gone in for a kiss, like, really gone for it and I came up with . . . nothing. Had I ever initiated a kiss before? Sure, I'd been kissed but that was different. This kiss was like something out of a movie.

I had known all night that Jean wanted to kiss me; he was all but saying the words out loud every time he looked into my eyes. And I wanted to kiss him too. I wanted to move closer to him, to let him know that somehow, when we were together, I felt both safe and like I was on the adventure of a lifetime. I'd never felt like this before. That was the kind of thing that happened to other people, not to me.

Speaking of other people, I looked down at the ring on my left hand. The stupid, clunky thing that had taken up so much more of my life than I'd ever meant to give it. It had only ever been a placeholder for a better life, an empty promise Jeremy had never planned to keep. He threw it my way to keep me from leaving him before he could leave me, never intending we'd actually get married. Why had I kept it on for all these years? Wishful thinking that he wasn't the scumbag that taking it off implied he was? Or an insurance policy, so I could always sell it and buy us a few more weeks if things got really bad?

If that was all it was, I could keep it somewhere else and live without the constant reminder of his failings. I turned my hand upside down and allowed it to slide off, clattering onto the counter. I flexed my fingers a few times, before I heard the recognizable shuffle of Linda's feet in the hallway. I shoved the ring down into the pocket of my jumpsuit.

"Howdy," I said as she entered the room. If I could have stared at my own self in disbelief, I would have. I had never said the word *howdy* in my entire life. I could feel all the wine we'd drunk tonight; it was making my heart race and my head swim. I couldn't remember the last time I'd drunk more than a beer. It must have been years. I needed to keep it together.

Linda rightfully looked at me like I was an alien. "Hello," she replied. "You doing okay, kiddo?"

"Fine!" I practically shouted. "I'm fine," I repeated at a more normal volume. "How are you?" Anything to get the attention off me, at least for a moment.

"Same old, same old," she said. "Just how I like it. You settling in okay? I feel like I haven't seen you as much lately."

"Totally. I think I've got the hang of this place now," I joked. Boy, oh boy, did I have the hang of it. I grabbed the counter behind me to keep my body from swaying. I would be waiting out in my car tonight until I was sober enough to drive home.

"Pretty sure the only reason you beat me here tonight was

I found a particularly sticky corner of room four. Some kid must have dumped out an entire juice box or something like that."

"Oh, yeah," I quickly agreed. "I'm nowhere near as fast as you."

"Mmm," Linda assessed. "Or, you're just more easily distracted. You still looking at the art every time?"

"Sometimes," I lied.

"That'll wear off at some point. You'll get used to it."

"I don't know," I said. "I don't see this getting old any time soon." *If only she knew*, I thought.

"Meh, a job's a job."

She had a point there. At the end of the day, this was work. And I had to keep the work up in order to keep having access to this place and these paintings.

"You doing anything for the holiday?" she asked.

"No, I'll just be here, working. I mean, I guess we're closed tomorrow, but I'll be here the other days. You?"

"I'm going to my sister's; she's local, though. It'll be a few hours of absolute madness and then I'll get to drive back and sleep in my own bed. You won't even go somewhere for dinner? Nothing festive?"

"We'll just stay home. It's too much food for our tiny family and I'm not much of a cook, so we'll probably just order takeout from whatever's open. It's okay, we don't mind. We love pizza." Did Linda notice that I always said "we"? It was habit at this point. Honestly, the only place I didn't fall into that word choice was with Jean, in the painting. In there, it was just me.

"Well, that's nice," Linda said. "Everyone has their own version of tradition."

I was hit with a wave of sadness that I wouldn't get to spend the holiday with Jean. I wondered if the people in the art even knew what Thanksgiving was, or if they lived by the same calendar we did. I imagined a grand spread, this colorful cast of characters pushing together every table they could find in this place, heavy with a hodgepodge of different painted foods. It would be loud and exciting, a contrast to Jean's quietness, but we'd be there together. I could see him, slowly coming out of his shell, getting into it the way he had earlier that night.

Then I tried to picture him in my own Thanksgiving, sitting on the couch between me and Gracie, a greasy pizza box half-empty on the coffee table, the apartment haphazardly picked up minutes before his arrival. It didn't work. Not because of Jean, I'm sure he would be as sweet as possible, but because the picture just never fully formed in my brain. It was too many different pieces—our overworn couch, the leather nearly splitting in places; the dark spots in the dirty light fixture that Gracie couldn't reach to clean; Jean's three-piece suit; his shyness that came across as formality when you first got to know him. He'd never see that home side of me.

"You look sad, chicken," Linda said, tapping my shoulder consolingly. "It's just a silly holiday. It's okay if your family looks different from the rest of the world."

"Yeah," I agreed, letting her think that was what was getting me down. And honestly, she wasn't far off from the truth. My reality, if you could call it that, looked so unbelievably different from the rest of the world.

"Well, I'm going to head out," she said as she unlocked her locker and retrieved her purse. "And you should too. I'll see you later, kid." She rummaged around in her bag, pulling her car keys out of a mess of headphone wires and gum packets.

"You too," I said, but she was already gone, back to the outside world. It was so strange: tonight, I was sure everything had changed. But Linda just looked at me and spoke to me like everything was the way it always was.

I poured myself a cup of the shitty coffee and wondered, not for the first time, was I really the only one who could see them moving around? Or who could crawl through the frames? I considered for a moment if I should show Linda what I could do. What if it wasn't just something special about me? What if we all could do it but no one else had dared to try?

She wouldn't get it. I liked Linda, I considered her a friend. But she would think I was out of my mind if I even started to try to explain it. And Linda liked rules. What if she somehow stopped me from going back? It wasn't worth the risk.

I pressed my hand against my pocket. I felt the outline of the ring through the fabric, touching the skin on my finger that now felt naked. No, not naked. Free.

JEAN

After that kiss, I couldn't bring myself to get back in my usual chair; it looked the same and I felt so different. But my legs felt weak all of a sudden and I plopped down onto the piano bench. My spine felt like it might dissolve into gelatin, so I lay down, allowing the bench to support me as my legs draped off the other end. I felt like adrenaline was dripping off my fingertips.

I wasn't alone for long. "I heard you caused quite the stir today. Should I be upset Andromeda got to meet her before I did?"

I lifted my head to see Marguerite standing inches in front of my bent knees. "How do you possibly already know about that? Where were you tonight?"

Ignoring my second question, she said, "News travels fast around here. So, did she enjoy *Le Bonheur*?"

"Yes, she very much did." I couldn't stop my ridiculous face from grinning at the memory.

"Do you ever doubt your trust in her, as you keep showing her all our secrets?"

I shook my head. "We don't have any secrets, Marguerite. We are publicly on display, all day, every single day."

An utterly French-sounding *pfffft* escaped Marguerite's lips. "That's an incredibly small-minded way of looking at our world. Don't undervalue your thoughts, Jean. Each time you share them, you're sharing a little part of yourself."

I was enjoying sharing myself with Claire. I thought back to before Claire knew I could hear her, how she told me that Linda trusted her and that was surprising because she'd never felt that kind of faith in her before, not from someone who had recently been a stranger. Nor had she ever placed her trust in anyone else. I wondered if she trusted me now. I wondered if I trusted her. I wondered how Linda was. It felt like a lifetime since she'd last been in our gallery.

"I like sharing myself with her," I assured my self-righteous sister. "I want her to know all the parts of me."

"It sounds like you know what you're doing," she said. It could not have sounded less like she had any confidence in what I was doing.

And I had absolutely no idea what I was doing, but I could not and would not confess that to Marguerite. I wasn't used to having the chance to drastically affect someone else and their livelihood. We had little room for choice in this world and when we did, those choices had little consequence. Suddenly, that was not the case. My actions no longer existed in a vacuum; I affected Claire and she had the same power over me. We had come quite far from the days when this was a low-stakes, unrequited infatuation.

Despite the heft of my thoughts, my body was full of bubbles from this evening. If I inhaled deeply enough, I would float up, my head grazing the ceiling, gravity losing all power over my physical state. I had absolutely no idea how I would make it through the next day with the museum closed.

But muscle through it I did. Come Friday morning, the museum reopened its doors and a steady stream of visitors flowed through the gallery. Cellphones were lifted up to us, their users capturing our existence on their glass screens, making us into a portable memory. A group of preteen girls even stopped right in front of us and executed a handful of coordinated steps and arm movements that looked like a choreographed dance. An older woman, presumably one of their mothers, recorded them, the smirk on her lips belying that she was holding in a chuckle. After finishing, they rushed over to watch the footage over her shoulder. Pleased, they moved on to the next gallery, carrying their winter jackets stuffed under their arms. The weather today looked cold and gray through the windows, but it was cozy and safe in our never-changing space.

That afternoon, a tour group swept through. We didn't usually have tours on holiday weekends, given how crowded the galleries were, so these must have been important guests, to someone at least.

This guide jumped right into the thick of it.

"So, I know we've talked a lot throughout our tour today about the *emotion* behind each of these paintings. They're not just illustrations *of* something, they're illustrations *about* something. This one is all about *fear*." Her group looked confused.

"Between the war, the typhoid, the draft, all the dangers of the time, the artist was afraid his family wouldn't survive." She pointed to my mother in the garden. "See the artist's wife here, pictured in a wheelchair?" She was not, it was a rocking chair. The guide described how my mother's position apart from the family signaled that her relationship with my father was in its decline. I let out a breath so strained it sounded like a growl. Her tone was brash; her wiseacre attitude stung. She acted as if we could not even hear her.

"I will admit"—her voice changed to a more playful tone—

"I have taken a liking to this little guy." She came right up to my line of sight, a few steps back from where Claire came to stand each night. "I love how I can come right up to him, stand at his eye level, see what he's thinking." I wondered if she was close enough to sense the frustration radiating off me.

Finally, she gathered her troops and moved them along to another room.

While the guide's assumptions that she understood us had irked me, she had forced me to think of my own fears. I still knew so little about Claire. I wanted her to open up to me, for her to feel like she could tell me things. There was so much of her life out there I couldn't picture. I didn't even know if I would be able to comprehend it if she described it, but I would try. We never discussed the ring, but I wondered about it daily.

When I let the worries fill my brain, they took full advantage. There was, of course, a chance this could all be over in an instant. Claire could be let go or move elsewhere. The museum could close. Linda could redo the room assignments. Our situation was so fragile and if it ended tomorrow, I'd never fully know her.

We eventually made it to evening and the gallery was once again empty. At closing, Marguerite and Pierre wasted no time rushing off to their nightly haunts. I stayed seated, waiting, as I was used to doing. Claire swept into the gallery, bucket clanging alongside her. From across the room, she lifted her left hand in a wave, right hand already clutching the mop handle. I waved back. Something seemed different.

Claire sprang into action, wiping away the day's grime. I wished, not for the first time, that I could climb out into her world and pick up a mop of my own, to keep her company while she went about her responsibilities. But I was not the special one. I was just the patient one. I waited.

After finishing her tasks to a level that would pass muster with most, though maybe not Linda, she rushed toward me and flung herself up over the frame before I could even offer her my hand. I reached out and caught her by the elbow, aiding her the rest of the way up into my world. As we both drew up to our full heights, I felt an unfamiliar warmth spreading across my cheeks. It wasn't painful, but it was certainly unusual, and I reached my hand up to feel my skin. I realized what was happening as Claire spoke it into existence simultaneously.

"You're blushing." She grinned as she said it.

"I don't think I've blushed in the last century," I confessed.

"What a guy thing to say," she mocked me, but reached her hand up to touch my cheek. I captured it with my own, holding it there.

"Hi," I said.

"Bonsoir," she replied, pronouncing every letter, including the silent R. I slid my hand along hers, entwining our fingers, and brought it down in between us. That's when my mind wrapped itself around what had changed.

All five fingers on her left hand were empty, no longer bearing any kind of rings or adornment. Her eyes followed mine, watching me come to this conclusion. I was unsure where the line was, of what I should say, or could say.

"I'll tell you about it later," she said, and I believed that she would.

"You don't have to," I assured her.

"I want to. I think. But not now. I've been thinking about what we talked about last night, about how it feels like there are two versions of me, the one out there and the one in here. And I decided that I don't want to let the girl I am out there hamstring the person I can be in here. While I'm here, I might as well be here. So, now, I want to—" She interrupted herself by leaning in to kiss me, and I was happy to do whatever it was the version of Claire in here wanted to do. I was really good at waiting. "Come on," she said, pulling me along by our still-connected hands. "Let's get moving."

15

JEAN

Claire didn't actually have any idea where she was going, despite the confidence with which she led me out to the edge of the garden. She did a small curtsy in the direction of Aurora, who responded with a pleased bow of her head. When we'd made it to the back of our property, she turned to me and said, "Okay, where to?"

I had enjoyed her leading and prompted, "You tell me— you've seen all the paintings in this museum. Where do you want to go?"

She thought about it for a moment, our world unfolding before her like a map. She looked absolutely giddy. "I've never been to a horse race before."

"Say no more," I commanded as I led the way into William James Glackens's *Race Track*. The sky was bright blue, a striking contrast to the inky black night we could see through the museum's exterior windows. It was peppered with fluffy white clouds, the colorful flags sitting still in the absence of a breeze. I fanned myself a few quick times, loosening the knot of my tie. The sound of the crowd was deafening compared to the near silence of my sitting room. The usual spectators had stuck around for the evening's entertainment and were joined by subjects from paintings all across the museum. I craned my neck to take in the throng filling every row of the stands. It was packed.

Our timing was perfect; a race was just about to begin. We waited as the horses and their jockeys crossed the path in front of us, strolling onto the track to find their starting positions. The gate swung closed behind the last competitors, and we took our places along the fence. The two men next to us gave Claire an intrigued look, but whether that was because of her janitorial uniform and unpainted skin or because she was so excited she was practically vibrating in place next to me was unclear.

"First time?" one of them asked, his Brooklyn accent strong. Claire nodded enthusiastically. "Which one did you put your bets on?"

"Oh, I don't have a bet! We're just here to watch," Claire responded.

"You've gotta have a bet! That's half the fun. Hell . . ." He turned to his companion for confirmation.

"It's more than half the fun," his companion agreed. "Here, you can have one of mine. I bet with my heart, not with my head, so no promises that he gets the job done, but at least he'll get you hooked." He passed his ticket along to Claire.

"Thank you," she said. "So—" She was interrupted in the middle of her sentence as a gunshot went off at the other end of the track and the horses burst forward from the starting gate. The cacophony of the crowd swelled into a full roar as people leapt from their seats to cheer for their sure-to-win steed. Claire's enthusiasm could be held back no longer; a whoop ripped from her chest, echoing across the field, and the two men next to her gleefully joined in. I could see it on their faces: they were proud of the fellow fan they'd adopted, and all three of them egged one another on.

Above the noise of the crowd, Claire yelled to the man who had given her the ticket, "Which one is ours?"

He hollered back, "That brown one right there, with the jockey in the yellow, in the middle of the pack."

"At least they're not at the back," Claire cried. "What's his name?"

"Great Sport, like you!" he replied as they genially bumped elbows.

"GREAT SPORT! GET GOING!" Claire's sense of shyness crumpled with each passing moment. This particular world was no more mine than it was hers; I spent no time over here. As she hurled herself into this time and place, we were making something that was ours together.

Claire squeezed my hand so hard I thought it might break. Much to all our surprise, Great Sport had pulled to the front of the pack right as they approached the finish line.

"Holy hell," the bet placer said. "He might actually do it."

"HELL YEAH, HE'S GOING TO DO IT!" Claire cried with such certainty, I actually believed her. Sure enough, with seconds to spare, Great Sport reached out his neck and extended his nose over the finish line, just before the horse to his right. A synchronized gasp escaped the crowd, and the masses were stunned into silence. Claire could be heard across the entire racetrack, shouting, "Yes! Yes! YES!"

"What happened?" I asked. "Why are they all so silent?"

Our new friends turned to us and one said, "They've run these races every single night for the last . . ."

"110 years, I do believe," the other supplied.

"Thank you—for the last 110 years and Great Sport has never won, not a single night."

"Why'd you bet on him?" I asked.

"I bet on him at least once a night, just in case," he said with a grin. "And I guess all that case needed was a lovely lady such as yourself to come along and surprise us all."

"Here." Claire quickly withdrew the ticket from her pocket. "Here's your ticket! I'm sure the winnings will be absolutely massive."

"That belongs to you, my friend," he said with a tip of his cap.

"Most definitely not. I am so, so grateful to you for lending it to me, but it was an honor just to be here." She returned it to him with a flourish. "But I'll make you a deal. You take this back, and I'll promise we'll come back another night."

He considered for a moment before relenting. "Deal. And please, don't make us wait too long."

"How could I resist coming back and stirring things up again?" She winked. "Thank you for having us, gentlemen." She gave each of them a kiss goodbye on the cheek. "Farewell!"

"Farewell!" they called in return. I'd never seen her so unencumbered. She took my hand in hers once more and led me back to the horizon.

"Where should we go next?" she asked me.

"How about the beach?"

"After you." She gestured for me to lead the way. We emerged on the top of a grassy bluff overlooking the beach at high tide. Soft purple clouds floated in the sky and a warm wind blew the waves onto the shore, where they crashed with a small patch of white foam on each swell. I took a deep breath, delighting in the way the salt in the air tickled my nose and throat. Claire imitated me, a smile spreading across her face.

"I think this is my favorite scent in the world," I confided.

"Did you spend much time by the shore when you were growing up?" she asked.

"Yes, this was a favorite place of my father's."

"I was wondering if this was one of his," Claire said. I nodded. "It's beautiful."

"Let's go put our toes in the sand." We trekked down the path to the beach below, helping each other get through the steeper parts. When we got down to the sand, Claire kicked her shoes off and ran toward the water. She squealed when she made contact with the waves.

"It's *cold*."

"Is it?"

She dipped her toes in again, "Wow, okay, not really. I think that was just shock. It's actually pretty comfortable." She yanked up the bottom of her pants so as to better splash around.

Watching Claire as she was now, I was reminded of all the stories she had shared before she knew I was listening. She might feel old, but the part of her she was showing now was still just a kid. We had that in common.

My relationship to aging was complex, to say the least. Within my world, no one aged and so I did not have an immediate foil, someone to fuel a sense of jealousy from watching a person I knew or respected grow into themselves. We were all equally frozen in time, for better or for worse. Some might call us "immortal" and others might call us "stuck," but we simply lived our lives. This was our reality. We matured, but we didn't age.

But we were not in isolation. We've watched thousands of patrons march through our rooms every day in ephemeral snapshots. We've seen people falling in and out of love, growing old, parenting, failing one another. We've become familiar with the staff, the curators, the guides, the members and repeat visitors. The collector himself.

I remember the last time I saw my father. He visited the museum in the context of creating a commissioned piece that would be shaped to match the unique space set aside for him. Fifteen years had passed since I'd last laid eyes on him, and while he was still as creative and intense as he had ever been, he was unfamiliar to me. His stance, his skin, his sound were all affected by the years that stood between us. It was like seeing a ghost. I wondered if he felt the same looking at me.

He left swiftly; in the relative nature of time, he had been there for barely a blink of how long he had been absent. Left in his wake was my favorite work of his to date: a series of people flowing across a punchy background of pink and blue and black. From where I sat, day in and day out, I could just see them leaping their way into and out of my field of vision.

But for the brief time that he stood in front of us, he inhabited the same position he'd been in as he put us here. I was overwhelmed with a sense of déjà vu. Once again, he was watching us the way he wanted us: safe and sound, together yet separated by the space in between us.

"Jean," Claire said softly as she wrapped her arm around my waist, "where'd you go?"

I bent down and pressed my lips to hers. "I'm here, I'm right here."

She laughed at me, gently. "You're cute when you space out completely."

"You're beautiful always."

Claire turned away from me and I wasn't sure if I'd said the wrong thing. There was still so much I didn't know about her.

"No one has ever talked to me the way you do. I like it so much, of course, duh, I just don't know what to do with it. It makes my cheeks burn, but also I hope you'll never stop."

"I never plan to stop." My brain was spiraling now. I had hundreds of unvocalized fears about how long we would be able to do what we were doing; now that we were here, having crossed every conceivable boundary, time felt like our villain, the thing that could bring our great love story to an end.

Claire turned back to look at me and suddenly, I couldn't have her fast enough. I was jealous of anyone else who would ever get some of her time. I felt pressure to make an imprint of her as she was right now with my eyes, to save the feeling of her body pressed against mine into my whole being, to memorize the way her lips tasted on mine. Her hunger matched mine; she was kissing me in the present, kissing me with no fear of what lay in the past, of what she had given up to be here.

The beach had mostly emptied out for the night, but there were still a few stragglers nearby. Eager for more privacy, I led Claire back up to the bluff and into one of the small cottages that overlooked the sea.

A gust of warm seaside air greeted us as we opened the door. The interior was plain: wood furnishings and white linen; a writing desk with a lamp; a few sheets of paper, their edges curling in the humidity. Most notably, we both spotted the small bed in the corner. I froze at the sight of it. We were moving too fast. This whole thing, it was senseless. It had been a really, really long time since I had done anything like this.

"Claire," I said, anxiety crackling in my voice. "It's been . . ."

"It's okay, it's been a long time for me too."

"I don't know—" I was flummoxed by my own words. "I don't know if things have changed?"

"We'll find out together," she said.

Claire walked up to the bed and turned back to face me. With a small smirk on her lips, she reached to her chest to unbutton her jumpsuit. She let it fall open, and the sight took my breath away. In a turn of the tables, she was the one waiting for me. I took the four steps to close the gap between us.

"I know this all seems like something out of a dream," she said. "But this is really real to me. I don't think I'm just dreaming. I'm here."

"This feels like— Sorry, let me start over." I attempted to

gather my wits. "This might be the only real thing I've ever done."

"Then let's do this together. Make it real," she said as she brought her arms around my neck, connecting us once again. I took a step into her, pushing the backs of her knees against the edge of the mattress. She let herself fall onto the bed, and I let myself follow her.

16

CLAIRE

My head rested on Jean's chest, my right ear close enough to his heart that I could hear it speed up as I ran my fingers up and down his arm. I drew invisible doodles along his bicep. My clothes, puddled in piles on the floor, were haunting, a reminder of the life to which I was pretending I owed nothing. My ugly but "practical" sneakers mocked me, tangled in the pant legs of my uniform.

"Do I have to leave?" I said, mostly joking. I was a human inside a painting.

"If I could ask you to stay, I would get down on my knees and beg. I'd have no shame in doing so. But I can't even imagine how that would work," Jean answered too earnestly.

"It was a joke," I reassured him, hearing the sadness in my own voice. "It's impossible; I know. Plus, I can't. I've got . . . people out there who need me." I saw confusion and maybe even a little hurt play across Jean's face. I had told him I wasn't ready to talk about it, and I knew he wasn't going to push me, but I felt guilty. I wasn't thinking about who Jean thought I was thinking about.

But he wanted to laugh it off, not contaminate this moment with those thoughts. "So, instead we have nights," he said. "I'm kind of a bore during the day, anyway, frozen in place as I am."

"And I have to sleep, like, kind of a lot, when I'm not here."

"Of course, sleep, I remember that," he joked. I pinched his arm and he caught my hand in his, holding my fingers in place. He leaned down to kiss me, and I felt like I could melt right then and there. I was utterly obsessed with him and it was freaking me out, how intense these feelings had grown.

"Speaking of sleep, I'm playing it fast and loose now. I better get back out there, check in with Linda." Jean nodded but made no move to get up.

"How is Linda these days?" he asked as he tangled his fingers in my hair.

"Same old, same old." I forced the words out, not allowing myself to get distracted by his touch. "She's normally done way before I am and is waiting for me in the break room, playing around on her phone until our shift is over. She sometimes makes jokes about how slow I am and I just let her. I tell her it's because I can't stop looking at the art and she totally believes me. But it doesn't feel like a lie; I *am* looking at the art." I gazed up at Jean again. "Just a little closer than she imagines, maybe."

"As long as she doesn't come looking for you, I think that's great."

"Oh no, she never would. Sometimes I describe to her a painting that I say just got me all caught up, and she'll listen and laugh. She has no interest in the art but I think she likes hearing about what makes me happy. She's a real friend in that way. I sometimes wish I could tell her about you." Or anyone, for that matter. What would I even call him? My boyfriend?

Jean wrapped his arms around me. "It feels unfair that the people in my life know about you while you have to keep all of this a secret." Well, at least I was good at keeping those. Maybe a little too good.

That imaginary alarm clock that seemed like it was built into my brain started ringing and I rolled over, putting my feet on the floor. It was time to go and we both knew by now that this part was easier if we just ripped the bandage off. Jean followed, though he had significantly more clothing to put back on. He pulled his shirt on one sleeve at a time, draping his tie around his neck. By the time I had buttoned my jumpsuit and scooped my hair into a poorly executed but serviceable top-knot, he had just started on his pants.

I tried to catch my reflection in the warped glass of the cottage windows, rubbing away the mascara that was making the dark patches under my eyes look even worse. Whatever sleep I was getting in this weird split life was not enough. Jean caught one of my eyes in the reflection. "It'll have to do," I said.

"You look beautiful, as always. Every day, you're more beautiful than I even remembered." I blushed viciously. I knew he was trying to flatter me and honestly, it was working. My skin felt hot all over.

We made our way back to Jean's house in a dazed, contented silence. "Remember when I won a horse race?" I asked when we were almost there.

"I'm not sure that's exactly what winning looks like in that context—"

I cut him off with a searing glare. I was not about to let the details get in the way of this story.

"Yes, absolutely," he corrected himself. "The team could not have done it without you. I'm sure your new friends will be eager to get you back."

"Well, duh, I'm a catch, but there's *so* much more to see. I get freaked out when I think of running out of time to take it all in." I panicked whenever I thought about this way of living coming to an end, but I wasn't going down that rabbit hole right now. I really did need to get going.

"Why would you run out of time?" Jean asked. I didn't know how to tell him I couldn't help feeling like something this good had to have an expiration date.

"No reason, I'm just daunted by the expansiveness of it all," I replied, trying to reassure him.

"You want to keep exploring the museum?" I could tell the gears in Jean's head were turning.

"As long as it's with you." I linked my arm through his and he patted my hand.

"Well, then, tomorrow night. It's a date," he said. I was distracted, wondering what he was cooking up, and I didn't realize his mom was back in her rocker, embroidery in hand, until we were right in front of her. It was clear from the expression on her face that she was listening to us.

"Good evening, Mother, have you had a nice evening?" Jean's measured tone made me feel like a kid again, embarrassed to be caught in the act. Could she tell from the dopey expressions on our faces what we'd been up to tonight? I shuddered at that thought.

"Oui," she responded. Clearly she understood Jean's English but had chosen to answer in a language just the two of them shared. Well, I could play that game.

"Bonjour, Madame Matisse." I tried to infuse my voice with a confidence I didn't quite have. I knew my pronunciation was rocky, but it sounded better than it had when I first started practicing. I crossed my fingers that this was working because I didn't have much French left. To my delight, Jean and his mother both looked utterly charmed.

"Bonjour, mademoiselle," she replied, one of her eyebrows crooked upward in an impressive arc. I'd have to practice that in the mirror later. "I gather you are the young woman my son has become infatuated with."

Jean's jaw dropped and I resisted the urge to slam my elbow into his side. I recovered for the both of us. "And I with him," I said. Jean turned toward me, a silly expression on his face.

"Well, aren't we lucky to hear that. My son rarely gives his heart away. I'm glad it appears to be safely kept." Speaking of hearts, I could feel mine thundering in my chest.

"To the best of my abilities," I said as I reached out and grabbed Jean's hand to stabilize myself.

She offered us a short nod; we were being dismissed. We made our way to the edge of our worlds for our usual framed goodbye.

"That went well, right?" I couldn't help myself from asking.

"Very well." Jean kissed the top of my head. "We have her approval, for now."

"I really don't want to, but I have to go." Even in this world, I couldn't shut off the logical side of my brain, ruled by rules.

"Good night, Claire," he said. "Rest well tomorrow."

"Goodbye, Jean, have a good day at work," I quipped back, giving him one more kiss before I dropped out onto the floor of the gallery. I grabbed my tools and pushed my way to the back halls of the building, winding my way to the storage area where we kept our supplies. That song about everlasting love, one of my grandmother's favorites, came to mind, and I hummed a little bit of it aloud. These hallways, white and sterile, having none of the coziness or color of the galleries, were meant to be the secret part of the museum. When the guests thought about the parts of this building that they didn't have access to, this was what they pictured. If only they knew what they were really missing out on.

I slammed my car door, tucking myself inside and dropping my purse on the passenger seat. It spilled to the side, dumping its contents between the seat and the door, and I just let it fall.

"What the actual *hell*?" I asked aloud, trying to process the events of tonight's shift. I pressed my hands against my cheeks.

I could feel a smile crossing my face. This was not the time for giggling, but I couldn't help myself. I knew I probably looked like an idiot, grinning to myself alone in my car.

I tried to put my key into the ignition, but my hands were shaking too much. I gave up and took a deep breath. My mind danced back to the newly made memories of tonight. Had it really only been a few hours since I was last sitting in this exact spot, getting ready for another night at work? So much had changed.

Life in Jean's world was a fairy tale, a conglomeration of colors and laughter and sunshine. It was never too cold or too hot; I never needed an extra layer and I never saw anyone sweat. I was never hungry or tired, and I weirdly never needed to pee. I didn't have to think about all the things that normally clouded my brain. For a few minutes, or hours, if we were pushing it like we did tonight, I could just be me. And, even better, be me with him.

Being with Jean made me feel like I could act my age again. I was twenty-one; in his world, it was okay to do something just because I wanted to every now and then. And it was okay to make mistakes. When I was with him, I could just let my feelings for him run free. And run they did.

Jean was so patient; it was like he had an attention span unaffected by all the things technology had done to ruin ours. He never looked away from me when I was talking, even if it took me a moment to figure out how I wanted to phrase things. He asked follow-up questions, trying to digest pieces of my life he didn't understand. He wanted to take the time to get it.

I'd calmed down enough by this point to get the car started and pull out of the lot without running into anything on the way. I waved to Terry, who ran the gate for the after-hours shift, and he released me to the world beyond. Reluctantly, I drove out into the night.

My euphoria rubbed off as I coasted farther away from that

dream life and closer to my reality. I remembered meeting Jean's mom. I should have assumed that would happen eventually, but there was nothing like meeting your boyfriend's mom for the first time. I wondered if she had liked me.

Was Jean my boyfriend? I had obviously never asked him. I was pretty confident no one was using the phrase *define the relationship* a century ago. But I also knew that for Jean, there was only me. He'd made that as clear as he could. So why did I need a word for it, to hear it from his mouth?

Because that would make it feel more real. Because it would put it in my terms, in my language. Because a boyfriend wasn't someone you just casually dated, saw when it was convenient, but who didn't cross your mind during the in-between moments. A boyfriend was someone you carried with you, even when you two weren't physically together. And that's what he had become to me. I thought about him all the time. I relived our nights together in the dull reality of my days; I imagined him inserted into various scenarios of my life.

I wanted to call him my boyfriend. I wanted to have a reason, an official reason, to define him in relation to me. I wanted to be in a relationship.

He'd never meet my mom, regardless of whatever term we chose to describe us, and that was for the best. She'd find a way to ruin this all—to insult me, and to hurt him. I was lucky he was safe from her.

I pulled onto my street. I'd been on autopilot for most of the drive but the need to focus on looking for street parking drew me out of my dreamy haze. It was either grab a spot or pull around the creepy alley in back and try to squeeze my car in. But it was barely lit back there, and I could never stop myself from sprinting the whole way to the back door. My fingers were crossed the parking gods would work in my favor tonight.

And sure enough, they did. A few blocks down, I found a

spot just big enough for my tiny old car. I completed an impressive parallel parking job, except there was no one around to acknowledge my feat of maneuvering. I leaned forward and gathered all my belongings that had scattered to the ground, sure I'd missed a Cheerio or crumpled-up tissue but telling myself I'd get them tomorrow in the daylight. Even though I probably wouldn't.

As I walked back toward my apartment along the silent, streetlamp-lit street, I noticed how this didn't feel any more real than life with Jean. This sidewalk right here could be something out of a painting. With no one around, there was nothing that reminded me that this life was the real one. I might as well be a player in a video game or a character in a movie. It wasn't until I reached my door, pulling my keys out and wiggling them around in my fingers, that a sense of reality struck. I probably had a few quiet hours, if I was lucky, before all hell broke loose, as it always did. I was always tempted to use those hours to do something for me, just for me, but I knew I needed to sleep. That would have to count as my self-care for tonight.

17

JEAN

I returned to the garden under my mother's expectant gaze. "You're happy," she said to me in French.

"I'm happy, definitely happy." A grin spread across my face.

"I'm glad. You've waited a long time to feel this way." There it was again, this refrain of my patience. While I'd always prided myself on it, believed it to be a virtue, I now wondered if others ever passed judgment on me. Did they think I had been standing in my own way for all this time?

The sun crashed through the gallery windows and I slipped my cigarette back in between my lips just in time for Susie and a new tour group to take over the room. I thought she was headed straight for us, but she took a sharp right and parked her group in front of a painting directly opposite us. She had a predictably eccentric outfit on today, a plethora of colors and textures, topped off with a remarkably silly hat. Shockingly, it remained in place for her entire monologue.

"Now that you're a bit warmed up, let's play a game! Any guesses who this is a painting of?"

From the thoughtful silence that followed, a tentative voice emerged. "Um, Beatrice?"

Someone in the back of the group stage-whispered to their closest companion, "Who on earth is Beatrice?"

The woman who had answered the question turned around, pink in the cheeks. "I don't even know. I just guessed it because it says 'Beatrice' in the top right-hand corner of the painting."

"Well, I could have read that," the loud whisperer said back with a bite.

Susie was there to get them back on track. "Yes, you are right! This painting is named for its subject, Beatrice Hastings. Modigliani, or Modi as I like to call him," she said with a wink, "met Beatrice when she moved to Paris in the twentieth century, and they began a tortured affair that would last years. It was quite the tumultuous relationship." The group giggled.

"Here, she's pictured in a box seat at the theater in a particularly plume-y hat, not dissimilar to my own. You can tell from the sharp angles of her visage that Modi was in his experimenting-with-Cubism phase. She's not my favorite, but that's a personal preference thing. What I do think is cool about her—gather up, everyone, I think you'll like this too. She was a journalist—a writer and a poet, and at one point, there was a piece of newspaper attached by Modi to this painting itself. Lean in close and you can just make out its text, right there, under her name."

The group followed her instructions, *ooh*-ing and *ahh*-ing. I wondered when Susie had decided she and Modigliani were on a nickname basis.

"Now!" she said as she pulled their attention in our direction. "To a painting I cannot leave this room without visiting: *The Music Lesson.*" The group huddled up around our frame.

"Today," Susie continued, "I want to talk about contradictions. This painting is full of them. See how that fountain beneath the sculpture bubbles blue? Why on earth does that clear water run down into a muddy brown pond? Or this garden—lush, forestlike, the stuff of fairy tales. Who on earth has a jungle in their backyard in an apartment in Paris? Or even something so simple as the light. When we look at this painting, we can see it is daytime. So why is this shadow here, behind this young man?" She waved her hand along my body, hovering just in front of me. She was so close; it was a wonder the motion sensor had not been triggered. I wasn't used to having anyone but Claire close enough to feel the warmth radiating off them.

"There must be light coming in through this window, so why would a shadow be pushing back toward it? Something to consider. Obviously, art does not have to all make perfect sense. There's a tension in this painting, between the order and the chaos of the world Matisse has built. With so many little puzzle pieces such as these, I can't ignore this question of what does the artist want us to notice or to know about this space that exists ever so slightly outside the bounds of reality? There's something inherently magical in it; Matisse created this painting in an act of fear of the war, out of a desire to see his family reunited once again. He is hunting for a way to keep his family safe and for a moment, frozen in time here, they all are."

The group's attention on us was rapt, as if Susie's words on our being had lulled them into some kind of a trance. A clap of her palms snapped them out of it.

"Okay! That's the end of our conversation for today. I've loved spending the morning with you—you've been an absolute delight and I hope you'll come back and visit me again soon."

"Susie, *you* are the delight," a woman cooed. They gathered around her to sing her praises, and little glimpses of their conversation snuck out our way. I latched on to one exchange in particular.

"Is there anything we didn't have time for that we absolutely must see?"

"I'm afraid we had to rush by Modigliani's *Portrait of the Red-Headed Woman* downstairs; that room was just too crowded. She's one of my absolute favorites; I'd pay her a visit if you have a few more minutes. Go downstairs and head toward the right, you won't be able to miss her."

A chorus of "thank you" and "we will" followed, as the women swept their way out of the room. I heard one of them say to another, "Well, she was just the greatest. Couldn't do it with anyone but her."

"Absolutely not. She's the only option."

I'd seen this so many times before: visitors invested in making sure their experience was the best one—the winner. I've never understood what it was about visiting a museum that inspired a need for competition, but there must be something in the air.

"How do you say it again?"

"Modigliani—it's like the G is silent."

"Ooh, got it, like Mo-Dig-Liani."

"No, no, no . . ." her friend corrected as they followed the group out of the gallery. Two women remained in front of us, looking at the painting directly to our left.

"I wonder if they're dead," one woman said.

"I'm pretty sure everyone in here is dead," her friend replied. The first woman nodded in agreement.

When they walked away, Jamie Leigh, the new museum president, was revealed behind them. Gone were the casual sweater and jeans of her first visit to us. Today she was dressed in a well-fitted suit, a crisp white blouse underneath. She was looking at us so closely, I felt compelled to slow my breathing and minimize any possible movements, trying to keep the illusion of stillness alive for her. It felt like she was challenging us.

Her red hair reminded me that I needed to make plans for what to do with Claire that evening. I would show her all the best the museum had to offer, a bit at a time, of course. I hadn't seen Odette in a very, very long time, but if Susie said she was not to be missed, that's where we would have to start. I knew Claire spent little to no time downstairs, and I didn't want her to miss out. We had a lot to catch up on.

18

JEAN

typically languished in the time between when the museum closed its doors to visitors and when Claire arrived, but tonight I sprang to action. Marguerite noticed.

"Where are you off to?" she called as I strode out into the yard. "And alone, at that?"

"Got some research to do!" I yelled over my shoulder. I didn't have to turn to look at her to know that her hand was reaching up to run her fingers along the black ribbon tied around her neck, as she always did when she was trying to figure something out. It covered a scar left on her throat by a childhood surgery. I couldn't remember ever having seen her without it tied into place.

I pushed my way through the lush trees that formed the jungle at the edge of our backyard and raced off through the other paintings.

Before last night's jaunt to the racetrack, it had been quite some time since I'd explored the first floor of the gallery. Acquaintances I'd not seen for decades tipped their hats as they rose from their assigned seats. I waved in return as I bustled through, stopping only for a moment to take in Seurat's *Models*, hanging high on the wall across from me. This was one of *my* favorite pieces in the museum, amateur appreciator of art that I was. I'd have to take Claire to see this one another night. But first, we were following Susie's guidance.

I capered my way through the rest of the works before landing in Susie's recommended gallery. There, I found who I was looking for.

"Hello, Antoinette." I'd gone not to Odette but to a work of my father's, *The Green Dress*, which hung directly opposite Modigliani's *Portrait of the Red-Headed Woman*. After all, you couldn't see a painting the way it was meant to be seen if you were standing inside it.

"Jean! My long-lost friend. It's been a while," she said, rising from her chair and placing a kiss on each of my cheeks. Her green dress draped perfectly along the length of her body, the billowing sleeves just gracing the edges of her wrists.

"Far too long," I agreed. "If you don't mind, I have a favor to ask of you."

She cleared her black stockings off the chaise lounge and gestured for me to sit. Her home was delightfully messy; despite her best attempts at order, her effects covered every available surface. "Please." I sat down across from her and explained what I had in mind.

"I'll help," she said. "Of course I will; it would be my pleasure. But before I do, you owe me an explanation."

"If I understood how the magic worked, I would explain it in a heartbeat." I exhaled. "But I can't describe it. Claire just tried to climb in one night and she could do it. I don't know any more than that."

"That's all very well and good," she retorted, "but that's not to what I was referring. I've been believing in magical things for longer than you've been around, out there or in here. I meant that it's time we talk about where you've been."

I picked at the skin around my left thumb, a splinter of paint falling to the floor. "I've been around," I said. "You know."

"I don't know," Antoinette said. "You used to come visit, maybe not often, but somewhat regularly. And that petered out into nothing. It's been decades since you've left your own home on a regular basis."

"It's just . . ." I'd never spoken about this before. "It's easier this way. What was ever the point? Drifting through the same world day after day with no purpose? When I stay put, I know what to expect."

"A whole lot of nothing, that's what you should expect with that attitude." Antoinette scoffed. "Jean, that's no way to live."

"Is that what we're doing in here? Living?"

"We're doing as much living as we're going to get to do, if you think about it that way. Or, if you think about it my way, we are going to get to live forever. We are immortal, which some people would kill to be. We have forever to figure out what we're doing here." I took a breath, preparing for a rebuttal, but she cut me off before I could even start. "You've been choosing the easy option, keeping yourself safe, but you're doing it in the name of protecting others. Thinking you're patient, when it's really just fear. I'm glad she's forced you to consider another way of living. I'll prepare myself for what you've requested of me."

Antoinette was quiet then, having said all she needed to say. I raced back the way I'd come to my living room. I could see by looking through the museum and out the windows that the sky outside had darkened. I wondered if Claire had beaten me.

As I jogged back through our garden and up the steps into the house, I saw that she had. She was cleaning, albeit half-heartedly, and I leapt up and down to catch her attention. She spotted me and rushed over. After she pushed the top half of her body through the frame, her words spilled out in a rush: "I was *so* worried you'd left, I mean after last night, that you didn't want to see me and wouldn't tell me and instead were just ghosting me by being freaking gone and that would just be the end of it—"

"Claire!" I tried to interrupt her dark spiral of thoughts. "Claire. CLAIRE!" Finally, she paused and made eye contact with me, though it was less to do with my calling her name and more because she was forced to catch her breath. "I didn't leave, I will never leave, and certainly never because of last night." I felt my blood surge with heat as that memory danced in my head. "I was planning what you and I are going to do tonight."

"Oh." Her demeanor was still shaken, but her eyes betrayed excitement.

"What was that word you used? You thought I might be 'ghosting' you?"

"Yeah, it's a thing out there. I'll explain it to you sometime."

"I'm looking forward to it. Now, are you ready to go for the evening?"

"I have a bit more cleaning to do."

"Not a problem, you get done what you need. I'll"—I took a seat in my usual chair and picked up my usual book—"be right here." She hopped back into her world and hustled her way around the gallery. I obviously read not a single page.

Suddenly, she was back in front of me.

"Well, that was fast," I complimented her.

"I'm not sure it would hold up to Linda's standards, but it'll do for now. I wasted time, worrying that this was all gone."

"Well, begone those ghosts from your mind. Did I use it properly?"

"Not quite," she mocked. "So, what's this grand surprise that you're planning?"

"Of course," I said. "Away we go!"

We wandered our way through a maze of paintings, me in the lead. We were slower together than I had been alone. Claire stopped in nearly every frame to take it all in, and I was happy to wait until she was ready to proceed.

Finally, we returned to Antoinette's chambers. I could tell she'd done her best to tidy up the place since I'd been here earlier. I was touched by the effort, even as I caught a glimpse of her stockings peeking out from beneath a pillow.

"Antoinette, you didn't need to clean on our behalf."

"Nonsense." She waved me off. "It's been decades since I had someone to spruce up for." Her gaze landed on Claire, and she said, "And you must be our guest of honor."

"Hi," Claire said, a hint of shyness in her voice. "I'm Claire."

"It's very nice to meet you, Claire; I'm Antoinette."

"Antoinette was one of my father's models in Nice," I explained. I had known her both inside and outside this world.

"Ancient history, that is. Now come along, have a seat." She seated both of us on the chaise lounge, which she had rotated to have a better view out into the gallery. "Welcome to my tour of, well, the works we can see here." She gestured to the wall across from her. Claire let out a little gasp as she turned to me.

"You got me an art history class?" she asked, her eyes sparkling with emotion.

I chuckled. "Professor Antoinette takes the floor. I wanted you to be able to see all that we have to offer. I know how much the pieces mean to you." We beamed at each other for a moment too long and Antoinette cleared her throat. Claire slid her hand into mine as we turned back to face our makeshift instructor.

"Now, as I was saying, let's turn our attention to this wall." She gestured across the room. Our eyes were drawn to the wall directly opposite, a plethora of artwork greeting us. Frames of all shapes and sizes hung in seven columns, showing faces, bodies, still lifes, landscapes, and more. Some were empty of their typical inhabitants, just a chair left behind. I had forgotten how charmed I was by the abundance of the collection. Just because this room was smaller than ours did not mean it housed any less work; it probably held even more pieces than ours did. I made a note to count the next day.

Antoinette spun tales of what we saw before us. Like the guides who passed through the galleries each day, her descriptions and anecdotes were undoubtedly embellished, but her rhetorical improvements shone with the light of actually knowing something of the artists and their subjects. She had just finished a rather riotous tale about one of the women we could see in a Picasso painting, which she followed up with a quick, "Also, this was a study for a work of his that some say was the true start of Cubism. Now, on to this fabulously blue boy . . ." Claire was eating up each word of Antoinette's discourse, which was more gossip-centric than education-focused. If Claire had a pen and paper, she'd be furiously scribbling notes, I was sure.

As if she could sense the spotlight our attention placed on her usual seat, Odette swanned back into her frame in the center of the wall. She reclined in her typical pose and gave us a little trill of her fingers. Antoinette returned her wave with a brief nod.

"She's beautiful," Claire whispered to me. Claire was right; Odette was transfixing. A collarbone as sharp as a razor blade set above a corseted black dress with voluminous skirts. Most unique was her vibrant red hair, which she kept in a curly bob, a few strands of bangs hanging across her forehead. Thin eyebrows arched above knowing eyes.

"Ah, parfait, Odette has returned." Antoinette clapped her hands together. "As you may or may not be aware, she is one of the most famous paintings in this gallery. Each tour group flounces through this room and claims she is an unknown woman whom the Italian artist met when he was trying out the 'bohemian' lifestyle in Paris—*pfft*—she is far from un-known, if they would just bother to ask us. Her name is Odette, and she was a musician in Paris. The artist met her while she was tending bar. With her flaming red hair and a look on her face that says, 'I see right through you,' of course she was des-tined to be a star, on the canvas and off. If you meet her, you must ask her to play the piano for you. Maybe her voice is nothing to write home about nowadays, but the way her sto-ries come alive . . . There is no one like her."

Unbeknownst to Antoinette, I had chosen this spot pre-cisely because we would be able to see Odette but get no closer than that. If I had it my way, Claire and Odette would never meet and we three would be all the better for it. When Odette could tell our attention had turned to another painting on the wall, she lifted her hand from the ripples of her skirt and pulled out a paperback book.

After Antoinette had wrapped up her lecture, Claire and I bid her adieu and wandered our way back up to our hall. Claire gushed over her newfound insider knowledge.

"How on earth did she ever come to know so much?"

"Well, we spend every day listening to tour guide after tour guide tell their version of what's happening in our gallery, so I am certain she's picked some things up there. But Antoinette was also an artist herself."

"There aren't a lot of women artists in here, not compared to the numbers of men."

"No, there are not. There are a lot of men represented on these walls."

"A lot of white men," Claire said pointedly.

We were just about to take the turn that would bring us upstairs when we saw Linda. Her galleries were, unsurpris-ingly, already sparkling from her night's effort. Claire grabbed my hand and leapt behind a nearby bush.

Claire whispered once we were both safely concealed, "You don't think she saw us, do you?"

I peered my head around the corner because it made more sense for Linda to see me in my own world than to know that Claire was there. "No," I reassured her, "I don't think so."

Claire laughed nervously while exhaling her anxiety. "Oof, that gave me a scare. I've thought about it before and don't know how I would've explained all of this." She gesticulated wildly at herself.

"What do you think would happen?" I asked. "If she saw you?"

"I don't know." Claire scratched that place behind her ear, the one she always favored when she was on edge. "I don't think she'd believe her own eyes. But I can't imagine it would be good if the museum found out; I don't think they'd like it if their staff was crawling around in their paintings. That's gotta be some type of security risk." She laughed lightly at her own joke before growing serious. "I think it would be bad. I don't think I'd be allowed to come back anymore."

I wouldn't stand for that, but I was also powerless to stop it.

"We have to be more careful, Jean," she warned me. I could tell that she was shaken by this encounter. We would be. I wasn't going to lose her.

"Come on, I know another way back." I pulled her in the direction we had come and took her along an alternate route. We ended up where we always did, strolling beside the murky brown pond in my backyard before being forced to say good night.

"Thank you again, for tonight's class. No one has ever arranged something like that for me."

"I'd get you a private boat along the Seine if I could, but I'm a little bit limited here," I joked, though another idea had already popped into my head.

"You're like a fairy godmother and a Prince Charming rolled into one unbelievable guy."

Now I was blushing again. She put me out of my misery, placing a kiss on my lips and sliding away.

19

JEAN

We passed the next few months in a flurry of make-shift art lessons with eccentric hosts and stolen hours alone in the empty corners of the worlds we had visited. We played cards with Cézanne's farmhands, shot the breeze with Seurat's models, and swam in the Mediterranean Sea. I revealed my horrific dancing skills to Claire, and she pulled me out of the heat of a crowded room and into a moonlit landscape where we could sway to a nonexistent beat in peace. I couldn't remember ever feeling joy like this.

Life outside our painted wonderland wasn't as easygoing. The skies visible through our room's colossal windows turned gray with a wintry chill. Claire's work was more laborious as she swiped away each boot print that brought the sludge of the sidewalks into our cozy sanctuary. The warmth of my world inside the frame contrasted with the bleakness of her exterior reality. I'd watched it happen every year; the change of the seasons seemed impossible, like winter would never end. And year after year, spring always came.

Early in March, there was an uncharacteristically warm stretch of weather. The patrons' clothing tipped me off—shorts and dresses with higher hemlines were wrenched from the backs of closets. Layers were stripped off as guests browsed by, having underestimated how warm they would get on their walk over.

Claire confirmed my suspicions when she crawled in through the frame that night. "It's different out there today, right?" I asked as I pulled her to her feet.

"What?" she responded, brushing her jumpsuit back down along her legs.

"It's warmer out there today? I thought, because of the way people were dressed . . ."

"Oh, yeah, you're totally right, it was really nice out today. Like, nicer than it should be for this time of year. I thought you meant—you know what, never mind."

"What is it?"

"I thought you were referring to this other thing, but there's no way. Anyway, it's definitely not a big deal and I'd way rather talk about something else."

Her tone worried me. There was so much about Claire's life I didn't understand, that I couldn't see, and that she refused to show me. I was desperate for her to let me in, but I was easily distracted by the fact that we were now together again, as I was every night that I got to see her. I briefly wondered if it had anything to do with our seeing smaller crowds each day, but I'd lived through decades of the ebbs and flows of museum visitors. It was probably another recession or something else to do with the economy; we were always the first thing to go when people started tightening their purse strings. Or maybe, I argued with myself, it could always be some kind of scandal with the museum or the administration. That would certainly keep things interesting. Marguerite might know more, if that was it.

Claire clearly didn't want to be the bearer of bad news and I didn't want to force that on her, so the tense moment passed. "What do you have in mind for today?" she asked, also eager to move along to another topic. I acquiesced.

"If you're not opposed, I would like to take you on a date."

"Jean, isn't every night that we're together basically a date?"

"Well, every night is special because I get to be with you, but I would say some of the art lessons tend more toward a seminar. I have a real, traditional date in mind. At least, what I used to know of as a date. But we can do something else, if you'd prefer."

"No, don't be stupid. Of course I'd love to go on a date with you."

"Terrific!" I clapped my hands involuntarily. I had always wondered about why people clapped with enthusiasm and suddenly, I was one of them. "Let us go."

I led her to a table set for two in a sunny restaurant. After pulling out Claire's chair, I filled the wineglasses up to their brims. I offered her a tear of the baguette and removed the lid of the tureen to reveal a cassoulet, one of my favorite dishes.

"Holy crap," said Claire. "That looks amazing. May I?" She waved her bread in one hand and when I nodded, she dunked a piece in the broth and popped it in her mouth. "Yeah, yum, that's as good as I thought it would be."

"I'm so glad you like it," I said, spooning some onto the two small plates in front of us.

"Whose is this?" she said, lifting the boater hat off the chair next to her. She looked around and then placed it on top of her head.

"It certainly suits you. I believe it should be yours now."

"Oh hush, as if that's how it works." Claire waved me off but kept the hat on. When wearing it, she had a delightful jaunt to the way she held her head. Our conversation meandered on from there, comfortable, not at all rushed. Not for the first time, I wished every moment of every day could be like this.

"This is what I always dreamed dates would be like," Claire said wistfully. "Fine food, a handsome man, wine that's so bitter I know it must be fancy."

"Oh, come on," I teased. "I'm not naïve; I know that I'm not the first man to take you on a proper date, much as I wish I was the only one you'd ever thought of." I'd seen the ring; I wasn't a fool. Claire looked at me somberly, the answer shining sadly in her eyes. "Or am I?"

"I haven't been able to date much in my lifetime," she said, purposefully revealing no more.

"Because you met him when you were very young?" I inferred. I was nearing my breaking point. I needed to see some of whatever it was she was hiding from me. "It's okay, Claire, you can tell me anything. It doesn't have to be everything. I just—don't know how else to let you know that I'm here for you. That I'm not going anywhere, no matter what you tell me about your past."

She was silent. "Please, Claire, please. It's just me. You trust me, right? Nothing you could say is going to change anything."

"People always say that but . . ." Claire was gritting her teeth, forcing whatever was on the tip of her tongue to stay inside. "There are some things that once you speak them, you can't un-tell someone. Sharing secrets isn't reversible."

"But it doesn't matter," I said, desperate to get her to understand. "You won't need to reverse it. I'm still going to love you just as much, no matter what."

Claire blinked rapidly a few times. "You . . . love me?" she asked.

My god, it had just slipped out. That was, of course, not how I'd intended to tell her. But it was the truth. I loved her so very, very much. And I wasn't protecting either of us anymore by keeping that to myself. "Yes," I told her. "I love you. I've been wanting to tell you that for a long, long time."

She was quiet for a moment. "There are so many things to tell you, I don't know how to begin. It's not that I don't trust you. I just don't know if I'm ready." I was disappointed, of course, but I thought I understood as well. Claire's life was so much bigger than mine. There was no way I could understand it all.

She didn't leave, but she didn't say much more. I tried to get a read on what was going on in her mind. I was sure she was angry with me for pushing her to reveal things she didn't want to reveal. I was angry with me. I hadn't wanted to tell her I loved her in a hurry like that. I'd had plans for a grand moment. The words had just fallen out.

When we went to bed that night, it was different, needier. We were both staking our claim on each other. A patina of secrecy still hung in the air around us.

We lay together afterward, both exhausted. We stayed there longer than we should have, limbs entangled, unspoken secrets swirling around us in the evening air next to my unreciprocated confession of love.

CLAIRE

What on earth was wrong with me? I sat in my parked car a few blocks away from the door to my apartment and stared out into the night. Sure, I was frustrated with Jean for pushing me. But I understood it, of course I did. It was obvious to him how much I was hiding. Why couldn't I just come clean and tell Jean the whole story? And tell him that I loved him too? I knew I loved him. I'd never felt this way about anyone before. I wanted to tell him that. I wanted to tell him everything, I swore to myself. I was only digging myself in deeper with every question I escaped, each answer I denied him. It wasn't that bad—I had blown this so far out of proportion in my mind. Right?

I tried to remember the last time I'd told someone the whole story, someone who didn't already know me. I hadn't made very many new friends in the past few years; I had just been focused on getting by. I'd even clammed up when Linda started asking harmless questions. She wouldn't have batted an eyelash; why should my drama have affected her? But I didn't know where to start and once I'd covered it up, I didn't know how to bring it back up.

Uninvited and unwanted, my mom's voice popped into my head. It had been years since I'd heard it, but it rang through clear as day, like she was sitting next to me in the car. The judgment, the disappointment. If I even began to confide in her about what was happening now, she'd just laugh. She'd never believe someone like Jean could love someone like me.

He'd said he loved me. And I loved him back, even if I didn't tell him tonight. I was too afraid, too frustrated by his pushing. But I did love him. And because of that, tomorrow, I'd tell him. I'd start by telling him that I hadn't seen Jeremy in years; I didn't even know if he was still in this city, even though I'd only moved here because of him. I hated thinking about that time.

When I first met Jeremy, I was sixteen. That was the first of many things my mother took issue with; I was still a girl, as she told me over and over again. And he was older, much older. I was too young to see that he was wrong for me but old enough to know others would think that. I kept him a secret from her and from Gracie for as long as I could. And when I couldn't hide it anymore, she let it rip.

When there was no home for me there anymore, Jeremy said there were opportunities in the city and he wanted me to come with him. I never asked what kind of opportunities. I just said okay. I didn't tell her where I'd gone; I didn't hide it either. She never tried to find me so I assumed I was right— she didn't care.

I thought life in the city would be something entirely different from home, that it would be the life I'd always dreamed of, a life of excitement and glamour. That's what he promised me, and I thought, *Okay, this is it.*

This was not it. When I was able to work, Jeremy got me a job at a friend's place around the corner from our apartment. I worked the counter every morning, ringing people up for their black coffees and breakfast sandwiches. I got home around noon and he was off to "work." He never answered any of my questions about what that work entailed and why he didn't come home until right before I had to leave in the morning. He never answered my calls, whether during the day or at night. It was like I was his employee, only good for a check at this point and a meager one at that. I didn't know anyone else here; I couldn't exactly up and leave. I was trapped.

One morning, he just never came back. I waited for him, watching the clock tick closer to the start of my shift and then barrel right on through it. I sat there for hours, simultaneously shocked that he was gone while also feeling completely unsurprised that this was how it had ended. I harbored no hopes he'd show up in a day or two. I knew he was never going to walk through that door again. Twenty-four hours passed and I was terrified, but finally I was free.

I worked up the nerve to call my mom to tell her he was gone and to ask if I could come home. She didn't answer. I didn't know if my voicemail would change anything, but I thought I'd at least hear back. I needed to know who it was she hated: Jeremy? Or me?

Nothing, radio silence, until Gracie showed up by herself a few days later, suitcase in hand. She never mentioned my mother or my message, just said she thought I might need her. And I did. So, she'd stayed ever since.

She took over the work at home and I moved from one job to the next. The deli refused to take me back after I'd missed almost a week of shifts with no warning. I moved on to a local bar in the area that always had a help wanted sign in the window. I wasn't experienced enough to be a bartender, so they stuck a spray bottle and a rag in my hand and let me pick up dirty glasses, clean dishes when needed, and try to keep the bathrooms in order. I soon learned why that help wanted sign was perpetually in the window—the clientele was terrible. Each shift was an exercise in trying to keep other people's hands off me. I kept the ring on for whatever protection it might offer me.

Gracie could tell I was miserable and urged me to look for anything else. Citing my deli experience, I was able to get a job at a trendy new coffee shop that had just opened. The work was dull, but the space was nice and the clientele was better. I could have worked there forever, but they announced suddenly that they would be closing up shop. One day, they were there; the next, they were gone. I'd always wondered how they'd made enough money to afford the rent until I understood they didn't.

I looked for something similar but struck out over and over again. I widened my search, inquiring at restaurants, bars, grocery stores, willing to accept the first job I was offered, until Gracie caught me by surprise. She sat me down and questioned how I wanted to spend the rest of my life. She wasn't asking about my dream job; if I'd said astronaut or princess or even doctor, she would have laughed in my face. She just wanted me to pick a place, any place, and want to work there.

I said the first thing that came to mind: if I could do anything or work anywhere, it would be at an art museum. I didn't care what the job was. She was understandably surprised; I hadn't mentioned art or museums since I won that contest as a kid. She asked me to explain and I told her about the picture Mom kept in the kitchen, how it always made me feel happy and safe to look at it and I was kind of desperate to feel happy and safe again.

Three days later, she returned from the library with a map of all the art museums in the area and the addresses and phone

numbers of their employment offices. I was so touched, I
didn't tell her I could have looked all of this up on my cellphone.

With each shift in the museum, I felt like I was coming
back to life a little bit more. I still couldn't believe these nights
with Jean were my life—glamorous parties, exciting new people, a never-ending list of places to explore, a love that felt bigger and bolder than I could have ever imagined. Of course, not
everything was a fairy tale. The days were still an exhaustive
list of responsibilities to manage. And once again, I was in a
relationship I had to keep a secret from everyone else. But
maybe that was why I'd kept everything about my normal life
so far apart from my world with Jean. Maybe I just didn't want
all of this to exist in the same place.

I thought of Jean's mother. Their relationship seemed so
different from mine with my own mom. No, there didn't seem
to be a passionate maternal love there, but she didn't ignore
his existence. She treated him with care and respect. She was
there for him, every day. Maybe his father was more like my
mother. They'd both abandoned us because that was what was
easiest for them.

I knew this because of all that Jean had confided in me.
When I pushed him to open up to me, he answered. That
wasn't fair, and my feelings were not the only ones that mattered. Tomorrow, I would start to make things right. We'd
start with Jeremy. It wasn't everything, but it was something.
And someday, I'd tell him the rest of the story too. I pushed
open my car door and stepped out into the unusually warm
night, heading back to my reality.

21

JEAN

The sun rose on another Friday morning. The day began as it typically does: a handful of school groups, teachers with nervous energy, kids bouncing off the walls as if they'd been shot out of a cannon. I wondered if it was just me or if everyone was truly a bit more frantic than usual today. Maybe it was both.

I couldn't stop thinking about the way Claire and I had left things the night before. Was I selfish for pushing her the way I had? I knew these were her secrets to reveal when she was ready. And I meant it when I told her that nothing she said would change my mind about her. So why did I even want to know? I would apologize to her tonight. I would tell her she could take her time. I would be patient. I would ask her to forgive me.

After the tour groups left around lunchtime, the gallery emptied out almost completely. Every so often, a young person or two would pass through, maybe alone, maybe with a friend in tow. But it was a small showing compared to what a spring Friday would normally bring. I noticed people going more than a few steps out of their way to avoid other strangers in their path.

That struck me as odd, but what came next was even more worrisome. In the afternoon, a few hours before our usual closing time, Jamie appeared, a small radio in her hand that crackled with indistinguishable conversation. She was informing patrons that the museum would be closing early, and they'd need to make their way swiftly to the exit.

"This is really happening?" a teenage-looking patron asked. Jamie bore a grave look on her face.

"I don't know much more, but this is what's happening today."

"I can't believe it," the only elderly patron I'd seen in the museum today said as she clutched her gallery guidebook to her chest. "I've never seen something like this." She stood still for a moment, as if saving a memory of us as we existed right then and there.

"I don't think any of us have," said Jamie. "I don't know if anyone ever has."

I watched as the handful of visitors hurried toward the stairs. After the last patron had left, Jamie stood between the two benches, directly in the center of the room. She spun in a circle, slowly, with the same level of attention to detail Claire showed in those first few nights. She gave us a small wave, then she followed behind the others.

We could hear the staff picking up their belongings on the floors below. After a few minutes of commotion, the doors were shut. The ceiling lights went out, though the sun still shone through the windows. It was eerily quiet. We held our places for a few additional minutes, but it was clear we were completely alone.

Marguerite was, of course, the first to speak. "Well, I am truly interested to hear what your friend has to say tonight."

That was a first. She had adopted an air of complete uninterest when it came to Claire, and I was not eager for the two of them to meet. My whole existence had become about making Claire feel welcome, about minimizing the differences between us. Something told me that introducing her to Marguerite would undo the work I'd put in.

"I am as well. I will, of course, ask her and report back."

She pulled out a cigarette. We were all a bit unsure if we were free to go about our evenings. It seemed there was a collective decision to hold tight for a moment to see if anything changed. "Have you met Jean's special friend?" Marguerite asked Pierre.

"Marguerite," I warned.

"What?" she asked, exhaling a plume of smoke. "It was just a question."

Pierre shook his head. "No," he said. "But Maman has. I saw them with her one night, in the garden." He looked at me and shrugged. I didn't fault him. It wasn't a secret. But I hated being reminded that everyone's eyes were on me—ironic, I know, given my day job.

After enough time passed to assure everyone that the coast was clear, Marguerite and Pierre stood up from their bench. "Well, have a lovely evening," Marguerite called out as she glided away, her words lasting longer in the room than she did. Pierre also pulled on a cap and ran along after her. My mother rose from her rocker, and once again, I was alone. Waiting.

I wondered what Claire would have to say about the weird behavior of the museum director today. I wondered if there wasn't something grimmer going on outside these walls; it could even be something as serious as a war. I worried for Claire's safety. I tried to ground myself. I was taking this too far. Claire would, of course, be fine. She would have mentioned if a war was imminent, wouldn't she? The issue must have been something more benign; maybe they were worried about a possible theft. Now that would make things interesting.

Each year they upgraded the security in our museum, the anti-theft technology getting more and more sophisticated. It wasn't as easy to steal things as it had been before. But if they kept upgrading the systems, theft must still be possible. I myself had never witnessed it, but that didn't mean the threat wasn't real.

I spent a bit of time lost in my fantasy about being a bystander to an extremely elaborate museum heist. In my mind, the thieves wore three-piece suits and smoked cigars as they carried the artwork out to where an old-fashioned getaway car—a horse, maybe—was waiting. There was even a musical score, something jaunty and suspenseful. Maybe something string-heavy.

I woke myself from my daydream. I wasn't sure how much time had passed, but I knew it had been quite a while. Claire still wasn't there. On the other hand, we'd closed early, so it would make sense that I had lost perspective on how long it had been. Maybe it was still early. I had no way to mark time except for the sky through the windows, which had been dark for at least some time now. My shoulders were hunched together with stress. I unclenched them and massaged my jaw. I wasn't tired, I didn't get tired, but I was feeling quite stiff. I switched my position and took a seat on the floor. I lay on my side, propping myself up on my elbow.

What if she never came back? What if the bad taste in my mouth from last night was how things ended between us? What if this was all over?

I rolled to my back. It must have been many hours by now. I was the patient one. I could handle this. Maybe Claire had a larger assignment now, maybe she needed to clean additional rooms along with ours. Maybe Linda had caught her up in conversation in the break room. Maybe they were receiving new instructions tonight and would be up later.

Later came and went. There was still no sign of her. There was no sign of anyone. Maybe there had been an emergency at home, something with her family, and she couldn't make it to work today. Remembering how distressed she had been the night I was meeting with Antoinette and she came in to find our frame empty, I resolved to maintain my post all night in case she showed up. It's not like I had anywhere else to be. It was funny how quickly my brain and body forgot that I used to spend every night like this. I had become so accustomed to Claire's presence, I didn't know how to be alone anymore.

The sun rose, flooding the gallery with cool morning light, illuminating tiny dust particles floating in the air. Marguerite and Pierre returned; they could see it written on my face.

"She never showed?" Marguerite asked. I shook my head. "Neither did Linda." My composure collapsed with relief. It wasn't just us; Claire had not left me. It was everyone who had not come. But relief was quickly replaced again with concern. What if something larger was afoot? What if there *was* a war out there?

"Wow," Pierre said quietly. "I guess last night we were really and truly alone."

"I guess so," Marguerite said. "How strange." Her fingers traced her black ribbon. "Well, it's nearly time." Out of habit, we all took up our usual positions, waiting to hear the reception hall come to life.

It never did. After a few hours, I noticed figures in paintings around us begin to drop their poses.

"What the devil is going on out there?" Marguerite asked.

"Maybe it's a massive snowstorm?" I posited. We looked through the windows to the sunny day outside. It was doubtful, even to the most naïve of forecasters.

"Well, I'm sure they'll be back in a few days," Marguerite

said through her third cigarette of the morning. Sensing my heightened anxiety, she added, "I'm sure *everyone* will be back."

"What if . . ." I could hardly get the sentence out. "What if something's really wrong out there?"

Marguerite thought about my question before responding. "Jean, if something really is wrong out there, what are you going to do about it?" With that, she walked away.

She was right. There was absolutely nothing I could do.

Pierre put a small hand on my shoulder. "I'm sure everything is okay, Jean. I bet she'll be back tonight!" I patted his hand with my own. I couldn't summon the same optimism, so I said nothing.

22

CLAIRE

"Hello?" I answered my phone, the dread audible in my voice. It was Monday. The phone number on the incoming call was still unsaved in my contacts, but this time, I knew who was calling.

"Hi, Claire, it's Jamie again," the woman on the line said, confirming my suspicions.

"Hi, Jamie, how are you?" I said, feeling a compulsion to be polite even though I knew the odds were slim that this call would go the way I wanted it to. I was no idiot; the news had been inescapable these past few days.

"Oh, you know, it's been a weird one. Not issues I'd ever thought I'd have to tackle in the first few months of this job or maybe ever but . . ." she trailed off.

"Yeah, I hear that. I don't think any of us saw this one coming."

"I'm sure someone did. Alas, I am guessing you've anticipated I'm not calling with good news."

"I figured as much."

"Now, we don't really have any sense of how long this will last or where we'll be when it's all over. We are temporarily closing the museum but it is just that, temporary. We are complying with the government mandates to keep all non-essential employees at home, so we're stripping back everything except security and anyone necessary to current conservation projects. Basically, we have to keep the art safe until we can all get back to normal."

I doubted we would ever return to what we'd thought of as normal before, but this didn't seem like the proper time for a debate.

"Okay," I said.

"So, now for the details part. We are going to lay you all off. I recognize that phrase sounds terrifying, but when we do, you'll be eligible to apply for unemployment, which I'd recommend you do as soon as possible. And I want to say as clearly as I can that we fully intend to hire you all back when we are able. We just don't know when that will be. I'm hoping this lasts for no more than a few weeks but . . . we just don't know." Her naturally authoritative tone was slipping with each bit of doubt she showed. I knew somewhere in the back of my brain that this situation must be a horror to manage, but I could only think about myself in the moment.

I couldn't believe this was how Jean and I had left things, me tight-lipped and refusing him the one thing he asked. Telling him the truth seemed so easy with so many days and one global catastrophe between us now. He didn't even know I loved him.

"I hope that's true," I said, not really hearing the words as they came out of my mouth. "I really hope I'll get to come back." It was an understatement.

"Me too," Jamie promised. "I will do everything in my power to make it so."

I had, of course, heard promises and been burned before, so

I took this with a grain of salt. I said my goodbyes and hung up the phone; I was sure she had many other calls to make. With a click, she was gone. Tears were already rolling down my cheeks. I'd known the whole time this was too good to be true and just like that, it was gone. I was mad at myself; this was not about me. People were getting really sick, lives were at stake. But how would I support my family?

I couldn't stop the stupid tears from coming. I let myself lean up against the counter of our tiny kitchen and I cried my heart out. Would Jean have any idea what had happened, or would he think we were all gone for good? Did he have a frame of reference for what this was? I'd heard them compare it on the news to the Spanish flu, but that had been 1918. If Jean had been painted in 1917, he would never have lived through it himself.

After my tear ducts had run themselves dry, I ran the tips of my sleeves under my eyes, wiping away any mascara that might have smudged and silently sniffling. I needed to pull myself together; I didn't want to scare anyone. I needed to make a plan.

I opened our cabinet and stared into it in horror. There was barely anything in there that could be pulled together to make dinner, even though it had only been three days since I'd last braved the hellscape that our grocery store had become. What on earth had I been doing when I was in there on Friday?

Well, Friday had been one heck of an afternoon, but I'd managed to get out of the house with a few minutes to spare. I shoved the apple in my hand in between my teeth, holding it there as I leaned down to put my car key into the lock. Oh, how I envied the women in the grocery store parking lot whose fancy cars unlocked at the mere signal of their approach. They didn't even have to open their purses.

Because Gracie had jumped in for me, I would have just enough time to do a grocery store run before work. I wouldn't be able to grab anything perishable but maybe I could scoop up a few more bottles of water and dry-food things. That's what they kept saying to do on the news, at least.

The car blared to life, the radio screaming with the voices of our local news anchors. I forgot Gracie had borrowed my car earlier. I turned the volume dial all the way down and switched over to the soft rock station; I needed a break from the doomsaying. The news was all panic these days.

I pulled out from the tiny spot Gracie had squeezed the car into and zipped on over to the highway, pulling up to the store a few minutes later. Twenty minutes left before I had to be on the way to the museum—this would be my own version of that show Gracie loved, *Supermarket Sprint* or something like that.

The grocery store experience was far more harrowing than I had anticipated. My basket holding the few nonperishable items I'd found left on the shelves looked silly compared to the other shoppers' carts stacked high with valuable items like Clorox wipes and six-packs of paper towels. Even the store-brand goods that I favored—because I couldn't afford anything else—were nearly all picked over. I grabbed some extra vitamin C and a few boxes of Easy Mac, a favorite in our household, and spent way too long evaluating which soup flavors I'd never heard of before would taste best. I went with split pea and ham. The chicken noodles were long gone. I was sure this wasn't enough, but I couldn't think of anything else to grab. What were the odds they'd shut the stores down? No matter what was happening or how bad things got, people needed food. Right?

I could admit it: I was distracted. My brain was not functioning on its normal wavelength. Instead, it was occupied by thoughts of how Jean was doing, what he was feeling about us, about the way things had ended the night before. I was psyching myself up to go in there and tell him everything. At first, I thought I'd just start at the beginning, but overnight I'd realized it was time he knew all of it.

Everything in the store was taking longer than expected. The aisles were crowded with people like me, confused about what to buy to prep for something none of us understood. The line for checkout stretched down the cereal aisle and was moving slower than normal, as both the cashiers and the customers were taking pains to stand as far apart as possible. One lady was wiping every item down with disinfectant before she put it in a bag. My skin grew itchy in that way it did when I knew I'd miscalculated the amount of time something was going to take. I reached into my bag to distract myself with my phone and found nothing. I must have left it in the car in my distracted state. All I could do was wait. I picked at the skin around my nails, a habit I was humiliated by but couldn't for the life of me break. Finally, it was my turn and I threw the proper change at the cashier.

"Sorry," I shouted over my shoulder as I barreled my way back out to the parking lot. "I'm going to be late for work!" I couldn't imagine I'd get in that much trouble for being a few minutes late, but I never had been before because I didn't want to miss a single second of potential time with Jean. And that night, I was practically sprinting in his direction, desperate to make things right.

I tossed the groceries into the back seat and turned the car on, only stopping for a moment to glance at my phone before I put the car in reverse. I caught a glimpse of three missed calls from the same local number and paused, putting the car back in park while I evaluated the situation. I thought that number might be the museum, though I had never saved it into my contacts.

There was a voicemail, left after the third call. I opened it up and listened.

"Hi, Claire, it's Jamie, from the museum. I hope I've caught you before you've left home, but it seems like you may already be on your way. If you get this in time, could you please give me a call? My number is . . ."

I swiped out of the message and hit the button to dial back. In less than half a ring, Jamie answered.

"Hello, Jamie Leigh here."

"Hi, Jamie, it's, um, Claire?" Did I need to describe who I was? I doubted the museum president, whom I had never met, and I were on a first name basis.

"Ah, Claire, yes, I've been hoping you'd call. Look, to cut to the chase, we are currently locking up the doors for the night. I'm sorry if you're already on your way here; I was trying to catch you before you left—"

At the end of the call, she promised to call on Monday with more updates. And now here it was, said Monday. Now I was fully up to date, fully unemployed, fully unable to get back into that painting, back where I belonged. But, then again, this was where I belonged too.

There was Gracie, a towel in one hand, holding the wall as she walked down the hallway. She was surprised to see me in this state and stopped her pursuit.

"Honey, what happened? Are you feeling okay?" She made to put her hand on my forehead, studying my face as she got closer. "Have you been crying? Is everything okay?"

"The museum is closing," I muttered. I could feel the tears welling up in my eyes again, threatening to erupt.

"Oh, honey," she said as she wrapped me in her arms. "I was worried something like that might happen. Don't worry, we'll figure it out together. We always do." I nodded against her shoulder. "Come on, put on some cozy clothes. You can get to sleep at a normal time every night this week. There, already a silver lining. Luna!" she called.

"Mommy!" a voice shrieked as Luna streaked out of the bathroom, a towel streaming behind her like a cape. She jumped into my arms and nuzzled against me, her wet hair wiping against my cheek. I breathed in her baby shampoo scent and felt instantly at home. "Do you want to pick out my pj's, Mommy?" she asked. I really did not want to start crying again, so I buckled the tears in.

"Why don't you let Gracie help you, nugget, while I figure out what the grown-ups are eating for dinner tonight? I'll be there in four minutes to read you a story before you go to sleep."

Luna looked disappointed, but Gracie swooped in as she always did. "I bet I can guess which ones you want to wear!" she said as she headed off to the bedroom we all shared.

"Cannot!" Luna called, running to beat Gracie to it.

I returned to the kitchen; Luna had already eaten and I washed her bowl out in the sink. I needed something to do to keep my hands from shaking. I needed a plan, a way to keep us all safe and fed. Gracie and Luna were my entire world. And I couldn't bring myself to tell Jean about them until it was too late.

It wasn't that I was worried he'd think differently of me. Jean was the opposite of judgmental. It was just that I spent my entire life, day in and day out, living for Luna. Of course I did, I loved her more than words could say. But my time with Jean, my time in the museum, those were the only moments of the past four years where I hadn't been defined as being Luna's mom. I could just be me.

At least there was a silver lining in all of this. And that silver lining was probably getting impatient for a bedtime story.

"Has it been four minutes?" I asked as I poked my head around the door of our room. Gracie had just tucked Luna under the covers of her twin bed, which we had nestled in one corner in between the closet and the wall. The double bed Gracie and I shared was on the opposite side of the room. It was different from Luna's not just in its size but in the absence of the pink unicorn blanket and sheets Luna and I had picked out together when we upgraded her from the crib. I picked up the corner of that blanket now and wrapped it around myself as I snuggled into her bed alongside her.

I took a deep breath. These were the things I could never feel in Jean's world. Under this warm blanket with my sweet, sometimes sticky baby girl, I was reminded of what my life really was. What it needed to be.

"Which book do you want Mommy to read?" I asked, trying to remember what we had in the stack. It had been a while since I'd taken bedtime duty. "What about that one with the dragons and their tacos?"

"No, Mommy, no." Luna shook her head. "Your story, Mommy."

I sighed, knowing she didn't mean a book I had written. When she was just a baby, I'd started making up stories to keep her entertained, and I was sorry to report that as she'd grown older, they'd become her favorites. I loved doing it but neither one of us ever wanted to quit, and the stories could get quite long-winded. I wasn't sure I had that in me tonight.

"Just a few minutes, okay, baby? Then we'll do a little more tomorrow too."

"Mommy, are you going to be here tomorrow and the next day and the next day?" she asked.

"Yes, honey. Mommy's going to be here a lot more. Work's closed right now." Oh god, was her preschool going to close? I needed to talk to Gracie. "What story should we tell tonight, Moon?"

"The little girl who can go into the art."

23

JEAN

She was not back on Saturday night, nor was she back on Sunday. No one was. Days passed and the galleries remained empty. I'd never known how reliant I was on the constant ebb and flow of museum visitors until the seas sat still for days on end.

We stopped assuming our positions each morning. The nights bled into the days; the days were no different from the nights. Before Claire, I'd romanticized my loneliness. I had no one, but I needed no one. I was most myself when I was alone. I'd made it my prevailing personality trait.

Today and every day now, my loneliness felt oppressive. It threatened to crush me, and I didn't have it in me to get out of its way. Marguerite and Pierre had tried to engage with me at the start, but it was increasingly clear that this time was in no way weighing on them the same way it affected me. If anything, this was something like a vacation for them, each free to spend all their hours however they pleased. They came back occasionally to check on me, always under the pretense of having forgotten something or of needing a break, but I saw right through them. Whatever they saw in me was not what they were looking for.

I had always been so good at waiting. I couldn't figure out what part of myself I had lost—why I couldn't sustain myself through this time like I had all the other times when isolation had been my normal. I couldn't read; I felt sick when I looked at the violin. I entertained myself for a while with games of the imagination, trying to picture what Claire was up to wherever she was, but that lost its charm quickly, as was to be expected. I couldn't envision what her life out there was like. I couldn't guess what anyone's life out there was like.

I took to wandering through the various landscapes, trying my best to avoid all other people. It wasn't as hard as it sounds, despite how many of us there were in the museum. The others tended to congregate in the usual spots: around the card table, at the races, by the pier. I never went near *Le Bonheur de vivre*. I took the long routes, winding my way through abandoned spaces. I came to prefer the landscapes on the first floor that faced the large, two-story windows. I watched through the glass for any signs of life outside. I rarely saw anyone pass.

I thought maybe there'd been some apocalyptic event and we didn't know that we were the only ones left. But I realized paintings probably wouldn't have survived the apocalypse either. And I knew that some people remained out there; every so often, I would see a car driving along the street, just visible through the tree line.

I missed the tour groups, with the guides trying to make the art accessible to students and the patrons striving to make their experience the best it could possibly be. I missed the chatter in the galleries, picking up on small pieces of the lives of strangers I would never see again. I missed the museum associates, careening from room to room with a sense of urgency. I missed Linda.

I missed Claire so fiercely, I sometimes wondered if I had made the entire thing up. One hundred years in the same place seems like it could bring on a bout of madness; maybe it had finally caught up with me. The thing was, I hadn't felt mad then. I felt mad now. I caught myself replaying the conversations we'd had, murmuring aloud the words we'd exchanged. It reminded me of how I had acted before she had leapt into my world, desperate to find a way to communicate with her. That was a shadow of a sentiment compared to the way I wished for her now. Knowing her had ruined me forever.

There was no respite; it was me and my wild emotions and little else. I never needed to be alone with my thoughts again. And yet there was no end in sight. Barring the museum reopening, which didn't seem to be anywhere on the horizon, I couldn't see a way out. I was trapped.

I was sitting on a bluff, staring out at the water. This was the same sea I'd taken Claire to after our first night at the racetrack. The same small purple clouds hung in the sky; the same swells crashed gently into the shore, each dotted with the same white foam. Everything felt the same and entirely different all at once. I was lost in my memory of us together in this place, one of the only past times I actively sought out these days.

Motion startled me back to the present. A great pouf of black took over the right side of my field of vision as Odette sat down next to me, tucking her voluminous black skirts around her. I hadn't seen her since Claire and I had been to visit her gallery during Antoinette's inaugural art history lesson. At first, we were both silent, as I had been before she joined me.

After many minutes, she turned to me and said, "You are sad." She was right. I nodded to show her so. "You miss her." I nodded again. "I have seen you, all these weeks, moving like a ghost through the museum."

I hadn't run into her once; I wasn't sure what she was talking about.

"From across the room," she clarified, gesturing at the gallery we were in right now, looking toward the paintings on the opposite wall. That made more sense.

"Did you follow me here?" I hadn't spoken aloud in days; my voice cracked with lack of use.

"I guess you could say that." She danced around the question. "You caught my eye from across the way. I thought you could use someone to talk to. We used to talk, you remember, I am sure, though it has been a very, very long time."

It had been more than half a century since I had spoken to Odette one on one. So much had changed since. I hardly even saw myself as the same person I'd been then.

"I remember," I responded simply.

"It is a neat bit of magic, what you and she have pulled off."

"It's not me who did anything," I said. "It's her. She's the magic one." I meant it, with my whole heart.

"I've been wondering: How did she think to try in the first place?" Odette asked.

"She says she's always had this feeling, since she was a kid, that she could just lean a little closer, stand a little taller, and fall right through."

"Accessible to all, maybe, who dare to believe it's possible."

"Have you ever heard of something like this before?"

"It's funny," she mused, not answering my question. "To think of a time before we knew of the inner lives of art. Do you ever think about what your relationship with paintings was like before you inhabited one?"

"Not in so specific a way. I think, in the past, I harbored jealousy for paintings and their ability to consume my father's attention so completely. But I had no sense of, no critical thought about, no ability to envision the movement beneath their surface level."

"What are you going to do, Jean?" Odette sharply changed the topic. "Wait?"

I always waited. "I don't know what else there is to do."

Odette let out a small *hmm*. I didn't know what she expected from me.

"And do you think she's doing the same?"

I had no idea. I'd lost track of how much time had passed, but the trees coming to life with green through the windows told me we were undoubtedly in spring. What if it had been too much time? What if she'd had to move on to someone new? Or back to her fiancé? I shuddered at the thought. What if waiting had hurt her as much as it was hurting me?

I hoped for the opposite; I hoped whatever was going on out there took her mind off me. I hoped she was preoccupied. I hoped, against all odds, that if it would help her to move on, she would do so. I only wanted what would make her happy.

"I'm sorry," Odette said. "It wasn't my place to pry. I only meant to say that humans . . . They can't always be what we want them to be. Things change, people make choices. And these are certainly"—she gestured to the empty gallery in front of us as she chose her words carefully—"unprecedented circumstances."

"That they are," I agreed gruffly.

I wasn't eager to share the darkness of my internal monologue with Odette, but I was surprisingly not annoyed that she was there. It was kind of reassuring to have someone force me to speak after so many weeks. I'd forgotten I was even capable of it.

"What have you been doing to entertain yourself?" she asked. "I'd never noticed how long a day could feel until the hours of freedom basically doubled. I've wished more than once that we needed to sleep after all."

"I haven't really done anything," I said. "I kind of just *exist* in here right now."

"Well, I've read practically every single book in this place. Many of them more than once; some are significantly better than others."

"I'd basically done that," I said. "Before all the . . . you know, before Claire."

"Yes!" she said. "I remembered you were a reader. I thought of you as I hunted down the various books of the museum."

"You can borrow my book sometime, if you want."

"Really?" Her eyebrows rose in surprise. "Thank you, Jean, that's very kind."

"I've read it so many times I can't even count."

"I bet you have." She laughed gracefully; everything about her was graceful. "I will absolutely take you up on that."

"Okay," I said. She let us fall into silence again. We watched the waves crash along the shore. A seagull spun lazy circles above our heads, finding a place to land near his colony that was already dotting the beach. "Do you think he notices anything different?" I asked Odette about our unhurried flying friend.

"Absolutely," she said. "He's watching the same world as the rest of us, isn't he?"

"What do you think is going on out there?"

"I have a hard time picturing anything of their world." I nodded; I struggled with the same blocked imagination. She continued. "But I'd be lying if I said I hadn't considered what it could be. Financial foreclosure was my first thought, trouble with the museum, but they would have sent people in here to appraise us by now. I've thought of war, but I'm not sure that's it. I feel like if it was war, the kind of war that kept even the curatorial and janitorial staff from coming in, even just once, I feel like we'd be able to see it. Maybe that's out of date but when I think about the Paris I left, the one of the war, this just isn't the same."

"I know what you mean," I said. "And I keep thinking if it was a war, we'd hear planes flying overhead, feel bombs hitting the ground. We'd maybe even be a target. And instead, we hear . . ."

"Nothing." She filled in the blank of my dangling sentence. "Some kind of mass illness, maybe? There was one, right at the end of my previous life, starting to cause trouble in the cities. But is shutting down the museum how they would have dealt with that? It seems hard to imagine."

"You know," I said, changing the topic, "in some of the paintings, they're reveling. If you're bored, you can definitely find a party elsewhere. I bet Marguerite could point the way."

"I'm sure she could."

"They see this as some big vacation."

"And why shouldn't they? Nothing else is required of them, not now." She ruffled her brilliant red hair, each piece of it falling perfectly into place in response. "But that will get old, I'm sure. The wine tastes the same night after night, you know."

"I'll take your word for it," I replied.

"Well," she said as she stood. Her skirt fell into elegant ripples around her, but she smoothed it out anyway. "I'd best be off, but I'll come find you again. To borrow that book, as you said."

I nodded enthusiastically. "Please do. Odette," I said, her name tumbling out of my mouth.

"Yes?"

"Thank you. For coming to find me. I think I needed this— to talk to someone else."

"Of course, Jean," she said as she tossed her head to the side, sweeping her bangs across her face without using her hands. "Something's going on and you shouldn't have to handle it alone. None of us should. What else are old friends for?"

With that, she sauntered off toward the horizon, her hands behind her back carrying a paperback book. I considered her words—"old friends." Was that what we were? I noticed that for the first time in so many days, my chest felt a little less like it might crack open at any moment.

CLAIRE

My head was going to explode.

The voice of Luna's teacher was booming through the speakers of the school-issued laptop that we'd picked up in the parking lot of her prekindergarten the week after the museum had closed. She'd since been engaged in "virtual school," which was currently a racket of shrieks and shouts as the dogged teacher attempted to teach them a song through the screen. Luna had quickly learned where the volume buttons were and enjoyed turning them up and down with abandon.

Gracie's crafty side had awoken in the last few weeks and she was currently bent over the sewing machine she had picked up in the basement of our building and nursed back to health. For days, she'd unscrewed, cleaned, and reinstalled each piece of the machine. When she finally dared to plug it in and turn it on, sure enough, it roared to life. And I mean *roared.* The thing made so much noise when she got it up and running that I wondered if its previous owners had discarded it because it was simply too darn loud, and our apartment was feeling smaller by the day.

And then there was me. For the first time in I didn't even know how long, I didn't have anything to be doing next. So here I was, lying on the couch, staring up at the ceiling, losing my mind.

Of course, the list of options of what I could spend my time on was endless. I could deal with the dishes from lunch that were just sitting in the sink. I could get a jump start on dinner. I could clean that weird corner of the tub where the grout would never go back to white. I could brush my teeth, which I wasn't sure I'd done this morning. The days were blending together; I was losing sense of what had happened this morning, yesterday morning, last week.

Chug, chug, chug went Gracie's sewing machine. Luna was now clapping together a pot and a wooden spoon, two of the "learning items" the teacher had asked us to gather for this week's set of lessons. What she was learning at this very moment, I couldn't quite say.

"Gracie, do you think you could wait to do that?" I shouted.

"What?" she yelled back, not taking her eyes off her work for a moment.

"Never mind," I said, mostly to myself. I went back to my ceiling staring. I wondered what Jean was doing at this exact moment, with no museum visitors to gawk at him. Was he frozen in place or could he roam free? Was he freer than me?

"Okay, everyone, that's it for today! I'll see you again tomorrow! Have a good night and go be helpful to your mommies, daddies, guardians!" Luna's teacher was incredibly sweet and incredibly underpaid for the work she was putting in to teach these kids through a screen. I bet she indulged in a good ceiling-staring session every now and then too.

Behind us, Gracie had packed up her work for the day and had gone into our bedroom. She normally napped around this time of the afternoon. With the absence of the crashing sewing machine and the enthusiastic preschool Zoom, the apartment returned to a state of calm. Luna climbed onto my lap, lying against my chest. I felt two small hands on my cheeks, dragging my eyeline over until I was face-to-face with my mini me. "What can I do for you, Miss Luna?" I asked.

"Hi, Mommy," she replied, keeping her tiny, tender grip on my jaw.

"Hi, Moon. What do you want to do now?" The buzzer buzzed, a noise I found particularly scary because it had been weeks since I'd heard it. "Hold on a second, let Mommy deal with this." I plopped her down on the floor and she tottered off. I wondered if one of the neighbor's boxes was mistakenly getting dropped at our door.

I pressed my finger to the side of the buzzer that allowed me to talk to whoever was standing at the door. "Hello?" I asked, quickly switching over to the listening button.

"Claire . . ." a familiar voice started. My hand dropped immediately, silencing whatever he was saying next. I turned to make sure Luna hadn't heard anything, but she was happily emptying her basket of toys I'd just put away back onto the floor. The buzzer rang again.

"Stop buzzing. I'll come down in a minute," I said into it, grateful I didn't have to hear a response unless I allowed it in. I walked over to Luna, leaving her mess be for now. "Moon, why don't you go lie down with Grandma for a moment?"

"But I don't want to sleep," she protested.

"Of course not, you don't have to sleep!" I was used to this one. "You can just lie there with your eyes closed. You can even take my spot. When you're done resting, we can play any game you want."

This little bribe appeased her and she zipped off to bed.

Once I made sure she was snuggled in, I whispered to Gracie that I'd be back in a minute. She waved me off and curled around Luna, both of their bodies looking small and safe under our comforter.

I put on shoes for the first time in days and decided to grab a jacket on my way out the door, having no idea what the temperature would be outside. Our neighborhood was crowded and hard to navigate without bumping into anyone, and an abundance of caution kept us indoors most of the time.

I opened the front door to find Jeremy leaning against the railing on the opposite side of the tiny porch in front of our building. My stomach lurched at the sight of him—the first time I'd laid eyes on him in years. He stood and made to step closer to greet me, but I held up an outstretched palm, an unspoken instruction to stay where he was. There were maybe six feet between us if we were lucky and although we were outside, the experts came up with new guidelines daily for how not to spread the disease. I wasn't taking any chances.

"What are you doing here?" I asked, no pleasantries possible in this conversation.

"Wow," he said. "It's great to see you. You look great."

"*What*," I repeated, "are you doing here?"

"Look," he said, rubbing his hand against the back of his neck. I remembered this, his tell. "I know I messed up."

I couldn't believe how unoriginal this conversation was. My life had become a fantasy and here I was, in a scene that could have been plucked from a badly written made-for-TV movie. It was harder to believe he was here, standing on my porch, so close to my safe space, than it was to believe I had the power to go inside a painting. But I wouldn't let him see my feathers ruffled by his sudden appearance.

"You didn't mess up," I corrected him. "You left. You left without a word and you never came back."

"Well." He tried for that charming smile that used to make

me weak in the knees, but I knew better now. I knew so much better. "I'm back now, aren't I?"

"No," I said bluntly. "No, you are not. We do not need you, we do not want you here, and there's a freaking global pandemic. Even if you were a better man, it's not safe."

"She's my daughter too, Claire," he pleaded. "You keep saying 'we' but do you really think that's what's best? For her to never know her dad? What would she choose?"

"I don't know what's best, but I do know you made that choice for her when you walked out that door. You're probably only back because you want something. And when you get what you need, you'll be gone again."

"It's not like that. I don't need anything. I've just—I've had a lot of time to think, these past few weeks. I miss her. And I want to know her again. It's okay if it's on whatever terms you say. I'll stay inside, quarantine or whatever. You tell me. Look," he said, pulling a slip of paper out of his pocket. "This is my number. You think about it and give me a call. I'll be around. You just let me know what works for you." He reached out to hand it to me, but I didn't take it. He left it on the ground near my feet like an offering.

I stared at it like it was a dead bug I'd need to deal with before Luna asked if it was okay and cried at the inevitable circle-of-life explanation I'd have to give. Jeremy was already making his way down the front steps. I called out to him. "You missed a lot."

He turned around. "Let me make it up to you, Claire, to both of you. I'll make things right. You'll see . . ." He turned again and walked down the street, out of our neighborhood. I hadn't watched him walk away the first time; he'd snuck out while Luna and I were asleep, tearing our lives apart in the most cowardly way possible. The abandonment had crushed me back then; now, more than three years later, I knew it was for the best. Long before he'd walked out the door, I could tell he didn't love me and he resented Luna. And he didn't deserve either of us. He'd only lasted a few months into life as a family of three. Luna was too young to remember any of it, though she asked about her daddy every once in a while.

Now he was back. And as much as I didn't want to admit he was right, it wasn't just up to me. I shoved the piece of paper into my pocket. His handwriting was familiar in that even though it had been years since I'd seen it, it looked like all boys' handwriting.

I wondered what Jean's handwriting looked like. I had never gotten the chance to see it. I thought it must be so different from this chicken scratch. If I ever got back in there, I'd make him write something down for me. Maybe I'd even try to carry it out with me when I left, some little part of him I could hold when he was gone.

JEAN

I was going to get out of here. Of course I'd heard the stories of others who had tried to escape, of their failed attempts. I wasn't the first one to want back their life on the other side of the frame. But none of them had the reason to get out that I had. None of them had a Claire to find. I had no idea how I would track her down once I was out, if I would even be able to navigate that world; I would figure that out on the other side.

I waited until the surrounding paintings were as empty as possible; I hadn't seen any of my family members in days, off as they were in their own corners of these halls. Most frames around me were deserted, the frames in our room not being the popular party spots. Anyone who remained was in a state of repose, drifting off in the daydreams surrounding them, paying me no attention.

I walked up to the watery layer of atmosphere that separated my world from the gallery. I had never tried in earnest to pass through it before. I might have, had Claire not walked so thoroughly into mine. I lifted a hand, nearly raising my fingertips up to the boundary, before I lost my nerve.

I was going to have to go for it all at once. I backed up, past the piano bench, until my calves brushed the radiator on the opposite wall. I removed my jacket and my tie, tossing them onto the piano bench next to me. I rolled my shoulders back and cracked my knuckles. It was time to go.

I took off running as quickly as I could toward the frame. It had been years since I'd run flat out and the sensation felt awkward in my muscles. I decided, in that split second, that I would try to jump right before the divide, hoping to land on my feet on the other side. At the right moment, I took off from the floor, hurtling toward the boundary.

I collided with what felt like a wall that expanded upon impact, sagging with the weight of my body and absorbing my energy before it flung me back into my world. I landed hard on the floor, my head and neck bracing for the impact. Every cell of my body hurt so intensely; I couldn't move. I stared despondently at the ceiling.

"Well, that was embarrassing," a familiar voice said above me.

I lifted my pounding head to find my sister sprawled across my usual chair, her hair a bit out of place, her shoes cast aside on the floor. Her black ribbon remained intact, swooping across her neck, but nearly everything else about her appearance was disheveled. If it were possible for Marguerite to develop dark shadows under her eyes, she would have them.

"What in the world happened to you?" I asked. "I haven't seen you for days."

"That's precisely the problem," she said as she fanned herself with my paperback book, which she had retrieved from the seat beneath her.

"You look terrible," I said.

"You're not looking so great yourself," she spat back. "Can I have a cigarette?"

I removed the case from my pocket, taking my time to roll her a cigarette I was proud of. Once I was satisfied, I offered it to her. She lifted her arm as if it was leaden and took the offering, holding it not quite to her lips. I lit it for her, and she took a grateful drag.

"I've never seen you like this before," I said, not as a critique but as the truth.

"Well," she said as she took another deep breath. "It's not something I care to make a habit of. Five straight weeks of revelry may be taking it a bit too far."

"It seems so," I agreed. Had it really been five weeks already? Time felt endless these days, but I could remember the feeling of holding Claire as if it were yesterday.

"What have you been up to? Please tell me you haven't been completely alone, making a martyr of yourself."

"I certainly haven't been spending any time with my sister," I spat out defensively. I meant it somewhat as a joke; I hadn't actually expected her to spend time watching me pine. But it had come out harsher than I'd intended. I tried to soften my tone. "I've been fine and, no, I haven't been alone. I was with Odette."

"You were, were you?" The cigarette was quickly becoming a prop dangling from her fingers as she assumed the role of all-knowing older sister. I could see that the gossip was reviving her from her hangover.

"We've been talking. Just talking," I said, even though I could see she wasn't listening.

"Right, right, of course. Well, as long as you haven't been lonely."

At that, an involuntary sob escaped my lips. We both looked up in surprise, but it was too late for me to regain control. Tears were streaming down my cheeks. I swiped up to dab at them with my tie. I didn't cry frequently; actually, I never cried. Even since the doors of the museum had closed, in the weeks since I'd seen Claire, there'd been no sign of a tear. But something about Marguerite's abject dismissal of my loneliness burst a bubble that had been growing in my chest, piercing straight through to my heart.

I collapsed onto the piano bench and put my head between my knees as the tears continued. I heard Marguerite rise from the chair and put out her cigarette. She slowly walked over to the other side of the bench, and I felt the fabric of her skirt against my thigh and her hand on my back, rubbing in slow, comforting circles. She said nothing; she was just there.

I pulled myself together and sat back up. Next to her, on this bench, with her hand still on my back, I felt like Pierre. I wondered what life would feel like if I'd been given someone to go through it with together, as they had. They were teammates; they spent the days whispering secrets to each other between piano scales. In my chair on the other side of the room, I'd been given solitude. I'd made that a part of my personality for so long, I'd forgotten it was never my choice in the first place.

I rested my head on Marguerite's shoulder as she said, "It's okay to miss her, Jean. I know what that's like. There's no point in trying to stop the feeling; it's going to be there regardless." We never spoke about Marguerite's own love life; I didn't know whether she was referring to someone in our world or someone she'd had to leave behind in the times before. She offered me a white handkerchief with small blue flowers embroidered along one corner. It matched her blouse. "We just keep going because we've got no choice to do anything but that."

I looked out at the world in front of me. Marguerite was right, there was no escaping my life here, for better or for worse.

"I've got no sage advice," she admitted, "no words of wisdom that will inspire you to do something so audacious as reach out to pull a complete stranger into our world. But I'm here if you need me. Or if you need a night of distractions."

"And I'm here if you need a night off from the wild woes of being incredibly popular," I offered in return. She kissed me on the cheek and headed off in search of her next adventure. I hoped, for her sake, it was something a bit more tame.

It was back to me and my thoughts. I didn't know what else to do. I thought of Odette reading every book she could get her hands on and understood what was driving her to do so. I wasn't sure my brain could focus on reading right now. I sat in my usual chair out of habit.

The days passed me by like a montage of blank space. I was aware that time was progressing; the sun streamed in through the gallery windows for longer each day. The blooms on the trees just outside the windows had turned to greenery. But in here, nothing changed. I was frozen, an inert object that would never move again unless pushed.

26

JEAN

was seated in that same chair when, weeks later, Odette came for me once more. It had been hours, days maybe, since I had seen my family, or anyone else, for that matter. I heard the rustle of her voluminous black skirts before I saw her, turning to watch her enter through the door to the kitchen. She paused, just within the room, standing behind the piano.

"Hello again," she said.

"Hi," I replied.

"I thought it was time I take you up on your offer to share your book." She peered around me, looking for it. I reached beneath my seat and pulled its soft, worn cover from underneath the cushion. She hesitated, not coming forward to get it. "How have you been?" she asked as if she already knew the answer and it was terrible.

"Oh, you know" was all I could think of to say. She sat down on the bench of the pink piano, purportedly my father's favorite color. She ran her hands over the keys but didn't press down with enough weight to make a sound.

"I think I do know," she said. "I've never felt so lonely in my life, and I'm alone most hours anyway. I hadn't realized until now the stock I've been placing in what it is to be the object of attention of a hundred strangers every day. I love it. It fuels me." She laughed gently at herself. "Though I've never really considered them strangers," she continued. "Do you?"

"I do." I nodded. They've always felt strange to me, too strange to connect with in their ephemerality, there for too-brief a time to feel a change.

"I don't," she said. "Even before I was here"—she gestured to our painted surroundings—"I would go to museums all the time, almost every day. The other girls I worked with slept all day long, burning off the hangovers of the night before, resting their feet in time to slip them into their heels once again. But I could never sleep past midmorning. I would walk, bleary-eyed, through the streets of Paris until my brain caught up to my body, which was already wide-awake. I'd stop for a coffee. And then I'd discover that my feet had taken me to the Louvre or one of the galleries, and I'd spend the day inside, surrounded by people I'd never met. But I always felt like we shared something. It was in the air; I could feel it on my skin. And when I sit, day after day, in my frame, I feel it in the crowds here as well. A sense of communion."

I was jealous of the sensation Odette had described. Maybe the next time we had people in the galleries again, I'd feel it too. If that time ever came.

"Without the people," she sighed, "it certainly isn't the same."

"At least you're keeping yourself busy," I said. She looked at me, confused. "With your books?"

"Ah." She waved her hand dismissively. "It's just a ruse,

something to trick my brain into thinking I still have a purpose."

"Oh," I said. We lapsed into silence, and I was hopeful we could stay that way. The sudden social interaction had left me exhausted despite its brevity. After a few moments, Odette placed her hands on the piano keys once again. This time, she began to play. It was simple, and she was stiff at first. It had probably been years, maybe decades since she had played. But as she soldiered on through the piece, she picked up confidence and comfort. Her hands weren't those of a novice; rather, they were those of someone who was once extremely familiar with this instrument.

Her tune lifted through the air, in a minor key but simultaneously a bit jaunty. A waltz rhythm, its ¾ time making me want to bob my head along. I let the impulse take me. When she finished, the end dangling on a hauntingly unresolved note, I gave her a quiet round of applause. She tipped her head to me.

"You are terrific," I said simply.

"What do they say about you when they give tours?" she asked. "The museum guides?"

"That we are the artist's family," I responded. "That our separation within our frame represents the divides growing within my family. That my father painted us out of fear or out of nostalgia. One of my favorite guides frequently tells guests he doesn't love my father's work. He feels like it never looks finished." I smiled at the memory. He was on the newer side at the museum but had quickly made a name for himself in my opinion. I felt a pang in my chest; I missed him too.

"How charming," Odette said.

"As I've heard the kids say, he 'tells it like it is.' What do they say about you?"

"That I'm an unknown woman, probably someone the artist met when he was living in Paris. Some take it further, offering up their own theories about who I might be, and why I might have been worthy of his painting. Some get quite close to the truth, speculating that I was a dancer in the halls on Montmartre."

I laughed along with her. I was in on the joke, as I had once known Odette better than any of them. Odette had been my first love or, at the very least, my first infatuation. She was actually the only other person I'd ever given my heart to. There was, of course, the former assistant curator but I'd be hard-pressed to call that anything more than a flirtation. At most, it was almost a friendship. We'd never even exchanged words.

Before Claire, there was just Odette. As Antoinette had explained, Odette was an accompanist in the dance halls before her painted life, playing the piano along to whatever tempo was demanded of the band. A part that might have been able to fade into the background of such boisterous venues, but she never did. With hair as red as hers, there was no disappearing. She was the object of fancy of most everyone she met, including me at one time.

Early into our tenure at the museum, maybe a decade or so in, we found ourselves together, alone, in someone else's living room. I had met her no more than a handful of times; back then, she ran in an adjacent social circle to Marguerite's, which I used to tag along with every few nights. We'd only ever exchanged a few words with each other, always part of a larger group. But here we were, just the two of us, and though we'd both been heading elsewhere, we decided to stay. We sat down at the small table that held a deck of cards, abandoned in the midst of a game. Odette picked up the hand closest to her and began to play as if it were her own. I followed suit.

"You're in the painting with the piano, are you not?" she asked me. We spoke entirely in French then. Odette spoke English fluently and would have been happy to make me practice; her mother was French and her father was English. But using French felt like home to me, and she understood.

"I am," I said as I laid a card down on the table. "Why? Do you play?"

"I used to," she said as she picked up my discarded card and replaced it with one of her own.

"If you ever want to play again, you could come use it," I offered enthusiastically. "Honestly, I mean it. Any time you wanted."

"Thank you," she said. "That's very kind." I had few friends of my own in this world, apart from Marguerite and Pierre, and I was looking forward to having a reason to see her again after that night. She was probably a bit older than I, just by a handful of years, but I could tell she had so much more knowledge of the world.

She placed her winning hand on the table. I held mine to my chest—I was nowhere near close to having completed the game.

"I'm glad I ran into you tonight," she said as she stood to leave. I could practically feel my eyes twinkle in response to the compliment. "Perhaps I'll come take you up on your offer in the near future." With that, she whisked herself out of the room, her skirts making their characteristic percussion as they brushed against one another.

She did come, the next night, to play. Before she began, she said, "You don't have to stay. I promise, I won't hurt it."

"I want to stay," I replied. "Really, if that's all right with you."

In response, she began a boisterous song, something I would learn was a frequent request from her days at the halls. It was lively and chaotic, like how I felt when I was around her. After she played for nearly an hour, she spun around on the piano bench to face me. She asked me more questions about my life and offered up information about hers, as I couldn't help but ask, "Where did you learn to do that?"

I delighted in our nights together, easing myself from instant infatuation to comfortable friendship. I had had so few friends in my life, only my family and those I had met in my youth, friends who were long lost to a different world. There was so much to know about Odette. I felt us growing closer with every story we swapped.

I knew I was attracted to her from the start but was surprised to find the ways my body could and would change without my permission when I was around her. It was like she was a magnet, and I was physically incapable of leaning away. Her hand might brush past my arm and I'd spend days chasing the high I got from the sparks caused by that moment of contact.

A thought interrupted my nostalgic reverie—I wondered about how time could dull certain sensations. Gone were the days where mere proximity to Odette could set my skin ablaze. What remained was a sense of familiarity, something an entirely different temperature from the heat we'd once known. Cooler, more stable, like an object at rest.

"Odette," I said in the present moment, when her second song had come to a close. "Why are you seeking me out now?"

A sly smile crept to her face. "Are you referring, Jean, to the fact that it's been quite some time since we kept each other company?"

"That is precisely why I'm asking."

"I've been feeling strange. This time feels aberrant. I craved something comfortable. You came to mind." I was surprised to hear her words echoing my own feelings. "What did you expect me to say? I'm on a tour of my ex-boyfriends?" She laughed. "Would you be upset if you thought there were others?"

"If anything," I retorted, "that would make it easier for me to understand 'why me?'"

"You think too much, Jean. You've always been overwhelmingly stuck in your own head. I don't always have such clearly identified motives. I just do what I like, within reason of course.

We have so little choice, those of us who live in this way. I like to take what power I have when I can."

"I've always admired that about you."

"I know."

It was she, not me, who had moved our relationship into another phase back then. I had felt locked in my brain, eager to push forward but unsure how to make the jump from friendship to something else. Odette had simply said one night, "I've been thinking about what it would be like to kiss you," and leaned in to answer her own question. A siren went off in my brain, my blood burning hotter than it had before. I'd been thinking about it too, to the point of absolute distraction, but had never thought to tell her so. How simple she made it seem.

27

CLAIRE

"Are you sleepy? Do you want to nap with Grandma?" We had just survived another day of virtual school by the skin of our teeth, maxing out Luna's attention span to the fullest. Summer break was still over a month away and I had no idea how I would fill the days enough to entertain her.

"No, not sleepy." Luna shook her head. "Can I have a snack?"

"Sure thing," I said. I wrapped one arm around her and swung us both up to sit, hitching her onto my hip and carrying her to our dining table. Pushed up against the wall, it had space for just three chairs, a perfect fit for our family. Luna always sat in the middle, which is where I deposited her as I started to open the cabinets.

"What are you in the mood for today?" I asked.

"You pick," she replied. She was amenable today, I thought with relief. Luna was hard to predict right now; hunger made her fickle. One moment, we'd be peacefully coexisting; the next, she would have a meltdown of ungodly proportions. It felt like a good time to have this conversation. Well, no time was really a good time, as she was only four and we were about to tread into concepts she certainly could not wrap her mind around. But I had been sitting on her dad's visit for weeks and I knew I needed to tell her.

I cut up an apple for us to share, making a little bowl of Cheez-Its for the side. These had been a comfort purchase for myself in my last grocery store run. As I surveyed our stock, I realized I'd have to do it again soon enough. I shivered. I hated going to that place. It still wasn't clear how we could best protect ourselves. Did we need to wear masks? Gloves? Face shields? Were we supposed to wipe every package down when we got home from the store?

My brain had never run so rampant with anxiety until I had Luna. True, up until that point I'd also been basically a kid, not even old enough to vote. But there was something about the way I now saw the world as a series of things that could harm her, that had induced a new-to-me near-constant state of panic. How could I optimize every moment to keep her as safe as possible? While I was still just trying to make it through myself?

The current state of the world didn't help. As much as I hated doing the shopping, it had to be me. Gracie wasn't quite yet in the age bracket that was considered the most vulnerable, but I wasn't about to take any chances. From what I could tell from the news, there were a lot of people who were getting super sick, no matter how old they were. At least Jean was safe from that.

Jean. If I let my mind wander, he was always there.

"Mooooooooooooom," Luna called from the table. I brought her the little snack plate I'd prepared. I really was a terrible cook and the last few weeks had put that on display. I watched

moms on TikTok take this time as a chance for culinary wonder, whipping up dishes for their kids that belonged in the
kitchens of Michelin-starred restaurants, building candy char-
cuterie boards because they could. Meanwhile, I could burn a
pan of scrambled eggs. Shockingly, none of my meals ever
seemed worth sharing on Instagram.

But Luna never seemed to mind. She chomped down on an
apple slice and smiled toothily at me in thanks. I took a handful of the cheesy crackers.

"What's next today, Moon? You want to watch a movie?"
We'd never been strict about screen time in our house; Gracie
and I agreed years ago that we'd do whatever was needed to
get through each day. But any semblance of guilt we'd felt
about plopping Luna down in front of the TV had completely
evaporated since lockdown had begun. We'd watched *Cars* almost a dozen times.

"No, thank you," she said, mouth full of Cheez-Its. She
swallowed hard, orange crumbs still dusting her lips. "Can we
color?"

"Sure." I grabbed the crayons and stack of scrap paper we
kept for moments like this one, a compilation of the backs of
bills, letters, and junk mail. I was grateful for something to do
with my hands. I picked out a letter that was mostly blank on
the opposite side, passed it to Luna, and emptied the crayon
box onto the table.

"What are we drawing today?" I asked as she picked out
two blue crayons.

"No, Mommy, do your own," Luna commanded. I was wary;
Luna's solo artistic endeavors often ended up covering more of
the table than the page, but I was determined to keep this
good mood, so I picked out a page for myself and grabbed a
green crayon. I could clean the table later. We lapsed into silence.

"So, Luna," I began.

"So, Mommy," she mimicked as she scribbled, using the piece of paper as a loose guide for where to stop her crayon.

"You know how some of the kids at school have a mommy and a daddy?"

"Or two mommies or two daddies," she corrected me.

"Right, right, of course."

"I have two mommies," she said proudly.

"Kind of," I said. "Gracie is your great-grandmommy. But she loves you just like any other mommy." Luna continued her coloring. "You remember I told you that your daddy had to go away when you were a really small baby?" She nodded. "Well, he got to come back and he would like to see you. Would you like that? To see him too?"

Luna stopped coloring. I could see her little face concentrating, searching for the right answer, and I wondered for the one-millionth time if this was too big of a decision, and I should have just made it for her. I had fretted about this for the past weeks before ultimately landing on the conclusion that I always wanted her to be involved in the decision-making process.

"Can you come?" she asked.

"Of course, Moon, of course I'll come." I did not relish the idea of spending time around Jeremy, not knowing if I could ever forgive him for leaving. But I certainly wasn't about to let Luna waddle off into his company without having any sense of where they were or what they were up to. "I was thinking we could meet him at the playground or take a short walk. Just to see how it feels. And if at any point you want to go home, you just say the word."

We had just started going to the playground again. We'd show up right before the sun was about to set, when it was sure to be as empty as possible. There were copious amounts of handwashing and wipes involved. I couldn't tell if it was safe enough, but it was necessary for our sanity so it was a risk we were taking.

"When?" Luna asked.

"I don't know yet," I admitted. "I'm going to call him after this and make sure he's safe from the sickness"—that's what we called it—"and we will set up a time. I'll let you know, okay?"

"Okay," she said. "Now, color, Mommy," Luna commanded. I obliged.

Against my better judgment, my mind wandered back to Jean, as it often did in moments of stillness. Did he think I'd abandoned him forever? Did he understand why I couldn't come? Did he know anything of a pandemic?

Oh, how our tables had turned. I had always been the one who was freer and now, here I was, locked in an apartment that was far too small for three generations of my family. Our neighborhood was so tightly packed, we hadn't even gone for walks during the first three weeks for fear of getting too close to another human. Meanwhile, Jean had hundreds of universes to explore. He could go as far as he wanted in a hop, skip, and jump.

"What did you draw, Mommy?" Luna asked, reaching for my page. I looked down, trying to decipher my mindless scribbles.

"I think it's a garden," I guessed as I passed it over for her inspection. It was, in fact, the garden behind Jean's house. I had even done my best to outline Aurora, the friendly statue next to the pond. "What do we have here?" I said, looking down at her page of unidentifiable shapes and colors.

"It's a zebra alien monster," she said, her tone implying it was obvious and I should have known that for myself.

"Of course it is!" I exclaimed, clutching it closer to my chest.

"Can we put them on the fridge?"

"Yes, we absolutely can," I assured her as I strode over to it. I surveyed the remaining real estate; the front of our fridge was starting to resemble the walls of the gallery, chock-full of art. Luna pushed aside some of her previous work and cleared a spot in the middle.

"Right here," she instructed. I followed along as directed, finding two available magnets to clip them on. We stood back to survey our work.

"Looks good," Luna declared before she wandered off toward the couch, where I could hear her freeing one of her toys from the bin we kept them in. It did look good, the fridge, in its own chaotic way. As I stared at my rough representation of Jean's world, I wondered how far my abilities extended. Could I crawl into this landscape, if I let myself just fall in?

I thought better of it. I didn't want to be in that makeshift version of the place I loved so much. That wouldn't get me any closer to Jean. There, I'd just be alone. Really and truly alone.

"What's his name, Mommy?" Luna asked from across the room.

"Jean," I said easily. Then I realized what she was actually asking. "Oh, your daddy's name?" She nodded. "His name is Jeremy."

She was satisfied with this answer and went off to create a new mess in the living room. Gracie was up from her nap, making a cup of tea for herself in the kitchen.

"I see you talked to her," Gracie said. I had previewed this conversation with her a few nights ago, letting her in on what had been taking up space in my mind. "How did it go?"

"As well as it could, I think. She wants to meet him, as long as I go too."

Gracie nodded in acknowledgment. As long as I was ripping off conversational Band-Aids, I might as well tackle asking her the question I'd been avoiding.

"She's okay, right? I know you're still in touch."

"Who, sweetie?" Gracie asked. She very much knew what I was asking, but she was going to make me say it out loud.

"Mom. I can hear you whispering to her on the phone in the living room when you think I'm still asleep."

Gracie continued to stir her tea, choosing her words carefully. "She's healthy. Seems to have avoided the virus so far, lucky, like us."

I tried to picture my mom, all alone wherever she was living these days. I'd never forgiven her for throwing me out and she'd never made an effort to get back in touch, but I did acknowledge that she existed and was somewhat comforted to hear she was okay.

"She always asks after you and Luna," Gracie added tentatively. It was rare that I mentioned my mom and opened space for us to talk about her. Gracie was proceeding with caution. I didn't believe her.

"If she cared about how we were, she would have let me stay." I felt a door in my heart slam shut as I said the words. I'd picked at an old wound and it stung. I needed to keep myself and Luna safe.

"You know it's not that simple," Gracie said. "All she ever wanted was a better life for you than she had for herself."

"My life is better because Luna is in it." I knew that when my mom looked at me, all she saw was her own failure. That's what she thought we both were: two failures who had gotten pregnant in high school and let it ruin our lives.

"I know," Gracie said. "I know." And I knew she knew. Gracie had picked us, after all. This wasn't her fault.

But it wasn't just Jean who was missing from this bizarre domestic scene. In a perfect world, free of judgment and grudges, my mother would be here, completing the four generations of our family under this crooked apartment roof.

I pointed to my cellphone and indicated I was stepping outside to make a call.

As the phone rang, I thought of all the ways this could go wrong. He could have disappeared again and then I'd have to explain to Luna that it had all fallen through. I'd thought of that before, but felt really strongly that I needed Luna's permission before I could open this door into our lives.

Jeremy answered on the third ring and I could tell from the hopeful tone in his voice that he had been wishing it was me. He'd been quarantining, he promised me, just on the chance that I decided to call. Still, I wanted to play it safe. I set a date for the next week and made him promise to see absolutely no one between now and then. He assured me it wouldn't be a problem, which made me wonder about his living situation, and if I'd ever believe he was telling the truth. But the circumstances were forcing me to trust him, and so I tried to do so.

After I hung up, I looked at the clock on my phone and realized it was nearly time to make dinner. These days could feel like an endless string of meals to be made and dishes to be washed. I made my way back up to the apartment.

"Mommy, come look!" Luna called through the doorway. I went off to give her whatever she needed.

28

JEAN

Our interminable isolation dragged on, no patrons swooping in to save us. I went searching for Odette. I didn't know where I'd find her. I started with her own gallery, but there was no trace of her. I walked through landscapes, still lifes, bedrooms, avoiding spaces where I heard the noise of a crowd gathering. The sheer amount of artwork in this museum was daunting; I wasn't sure I'd ever seen so much of it in one day, but I pressed on, avoiding the crowd.

I found her in front of a fishbowl, watching a troubling of goldfish swim in lazy circles. She spoke to me without looking up: "I used to come here because I thought they might be the only creatures in our world more constrained than we are. But now I don't know. I wonder if confinement is relative; who's to say this gallery isn't just one big fishbowl and we're all swimming in circles for some other viewer's distraction?"

"I think my father aspired to that kind of absorption in

something else, the kind only being painted in place could ensure."

"Do you think he ever thought that we'd have another life in here? Could he imagine something close to what this is really like?"

"No," I replied. "I actually think he imagined the opposite. That painting, or creating, was a way of freezing time. Of making absolutely sure that his subjects would be protected and safe forever."

"Until now, I would have said he was wrong, but with no way of knowing what's happening out there, maybe he was right. Maybe we're safest in here, together," Odette mused. "I don't spend much energy keeping track of how much time has passed; I lost interest in that long ago, but I do know it's been long enough that no one I knew in that life is still out there. I don't have anyone out there to be worried about." A physical pain the size of a fist rose up in my chest and attempted to strangle my heart.

"Oh my goodness," Odette said quickly. "I completely forgot myself. I didn't mean to say that, to draw attention to your, oh my goodness. I've really put my leg in my mouth, haven't I?"

"Foot," I said as I took a deep breath.

"Excuse me?"

"The Americans say, 'put my foot in my mouth.'"

"I've always thought that was a ridiculous turn of phrase anyway."

"And about that, you are right." I sighed, putting my palm to my heart as if it could push back against that pain. "I don't want to talk about it tonight. I physically do not think I am capable of talking, or thinking, about it anymore." I walked around the table to the side where she was sitting and reached for her hand. She watched me as I took it in my own palm. It felt smaller than I'd remembered. It had been decades since

I'd held it. We'd split for the most predictable of reasons: I was not in love with her and she was not in love with me. We were attracted to each other and, over time, came to care deeply for each other. But with the possibility of forever stretching out in front of us, it was impossible not to admit, after many years had passed, that we both wondered if there was something else out there. We'd mutually agreed that it was time.

I held her small hand in mine. If time shrank memories, there might be hope for me in the future.

When I walked into our living room later that evening, Marguerite was draped across my seat again, flipping the pages of my book. I couldn't remember Odette returning it before tonight.

I shuffled a bit farther into the room, making my presence known. Marguerite spun around to face me and tossed my book to the side.

"*There* you are; I have been waiting for you for forever. Wait, what's going on with you?"

"Nothing is going on with me," I refuted half-heartedly. Something was clearly wrong with me.

"Anyway! It doesn't matter!"

"You're right about that, at least."

"No, no more of your 'nothing matters anymore' thing. I have news." She was practically vibrating in her chair. She stood up.

"Oh?" I said, opposing her energy as I sank onto the piano bench.

"Yes," she repeated. "I absolutely have news."

"Cut to it, Marguerite."

"People have been in the museum," she blurted out. "Today."

"What?" I said sharply as I snapped to attention. "You saw them? Who was here?"

"Well, no, I haven't seen anyone yet, but Andromeda came running in today and said she'd just seen the other custodian—

not Claire, the one who normally works downstairs—what's her name?"

"Linda," I whispered.

"Yes! Linda! She was here with Jamie, the museum director. Anyway, apparently they were walking through the galleries and discussing a big cleaning job. And then!"

"And then what?"

"Oh, I don't actually know, that's all Andromeda heard them say before they walked out of our wing. But! If they're cleaning, don't you think that could mean people are coming back?"

I had little idea what anything meant anymore. Marguerite absolutely might be on to something, but I didn't feel hope brewing inside me. Not yet, not until I could see it with my own eyes.

"It's got to be that," she continued giddily. "We're going to spread the word, let everyone know they should start returning to their posts in the mornings. It might be too eager, but it doesn't hurt to be prepared. I doubt everyone will listen to us, but at least they'll have it in mind to be somewhere nearby. We're all a bit out of practice, I guess."

"Did they not notice you were all in the wrong spots today?"

"Oh, they weren't looking at the art, just the common spaces and talking about the air filtration system or something. But I guess we ought to be a bit more careful. Though I've never known what they would do if someone noticed. They can't come in here and force us to do anything, Claire aside of course." Pins and needles pricked my skin at the mention of her name.

"They could take us down."

"I guess you have a point there. I'd never considered that as an option for punishment. After all these months, I can tell you I definitely would not like that, not one bit. Well, in that case, all the more reason to spread the word. Can you believe it!" she exclaimed, her question rhetorical. "The end might be here." Marguerite paused for a moment, studying my expression, or lack thereof. "I thought you'd be more excited, to be honest."

"I think I'm in shock," I said. The emotional hurricane brewing inside me pushed back against the walls of my rib cage. I needed Marguerite to leave so I could begin to pick through this storm of emotions by myself.

"Okay," she said suspiciously. "If you say so. I think I'll find Pierre first. Do you have any idea where he is?"

I did not. I never thought of anyone but myself, did I?

"I see you transitioning into self-loathing and I'm going to ask you to not take this there," Marguerite commanded. "I'll find him. If you see your mother, please pass along the news." I nodded, reassuring her that I would. She trotted out of the room in a rush.

Claire might be coming back here. To our museum. I walked to the edge of our frame and sat on the floor facing the gallery, where I used to wait to be as close to her as possible while she cleaned.

"Oh! I forgot." Marguerite hurried back into the room, straightening the black ribbon across her neck. "Andromeda did say one other thing. Apparently, they were wearing masks."

"Who was?"

"Linda and the museum director."

"Masks? Like the kind you wear at a ball?"

"No," Marguerite corrected me. "Like the kind a doctor might wear at a hospital. The ones that cover your nose and mouth." She shrugged, offering no more thoughts on what that might mean, and left in pursuit of her mission.

As I considered this news, the first image that came to mind was Claire's face, partially obscured by a cloth covering. I could see only her eyes, and they were staring right back at me, knowing all they needed to know.

"It will feel so different," a voice said behind me. I turned to see Pierre standing next to the piano. From my position on the floor, his silhouette was backlit from the light coming in through the window, making him appear three times his normal size. "For these rooms to be full again. For so long, it felt like we were a part of their space. Now this feels like it belongs to us. I wonder how the power will shift again when we're no longer alone."

I marveled at Pierre's maturity. I still thought of him as a boy, as older brothers always do, but I was reminded that he had more than a century of wisdom stored up in there.

"It's like," he continued, "we finally had a kind of control, the kind we have at night, but whenever and wherever we wanted it. I wonder how many people in this time did things they would never have done otherwise."

"Are you speaking from personal experience?" I asked.

"I'm not looking to confess, just proffering a theory." He sat on the bench, not in his usual seat but on Marguerite's side, closer to me.

"Which do you prefer? Our life on our terms or the other version with the constraints of belonging to the public eye?"

He considered my question, answering, "I think I crave the structure a crowd gives us. With too much free time on our hands and no physical need for sleep, we are pushed outside our limits to try to fill the endless hours."

"I wonder if you'd feel the same if we'd had such options from the start."

"A fair question, but we have never lived in that version of the world. We were created for this. And before it was this, we were never truly free either. We still had the expectations of family and of society out there, so I hesitate to romanticize that."

The sun descended in the sky. The light crept away across the gallery floor, eventually pulled back out the windows through which it came as day faded into night. There was an unspoken invitation from the darkness that seeped its way across the room, a final hurrah being offered to those who wished to take part in it.

"What will you choose?" Pierre asked. "How will you spend what might be your last night of this thing that feels like freedom?"

"I think I'll just wait here."

29

JEAN

There we were, all four of us, together again. We had not all been in the same room since we had descended into this lawless life. How natural and unusual it felt at the same time: our untraditional family, without the man who related us all, scattered across one room. I didn't know what to do with my hands or my eyes. Where did I normally look?

Pierre and Marguerite were whispering at the piano bench, giggling and shushing each other as if nothing had changed. My mother reclined in her rocking chair, not yet stitching her embroidery, though she held it in her hands. Her gaze was upward, toward the sky.

Across the gallery, I could see others in their frames resuming their positions as well. Some rested near where they were meant to be, leaning against a wall or a doorframe, waiting for a sign that this was, in fact, going to happen. As the light rose in the gallery, I felt us all take a collective inhale of expectation.

Moments later, we heard the recognizable trundle of the wheels of a cleaning cart rolling into the main hall on the floor below us, the noise carrying through our open doorway. Marguerite let out a soft "mon dieu." Pierre's head snapped up from where he had been resting it on the piano in front of him. I leaned forward, pressing my ear to the divide, and could hear her dunking the mop in the bucket and slapping it down against the floor one story below.

Could it be Claire? It must be Linda, I reminded myself, based on her location in the museum. If it was Claire, she'd come right up here, I was sure. Or maybe she wouldn't because it was still daytime outside. Did that have any effect on her magic? It didn't matter, it was probably Linda anyway, like Marguerite had said.

The act of listening to someone clean a room we were not in lost its fascination as time went on. We heard whoever it was slowly progress into one of the first-floor wings. Marguerite and Pierre had begun a game that involved spinning the ring she wore on her thumb against the lid of the piano and guessing in which direction it would fall. I lit a cigarette.

The gossip network of first-floor paintings confirmed that night what I had suspected—it was, in fact, Linda. Claire was nowhere to be seen.

The next day passed the same; we heard Linda roll into the gallery beneath us. This time, she turned in to the other wing of the first floor. Once again, we stayed in place, but relaxed a bit more than we would on a typical daytime shift. As the light faded at the end of the day, we could hear her roll out.

"She must be cleaning these rooms within an inch of their lives," Marguerite remarked as she stood up to stretch. "They're not very big. How could it be taking her so long? And if it's such a large project, why did they bring her in alone?"

"I've been thinking," I replied. "They can't be very dirty either. No one has been in here. What's there to clean besides dust?"

"I hope this isn't some sign of the end," Pierre piped up. "What if they're making it all spotless because they're bringing in a potential buyer or something? What if life outside the museum has gone on as normal, it's just that we're in trouble, legally or financially or something of the like, and that's why we've been shut down this whole time?"

I panicked. If that was the case, I would never see Claire again. They'd chosen Linda for this final cleaning. What if this was the end?

"Maybe," I mused to make myself feel better, "the building is condemned and it's a hazard for them to let anyone inside anymore and we're all getting moved."

"Then why would they send Linda in to clean," Marguerite asked, "and why wouldn't they take us out immediately? We know the value of some of the pieces in here is astronomical. They wouldn't just leave us here in a room that might collapse at any moment."

She had a point there, as did Pierre. But what if they did take us out? Would they tell Claire? What if one day Claire returned and we were gone? Would she try to follow us?

Finally, it was our turn. Linda appeared the following day, stomping into our gallery and beginning her work. As Marguerite had supposed, Linda took her time, really cleaning each and every nook and cranny. The gallery glittered with the residue from her cleaning solution and the sunlight dancing through the windows and across the surfaces. I felt impressed by how we looked; we were ready to be seen.

Linda's presence brought life back to the gallery with a jump. She danced and hopped her way across the room as she brought it up to her standards of cleanliness. Just like Andromeda had described, she wore a mask that covered the lower half of her face, though it frequently slipped below her nose and she left it dangling there, only partially obscuring her mouth.

I got the sense that Linda had missed us too; she spent

some of her time just taking in the room, her eyes sweeping across the walls, the doorways, the windows, the ceilings. It was a contrast to the alacrity with which she normally did her cleaning, moving as quickly as possible so she could get back to the break room. She even took her cellphone from her pocket, the one that I'd seen her use exclusively for gameplay, and snapped a few photos.

I wished I could ask her if she'd heard from Claire, if she was doing okay, why it was just Linda who had returned to us, if we would get to see Claire again. Instead, we just watched Linda work. As evening crept in, she surveyed her progress on our wing. Pleased with the state of things, she pushed her cart back out toward the elevator.

"What do you think happens next?" I asked.

"It seems like she's nearing the end, so I think we'll soon find out," Pierre supposed. "There aren't many rooms left to clean. Either the galleries are about to reopen, or we're headed toward whatever is out there, waiting for us."

"At least we're pretty and clean in the meantime," said Marguerite. "I didn't realize how much the dust was dulling our shine." They both rose, heading off to their nightly activities. On their way out, Marguerite stopped to say, "Have a nice night, Jean. We'll see you in the morning." It was touching, and out of the ordinary compared to the way we normally interacted. I could see it was bringing all of us comfort to be together regularly again.

We had just reassembled into our assigned positions, morning having newly begun, as the gallery below filled with voices. I could hear the stiffening of fabric around me as we all straightened up into our assigned positions. Moments later, a group of museum employees walked into our room. Jamie was there, as expected, accompanied by Lisa, Henry, and Christie, the board members. Our painting, the largest in the room, was centered along the longest wall. We faced directly across from an open doorway, looking toward the windows.

The four of them assembled in a clump between the windows, opposite the four of us.

"I think this spot will be perfect," said Lisa, her dark hair streaked with gray. Her face was covered by a mask with bright splotches of color across its white surface. I wondered if she'd made the pattern herself at home.

"Can we have this dresser removed?" Henry said as he rapped his palm against it. The sound of his ring hitting the lacquered wood was grating and made everyone jump. "Sorry," he apologized, wringing his hands before he tucked them away into his pockets. "I'm not quite myself yet in public."

Christie reached out to him, her touch falling a few inches short of his shoulder. "None of us are right now."

"Is there enough of a flow, in case we start to get crowds up here?" Henry asked.

Jamie nodded. "These are two of our most visited galleries; we're used to heavy foot traffic up here. We can always put stanchions and a guide right through that doorway, if we need to create a queue. I'll also say that we have no idea what kind of patronage we'll be seeing in the next few months. We'll cut the total capacity down, of course, to allow for social distancing in the galleries. But we don't even know how many visitors, if any, will want to come back, at least right away."

A worried silence fell upon the group as the words set in. "Well," Lisa finally said, "we'll just have to see."

"I would want to come back," Christie said. "Even today, being back in these halls, I have chills. I forgot just how full to the brim it is with art. How much I've been missing it."

"Let's hope the rest of the city feels that way," Jamie cautioned as she led the group out of the gallery. "I'll see what can be done about moving that dresser into the restoration facilities before tomorrow . . ." Her voice became too faint to hear as they descended the stairs.

"What do you think they're putting in there?" Pierre asked.

"I have no idea," Marguerite and I said in near unison. "They never move things in this room. Or in this museum," she added.

"Do you think this has to do with why it's been empty for months?" Pierre said.

"It's hard to say—maybe that, or maybe they're using this time as an excuse to make a change," I thought aloud.

"It can't be a painting," Marguerite said with her typical certainty, "or they wouldn't be looking at that space. I can't imagine they'd ever hang another painting in here. It must be like . . . a thing."

"A thing," I joked back at her. "Of course, how astute of you."

"Oh, *pffffft*," she said. "You know what I mean. It's an object, maybe of some historical importance to the collector. Or to the art in here in some way. I doubt it's art itself."

"I guess we'll all see, seemingly soon."

"Lucky us," Marguerite said. "It's all going to unfold right before our eyes." She had the glint of gossip that was hers to trade in as she sashayed out of the room with a wave of her hand.

30

JEAN

Our world burst to life the next day with the sound of a drill as two men in unremarkable uniforms assembled a wood plinth. The wood was a warm brown color, almost an exact match to the dresser they'd moved into the elevator earlier that morning. The new plinth was now standing in three dimensions and had inspired an argument among the four decision-makers of yesterday, who had returned alongside the construction crew.

"Do you think it would be better centered in this room, so viewers could walk all the way around it?" Lisa asked.

"Absolutely not, it would be far less protected that way," Henry said.

"Not if we encased it in glass," Lisa countered.

"Wait," Christie piped up. "We weren't planning to encase it in glass? How on earth will we keep it secure?"

"Hardly anything in this museum is in glass," Henry argued. "Only the objects in those little curio cabinets. Glass would go against the entire aesthetic."

"But most everything of value in here is glued to the walls, it's not going anywhere. The things in those cabinets and out on the shelves, those are just glorified knickknacks compared to the rest of the collection."

"Is glass how the collector would have wanted it displayed?" Christie asked.

"This is the only thing we've ever added to the collection that the collector didn't bring in here himself," Henry said.

"I can't believe we're even considering no glass." Christie shook her head at their collective naïveté. "What if someone trips and spills coffee on it!"

"No food or drink will be allowed in the museum, because of the . . ." Henry gestured to the covering on his face. "We won't even have the concessions stand open."

"What if people try to turn the pages?" Lisa asked. "Maybe we can find a cabinet for it that matches the aesthetic of the others."

"If we put it against the wall, we'll be able to put a low bar with an alarm sensor in it around the perimeter. It will let out a warning sound to alert both the patron and the nearby associate that someone has gotten too close. And if the journal was ever lifted, the museum would go into full lockdown mode, same as any other security alert."

"Okay," Christie said. "I believe you that you've thought about this every way you can imagine, but why? Why take this kind of risk with something so newly discovered that we don't even know what the value of it is?"

"Because these are the donor's demands," Jamie answered, breaking her silence. "They required that it be placed in a location that is accessible to all guests, that it must be unobscured by glass or covering, and that one page must be turned each day. If we can't meet all these requirements, we will not get to display it. Maybe no one ever will."

"But you'll at least put it in a secure location each day after closing, of course," Christie said.

"No." Jamie shook her head. "The donor was very clear—this is for the people who work the night shift too."

Christie let out a low whistle. "You must really trust the janitorial staff."

"Don't"—her voice grew unexpectedly sharp—"insult the janitorial staff. They are trustworthy."

Certain this was a bad idea but positive her concerns would be considered no further, Christie apologized and stood to the side as the two men in uniform secured the wood plinth to the floor.

There was another round of discussion about how far from the stand the low-lying bar on the floor should be placed. The consensus was just out of fingertip reach, but close enough for those with good eyesight, natural or corrected, to read. The four members of the group took turns standing at different angles and reaching out their arms, backing up inch by inch until they could no longer reach the platform.

Linda arrived soon after, and the group directed her to their new piece of construction. Still there was no sign of Claire. Linda swept up the sawdust. She wiped down the surface, cleaning it thoughtfully of any debris. The group thanked her profusely, and she dropped to the back of their cluster. I could see from the way she checked over each shoulder that she was hopeful no one would complain if she stuck around. She took a seat on the bench nearest to me, tucking herself out of the way of the immediate action, but granting herself a ringside view for whatever was about to unfold.

A large black storage chest was rolled in from the elevator and wheeled right up to the display stand. Jamie stepped forward and lifted the two large metal buckles on its exterior. From within the case, she pulled out a smaller suitcase that looked like something I might have carried in my previous life—vintage, I'm sure they'd call it now.

Jamie lowered the suitcase, resting it on the lid of the black trunk. The gallery was silent; every pair of eyes, even those on the walls, was focused on the suitcase. Linda and I simultaneously shifted forward in our seats, surreptitiously angling to get a better view. Jamie was charged with this concentrated energy, the knowledge that all eyes were on her, her understanding of the weight of the moment.

She lifted the clasps one at a time, right first, then left. She cracked open the suitcase and pulled out a small notebook. It was hard to see from our vantage point, but it appeared unremarkable. It had a worn brown cover, notably distressed but not tattered.

"That's it?" Marguerite said under her breath. Pierre and I both shushed her, but we were all thinking it. We were in a room full of masterpieces; a journal was what they had to offer in addition? All this fanfare for that?

"We'll be attaching a protective slipcover over the jacket, so we can secure that down to the display surface," Jamie narrated as she pulled a thick piece of plastic out of a cardboard sleeve. She took care in adhering it to the journal, and then the journal to the stand beneath it. After a few minutes, the job was done.

"We'll start at page one tomorrow. For each day after that when the museum is open to the public, we'll turn one page. When we reach the end, we'll return the object to the donor."

"I can't believe we get to be a part of this," Christie said. "What a year this is."

"It's not just once in a lifetime," Lisa said. "It's once in their lifetime." She gestured to us on the walls.

"I wonder," Marguerite whispered, "if we can read it if we stand in that painting right above it. What makes this little journal so important?"

"It's probably in English," I said. "Can you even read in English?" I was mocking her, but I too was curious why this diary was special and was eager to find out for myself.

"A little bit," she retorted. "I'm sure someone in here can." Pierre shushed us both, not wanting to miss what was unfolding in front of us.

"I can't believe people will finally be back in here tomorrow," Lisa said.

"I can't believe they haven't been here in over four months. Is that the longest we've ever been closed to the public?" Henry wondered.

"I had that same question," Christa said. "And the answer is quite interesting . . ." Their voices trailed off as they wound their way out of the gallery. The men who had constructed the installation packed up their tools and followed the larger group out.

That left just us and Linda, who busied herself with making sure everything in the gallery looked as spotless as it had before the day's commotion. I caught myself thinking the new addition was quite the eyesore, though I was unsure if I was just unused to seeing anything new in these galleries and knew it might be less "ugly" and more "unexpected."

After she was content with the state of the room, Linda put her equipment aside and came to stand directly in front of the journal. There was an air of ceremony to the moment; she was the first to have this experience.

"I wish Linda shared Claire's tendency to narrate all her thoughts out loud," Marguerite said.

Pierre said, "Me too." I silently agreed. But that wasn't Linda's way. She took in whatever it was she was privy to over there, shrugged with a small *hmm* sound, and began to pack her things up to head out of the gallery. As she was nearly at the exit, something struck her. She turned and pointed her phone back at the new podium, a synthetic camera shutter sound implying that she had captured a photograph.

"Aw," Marguerite cooed in a whisper. "Even Linda missed the art." Linda pocketed her phone and left the room.

As soon as we were alone, Marguerite was on her feet. She was practically vibrating from the many revelations of the day, mixed with the excitement of that which was yet to come. I had expected her to race from the room, but she paused before doing so and turned to me.

"People are coming back tomorrow," Marguerite said. I nodded; the knowledge of that had struck me as well. "I wonder if that means Claire will return?"

"It could mean that," I responded. I felt a bubbling in my stomach, an unstable solution of excitement and anxiety. Would Claire actually come back? Jamie had said that patrons might not even return. Would the museum have filled the staff back up right away? I resigned myself to the fact that it was probably best to just expect the worst.

"Hard to know," Marguerite continued, "as everything has been so unknowable lately."

"Right," I said.

"I know you won't get your hopes up, but mine are up on your behalf." She smiled and gave me a single pat on the shoulder on her way out of the room. Pierre followed, a bounce in his step.

I pictured Claire, standing in front of my frame. It was a Claire of old times, when she used to pass by just to say hello, before we ever knew what she was capable of. My vision of her was so clear. I got up to stand at the edge of her world and mine. At some point in our isolation, I'd given up this memory game; it had been too painful. But as I extended my hand as far as it could go, I felt myself come out of emotional hibernation, my skin tingling. For the first time in a very long time, against my better judgment, I allowed myself to hope.

31

CLAIRE

The first park date had gone shockingly well. If anything, it was underwhelming. I'd arrived early, nervous about any upcoming disappointment that might be heading in Luna's direction. I had convinced myself that there was no way he was going to show.

Jeremy arrived at the agreed-upon time, wearing a mask. He made a show of sanitizing his hands before he reached out to fist-bump with Luna.

"Hi, Luna. I'm Jeremy," he said gently.

"I know," she replied in her confident way.

"I brought you something," he said.

"Okay." Luna wasn't used to getting gifts when it wasn't her birthday or Christmas, as we didn't often have anything extra to go around. Jeremy looked at me as if to check what her answer really meant. I gestured for him to continue.

He pulled a stuffed animal out from behind his back. Well,

I'm not sure "stuffed animal" is the right term. It was actually a fluffy white stuffed crescent moon with a kind face and legs that dangled down. It was beautiful.

"Get it?" he asked. "It's a moon, like your name. It's a Jellycat, I heard they're the special ones." Luna took it and tucked it under her arm, heading off with determination toward the swing set. She knew I wouldn't let her stay here long after dark and that her minutes were numbered.

"A Jellycat?" I hissed at him when he stood back up to his full height. "Aren't those things stupid expensive? Jeez, next time just pay for our groceries or something." He shrugged and I knew I wasn't being entirely fair. It was a gift for Luna, not for me, and it was actually pretty thoughtful.

As if she'd remembered what the purpose of this trip was, she came wandering back over. "Would you like to swing too?" she asked in her most polite voice. He nodded and she thrust the moon up at me before she led her father off with her.

I took a seat on the bench, petting the moon in irritation. *Damn*, I admitted to myself, *it is really soft.*

We'd had a handful of additional successful outings after that one, the three of us. We'd shared a box of pizza in the park, packing our plates and Luna's plastic silverware from home so I could cut hers up into manageable bites. We'd visited all the playgrounds within walking distance. I was sure in normal circumstances I would have resented anything to do with Jeremy taking up so much of my time. But right now, I had nothing but time. It was as fine as any way to spend these many unspoken-for hours.

The jury was still out on what Luna thought of him. She treated him with more familiarity than your average stranger, but no more affection than she had for, say, one of her teachers. She was cautious with her heart. I was nervous I had taught her that.

When she was off in her own little world, conquering yet

another slide, Jeremy feigned interest in my life. I knew it was fake because he'd never indicated a smidge of care about my life since we'd moved in together all those years ago, but today, he asked about the museum, how I liked it, what I did there. He asked after Gracie's health and even dared to ask if I'd heard anything from my mother. He asked if I was seeing anyone. At that point, I told him we didn't have to talk anymore. So, we didn't.

Today was a big day. Last week, Luna had told me politely that I didn't need to go along with them anymore. I clarified with her—did that mean she didn't want me there? No, she'd told me, I could go if I wanted to, but it was okay for me to not go. As always, I wanted to respect her growing independence. It was amazing how much older she seemed to me after these few months. I was watching her become her own little person.

I'd called Jeremy to tell him what Luna had said, and he was just as stunned as I was. I found myself assuring him it would be fine and that he could call or text if he needed anything. We'd agreed he'd pick her up at the usual time and take her to the playground near our house.

Luna had asked me to braid her hair today, and I wrestled her boisterous curls into plaits. She had definitely inherited my hair. We sat on the porch with her stuffed moon, which had been named Moona, and we waited. And waited. And waited. When he was twenty minutes late, I started calling him. They all went straight to voicemail. Of course they freaking did.

The sun slipped lower in the sky. In the normal times, I would already be on my way out the door, heading off to the museum. I was grateful I was here now to hold her hand. I didn't want to freak Luna out, so I sealed up my anger inside my body and suggested we go upstairs and watch *Cars*. Even that classic hit did nothing to brighten her spirits as she headed sluggishly inside. I got her snuggled under our coziest blanket and allowed Lightning McQueen's voice to take over our living room. I watched out of the corner of my eye as she undid her braids with her tiny fingers. If I ever saw that man again, I was going to punch him square in the face.

Unless, of course, something was wrong. Oh my god, was I a terrible person? What if something had happened to him?

My phone rang, an unknown Philadelphia number. If this was Jeremy calling from some bar, I was going to let him have it. I got off the couch and walked into the bedroom, shutting the door behind me.

"Jeremy, I swear to god," I answered.

"Erm, no, Claire? Sorry to interrupt. It's Jamie, not Jeremy, from the museum?" A voice cut through my tirade from the other end of the line. It was like time stopped, my heart pausing its beating in my chest.

"Oh, hi, yes, sorry for that confusion!" I said, my tone newly polite. "How are you? How have things been?"

"You know," she replied, and I did know. "We've been keeping on as best we can. But I'm calling with good news—great news, actually. We're reopening the museum to the public next week and I was wondering if you'd be interested in taking your job back?"

JEAN

I should not have been as surprised as I was to hear a familiar voice first thing the next morning. In hindsight, of course it made sense that a special group would be the first to experience the new installation. Jamie had silently slipped into the gallery in the early hours of the morning. Ever so gently, she turned a single page. She'd read what was there before leaving just as silently as she'd come.

In cacophonous contrast, the recognizable peal of Susie's voice came bouncing in from down the hall. "Now," she commanded, "please make sure your mask covers both your nose and your mouth the *entire* time you are inside the museum." Ironically, I would later notice that Susie's own mask slid beneath her nose every time she opened her mouth a bit too animatedly, which was nearly every time she spoke.

She shepherded her flock of patrons into the room like it was second nature, as if she'd never stopped doing it, careening about the room as if she owned the place. The group was on the smaller side and they entered the gallery timidly, standing apart from one another in awkward clumps.

Susie positioned herself next to the new podium, as close as she could possibly be without stepping over the guard bar. "Come closer, come closer!" she encouraged as she waved the group in. No one moved. "Not too close, of course, you know what I mean. No need to get me in trouble." She laughed boisterously as the group tittered nervously back at her.

Susie radiated a *here making history* energy today. "All right." She turned to face the journal for the first time. Whatever words she was about to say evaporated in her mouth. She was, for the first time in my knowing her, silent, staring dumbstruck at what lay before her. Time passed—so much time that the group began to stir and even I felt some discomfort on their behalf. Finally, she snapped herself out of it. As she turned back to the intimate crowd, small tears dotted the corners of her eyes.

"Wow," she gasped. "I knew this was going to be a big one, but I didn't expect this reaction! I'm so embarrassed!" Susie exclaimed. "I guess maybe I should have come in here by myself first, but when they gave me the chance to be part of the first group, I couldn't say no. Anyway! Okay! Now that we've gotten that out of the way, what do you know about what we're looking at here?"

The group was coming more clearly into focus for me now. I realized I recognized a handful of its members as our regulars, visitors in their sixties and seventies who came together every few months, who knew the museum well enough to have favorites they liked to check in on occasionally.

One of the women in the group raised her hand, and Susie encouraged her with an enthusiastic nod. "It's, um, a journal that no one knew existed until lockdown."

"Precisely," Susie said. "A woman in Massachusetts discovered it this spring as she cleared out an old attic full of her deceased relatives' personal effects. She chose our museum specifically to donate it to—there was no auction. She has reason to believe its author might be represented here, in one of these galleries. It was then delivered to the museum this week with strict instructions—turn one page a day, each day that the museum is open, until we reach the end."

"Do you know if the museum is expecting people to come in every day? Like, to keep coming back, to read the entire thing?" another member of the group asked.

"I don't know," Susie admitted. "I'm just an independent contractor, but I'd imagine no one really has any idea what to expect, given the unprecedented times. Now, where was I?"

"You were about to tell us what's so special about this little thing," whined a man I recognized as the husband of one of my favorite regulars (a favorite because I had oft heard her describe us as *her* favorite work in the collection). His wife covered her already obscured face in embarrassment.

"Right you are." Susie was unbothered by his snark. "As Elise Durand was sorting through all her grandparents' belongings, she found this singular journal tucked in a trunk. The pages were full from cover to cover." Susie was picking up steam now. She continued.

"Written in a mash-up of English and French, the pages supposedly detail a handful of years of the grandmother's young life, spent between Paris and Nice at the end of the 1910s. She had a myriad of artistic talents, it would appear, including a penchant for painting. But successful women artists were few and far between in the late nineteenth and early twentieth centuries—not from a lack of talent but from a lack of opportunity. Unless they had a wealthy father or husband who approved of the pursuits, for most women, art was not a viable career.

"The author of this journal supported herself through her

career as a musician, but still craved a life full of painting. So she moved to Nice with as much savings as she could set aside, and she sat as a model for the great male painters of the era, offering them her time in return for access to canvases and paints. In the journal, she names a dozen of the men whom she modeled for, many of whom are featured in this very museum."

"Now," one of the men interrupted, "how, if it's nearly a century later, can any of this be substantiated?"

"I had the same question," someone else in the crowd said. "How do you know this isn't all made up? A lady's clever pandemic project?"

"The foundation has, of course," Susie supplied a scripted answer, "substantiated everything to the best of their abilities." This was followed by a predictable scoff from the skeptical member of the audience. "With modern technology, we are able to know mostly everything about when the paper was created, how old the ink is, if the handwriting matches from page to page, et cetera. Plus, the journal is not being presented as a research document; rather, it's another work in the museum. Apparently, the pages include her artwork as well: sketches, doodles, smaller pieces of her larger projects. If it is real, and we believe it is, this journal gives us a new window into the lives of a handful of great artists *and*—more important, in my opinion—it reveals a female compatriot of theirs who may have been just as great, were it not for her unfortunate luck of being born a woman and thus lost to history."

"I'm sure the museum only agreed to it because they were worried about attendance numbers and wanted to ensure they'd be able to get people in here after reopening," the snarky member of the audience responded.

"What do you think it says in there?" a woman asked.

"I don't even know where to begin." Susie exhaled. "I can't tell if I want it to be a revelation, maybe a brand-new way of looking at art, or if I'd just prefer something more quotidian. I think my internal monologue feels that if it's quiet, interesting to only us, no one else will want to take it away from us. If it's something larger, history changing, there could be historians, journalists, who knows who, people who might want this for a larger posterity effort. It could get out of our control. So, I don't know what I think is in there, but I hope it's something comfortable that gives us small hints as to what the lives of these artists, these men, looked like through her eyes."

"I'm most excited," the woman who asked the question said, "to see the small pieces of her art as well. What if her modeling is featured somewhere on these walls? The art is finally being reunited with its artist."

"I never would have thought of it like that," the snide man said. Susie and the woman shared a glance.

"Well." Susie clapped her hands together. "Get after it! One at a time, come up and have your moment to look before the museum opens to the public for the day. Plus, I know it's everyone's first time back in so long, so I'm sure we have some favorites we need to visit."

The sound in the room faded into the dull hum of a few pockets of conversation melding together indistinguishably. The regulars stepped up one at a time, as Susie had instructed, some staying for a full minute or even two, others giddily walking away after just a handful of seconds. One woman drifted our way after her turn had ended.

She looked us over like she was trying to memorize every nook and cranny, like a child who had been gifted a detective's magnifying glass and only wanted to look at things as closely as possible. I felt Marguerite and Pierre sit up a little straighter, and knew I was basking in the glow of her attention too. After so long, it felt so good.

She was called away by her partner as Susie moved them on to other rooms to visit other paintings. Not long after they'd left, our first unaccompanied patrons arrived, two young men in shorts and the bright shirts of American summer, their faces covered with cloth masks someone must have stitched by hand. They walked quickly into the gallery, striding confidently, but they stopped still when they realized they were alone in here. The leader gently took the other by the hand, peering toward the journal before he led him over to it. They looked together, hand in hand.

The visitors continued to arrive, the crowd never rising at that of a popular day before the hiatus but ebbing and flowing comfortably as the hours moved along. It felt so good to have people to watch; I wondered how I'd ever before taken this for granted.

33

JEAN

I expected night to fall suddenly, weighed down with anticipation, but the sunlight stretched on long after the final patron had shuffled out into their own world. Either this was
the longest day of the year, or my anxiety was transforming
seconds into minutes, or both.

The sound of footsteps froze my blood where it was in my
veins; I could tell it wasn't Claire. Because I recognized the
sound of her tread, I was not surprised to see Linda appear
moments later, but I was disappointed. I guessed this was all
Linda's domain now. Oddly enough, she didn't have her bucket
and supplies with her. She walked, empty-handed, toward the
journal, and stood above it, transfixed.

Claire's appearance in the doorway moments later startled
both Linda and myself.

"Oh my god, Linda," Claire said, her hand over her heart. "I
did not expect to find you in here. You don't, um, we haven't

switched gallery assignments, have we?" Claire's voice was like music to my ears, sending my heart dancing around my chest. She was here, she was back. We were together again—almost.

"I'm sure Jamie explained that they chose to put this installation in one of your galleries," Linda replied as she pointed toward the journal. I could feel the effort it took Claire to follow Linda's gaze, to feign interest in the journal instead of looking straight at me.

Had someone ever been so familiar and unfamiliar all at once? She was just as I'd remembered, just who I'd been picturing, but she was even more beautiful. I studied the differences in her face. A light blue paper mask covered the lower part of her face; the dark circles under her eyes looked deeper than I'd seen them before. The fluorescent light from the ceiling flickered off a few silver strands now woven through her hair, which was longer than I'd ever seen it. It was tied in a simple braid down her back.

"She did," Claire said. She peered over Linda's shoulder at the pages beneath her.

"I asked, obviously, if she wanted to redo the assignments, as this piece is of high value and I'm the more senior of us."

"Oh—" Panic flashed across Claire's face. "She didn't say anything about my taking on different rooms."

"That's because Jamie said that things would be fine the way they were," Linda informed Claire. "But I let her know I would report back if I got the feeling there was need for a change."

Was Linda jealous of Claire's proximity to this shiny new object? Did she view this as a demotion?

"I'll take good care of this space, as always," Claire assured her. "It's my favorite." Claire allowed herself one look around the room to illustrate her point, catching my eyes with hers for the briefest moment. "I heard each page is only visible for one day," Claire continued. Linda nodded in acknowledgment. "If anything, it's kind of cool that it's so temporary and that we'll get to be in here every day."

"If you're into that kind of thing," Linda replied.

"I think I am." Claire shrugged. Linda patted her on the shoulder.

"You're cute; I forgot that. I missed you, kid," Linda said on her way out of the room. "Catch you in the break room later?"

"I owe you a cup of coffee," Claire said.

"The coffee's free, baby."

"Exactly." Claire's smile hid a wink within it. Linda continued her walk to the staircase and out of sight. I forced myself to breathe.

From across the room, she finally looked me in the eye. "Hi," she said, as she took the mask off her face.

"Hi," I said back, knowing that to her it looked like I'd just mouthed the word.

She began to shuffle toward me, taking off in a full run after just a few steps. I crouched down to offer her my hand as she hurtled herself into the painting, crashing into my chest instead of meeting my grasp. I wrapped both arms around her and we lay there for some time, crumpled into each other on the floor.

"You smell the same." She broke the silence with a laugh.

"Did you think that might have changed?" I asked.

"No, but nothing out there smells like you. I've spent months trying to remember what this was like."

"You smell the same too," I said, thinking I could bury my head in the space between her neck and her shoulder forever. To my dismay, she pulled away as she sat back, rising up straight.

"Jean," she began. "I am so, so, so sorry for—"

"No," I interrupted. "I'm the one who is sorry. If you only knew how many hours I've spent over the past months worried that would be how we left things forever. I never want to push you, Claire. I love you so much and I trust you and I don't need you to tell me anything you don't want to share—"

"But I want to," she cut me off. "I want to tell you everything. I wanted to do it that night, as soon as I left. And I've just been waiting and thinking and planning all this time how to share it with you."

"There's no rush," I said. "We have time again. You can tell me all of it; I want to know everything you have to say. But let's just be here, together, first."

She lay against me on the floor, exhaling a sigh she must've been holding in for weeks. I wrapped my arms around her. I didn't think I'd ever be able to let go.

"So," she said as she reclined into me.

"So," I responded. "What happened?"

"What do you mean?" Claire laughed a laugh filled with anxiety. "You mean, like, what *happened* happened?" She sat up to look me in the eye. I nodded apprehensively. "Oh my god, you actually have no idea."

"All we know is all of a sudden, everyone was gone."

"Okay, wow, I haven't actually talked to anyone who doesn't know—like, literally where do I start? Okay." She gathered her thoughts. "So there was—I mean, there is—a global pandemic."

"Mon dieu."

"Oh my god is right. Basically, it blew out of control, like, super fast, and no one knew how it was spreading so they just . . . shut the world down. Only essential workers were supposed to leave their homes and everyone else just had to wait. It's been a huge mess. So many people have died."

"But you're okay?"

Claire shrugged. "I've been healthy—thank god for that." I pulled her back into me, realization dawning about how lucky we were to have this moment. "Jamie called last week to say you were reopening, and would I be comfortable coming back to work, and I actually started crying on the phone. I think I really freaked her out. Or maybe everyone is so freaking broken right now that she expected it."

"I'm so glad you are healthy."

"What's life in here been like for you?"

"It's been—" I wasn't sure how to finish my sentence. "It's been quiet. And loud. For a while, it was like every day was a party. *Le Bonheur de vivre* was going full steam, twenty-four seven. Even Marguerite was beginning to show signs of exhaustion."

"No way."

"Yes way," I responded, as Claire had taught me to do.

"Did you join in? I know how you prefer your solitude but that's a long time of just . . . you."

"Mostly, I just missed you."

"Oh, come on. I would have given up pretty much anything for this to be my quarantine location." Claire sighed and continued. "There's this book I used to love as a kid about a brother and a sister who sneak into one of the big museums in New York City, I can't remember which one, and they stay there overnight for like a week. They sleep in the historic beds and shower in the fountain and eat out of the vending machines, and there was more than one day over the last few months when I caught myself picturing that life, but it was me, figuring out how to stay alive in this place."

"I wish you'd been here too. I wished that every day." Something crossed over her face at my words. "What?" I probed. "What are you thinking?"

"Nothing, it's just . . . I was kind of worried about you. Very worried, actually. I knew how much my being able to be here blew your world open. I was a little worried about how you'd feel when it sealed back up. And anxious that maybe you'd think I'd chosen not to come back. I worried every day about how we left things and if you thought I was just running away."

I hugged her tightly. I didn't know how to deny her fears; I hadn't been okay. So I didn't say anything at all.

She reached her hand up into my hair and tightened her grip, strands locking into place between her fingers. She pulled my mouth to hers and any words I might have said flew right out of my head. Claire kissed me ravenously and I knew this was something she'd missed, just like I'd missed it too. I slid my arms around behind her back, lifting her and lowering her down against the floor. She lifted her leg and ran her heel up and down my calf, a move that inexplicably turned me on more than anything else. I began to lose control.

"Jean," Claire said, pulling back.

"Yes?" I all but panted at her.

"We are literally lying on your living room floor."

"It would be a first for me too." She punched my arm.

"I'm not having sex with you when your mom or sister or, god forbid, Linda, could walk in at any moment."

"Fair point," I said as I scooped her back into my arms.

"I want to tell you everything," she said between kisses.

"We have time," I said. "After," I promised. I stood and swept her out of the room, catching a glimpse of the plinth across the way.

"Oh!" I exclaimed. "We didn't even talk about the journal!"

"After," Claire instructed.

"After," I agreed again as we raced off to somewhere more private.

34

CLAIRE

Jean was moving fast. He kicked the door of the cabin closed with his foot, putting me back down on the ground but grabbing my hands to pull me close. He spun me, pulling me in and backing me up against the wall. I laughed into his kiss from the thrill of it all. I had spent so much of the past few months feeling old, my responsibilities adding years to my life. Jean made me feel my age again.

We kissed like we were doing it for the first time, sloppy with enthusiasm, not a drip of self-consciousness. My fingers tightened in his hair and I bit down gently on his lip; I could feel his heart rate spike as he moaned. He put his hands under my legs and picked me up again, wrapping me around him. I was desperate to get my uniform off; ironic, as I'd been so excited to put it on a few hours earlier.

"What's so funny?" Jean asked as he kissed my neck. "You keep giggling."

"I'm just"—I gasped as he nipped at my neck—"so happy to be back."

He smiled and lowered me onto the couch, keeping his kisses going as he undid my jumpsuit buttons as fast as he could. I sat up to help him undress me, shimmying out of the top and freeing my arms. He pulled the whole thing off from the ankles.

And then he paused. Where he had been frantic and frenzied, he was now slow, taking his time to step back and look at me. I knew what he was doing but I was impatient, my body craving as much of his touch as it could get. He ran his fingers along my calves, drawing small, slow circles. I wished I could take a picture with my memory.

"Jean," I begged when the anticipation was too much.

"You're beautiful," he said as he lowered himself to his knees and pulled my hips up to meet his mouth. He was so different from anyone I'd ever known before, both in the way he spoke to me and in the way he treated me. He was the one who asked me to show him what I needed. He was generous and attentive, uninterested in climaxing himself until he was sure I was taken care of. I wondered if he had an ex-girlfriend to thank for that education. I could tell it was what turned him on above all else.

I cried out in pleasure. Jean didn't stop until I physically sat up and drew him by the shoulders to meet me. I was shaking and he was so aroused, I thought he might rip his pant seam. I wanted today to last forever and also to move so quickly. I began to strip away his jacket, his shirt, his pants; he was fully clothed compared to my complete and total nakedness and I made quick work of leveling the playing field.

I switched our places and he grinned in surprise as I pushed him down onto his back. I lowered myself onto him and he immediately reached down to that spot that made me shiver, rubbing in slow circles. He couldn't hold out for long and came quickly, and moments later I did again too.

I collapsed onto his chest, trapping his arm between our bodies. Again, I got to smell his perfectly distinct scent, one I had tried so hard to keep ahold of in my memory: a little tobacco, a little oil paint, a little of that classic guy smell. I inhaled as he kissed the top of my head, and I heard him whisper, "I love you."

"I know," I said. "I love you too."

"I know," he echoed. I rolled ever so slightly to the side and laid my head on his collarbone. I could feel his chin on the top of my head. We fit together like a puzzle and I never wanted to leave.

But Linda had freaked me out earlier, and I knew it was possible she'd come back to check on me soon. As much as I didn't want to get up, I didn't want to get fired even more. I forced myself to sit up. I didn't even have to say anything, Jean just followed my lead, passing me my jumpsuit.

"It's always too short," I said as I got dressed again.

"But we have so many more nights ahead of us," he reassured me.

As I helped him do the buttons on his shirt, I remembered he had mentioned the journal earlier. I reminded him of this.

"Oh!" he exclaimed as he pulled his shoes back on. "So you've heard of it?"

"Of course I have," I said. "It's everywhere on the news, online, everyone's talking about it. They said it's possible the writer is one of the anonymous models on the walls."

"I heard the same," he confirmed.

"Don't you feel like we could figure out who it is?" I asked. I'd been puzzling over this mystery ever since the announcement—the chance to reunite the journal with its true owner. A genuine historical riddle, and I was perhaps the only person alive who could investigate from within the paintings on the walls—the only one I knew of, anyway. I hoped the journal belonged to Antoinette, my occasional professor and favorite person in the museum besides Jean, but I didn't want to reveal my theory yet, in case I was wrong. Jean knew her much better than I did.

"I hadn't thought of that," Jean mused. "There are so many figures in the museum, I think it would be impossible. Or if the person wanted to be found, then they would reveal themselves."

"Can we at least go try?" I asked.

"Yes, yes, we absolutely can." Jean draped his tie around his neck, to be tied later, and left the top buttons of his shirt undone. I loved seeing him like this. I knew he wouldn't age, not like I would and had in the last few months, but when he was mussed up like this, I could picture a Jean two or three decades older, growing hotter and hotter in middle age.

"Ooh," I cooed. "It's casual Jean today."

"Only for you," he said, stealing one more kiss.

We walked together out into the daylight of this painting's bucolic scene. Jean led the way through parlor rooms, estates, and seascapes until, in a matter of minutes, we were in the painting that stood above the journal. We crouched to better inspect the page beneath us.

I read aloud as best I could. The handwriting was loopy and blurred with age. "*April 15, 1918. To begin in a sincere place, life has not been all I've imagined. After so many years of just scraping by in Paris, I've decided to leave. I want to work on my art and my own music. I've always thought I'd get to make some sort of stamp on the world, instead it's been keeping me in place. So, I've escaped. I've just arrived in Nice, with Pierre and a few others of his cohort. This is supposed to be a place for* . . . What does that word mean?"

Jean looked closer. "That's the French word for 'storytellers,' if I'm reading the letters correctly."

"*I've made it clear to all that I'm here to pursue my work but I'm not sure Pierre's been—* Is that French again?"

"'Amenable,' I think she means."

"Who do you think Pierre is? Your brother?"

He shook his head. "Renoir, maybe? He would have been pretty old. It was a common name. Keep reading." I could tell Jean was getting excited about this too. We had a front-row seat to art history.

"*—Amenable to my message. We've settled in amongst a series of apartments in a neighborhood that seems to be favored by others of our sort. A man stopped me on the street today and asked if I would sit for him. I'd anticipated this kind of thing and said I'd do so only for a trade—I'd take a canvas and the other materials I needed to get started. He agreed. I'll sit for him tomorrow. Tomorrow, I'm going to start to make the life I always thought I would have.*"

I heard a noise and stopped abruptly. It was the red-haired woman that we'd seen in the gallery downstairs during the first of Jean's art history lessons. I thought she was stunning then, but I had underestimated her. She was so beautiful up close it overwhelmed me. While Jean had come to feel human to me, she felt like a real work of art.

"Oh," she said. "I'm sorry, I didn't realize you"—she looked at Jean as well—"I mean, anyone would be here."

"Hi," I said, somewhat starstruck to see her in person. I didn't know why; it wasn't like she was any different from anyone else I'd met in this world. "How are you doing?" I asked, trying to seem normal.

"I'm well, thank you for asking," she said as she backed out of the room. "I'll let you have your time; I'll come back later."

I started to tell her that wasn't necessary, but she was already gone. "Oh, I do really need to get going," I admitted to Jean. "Are you okay?" I asked. He looked sad, so sad.

"I'm going to miss you again," he confessed.

"I know, but I'll be back tomorrow. And tomorrow, we'll talk. I'll tell you as much as I can."

"No rush," he said. "We will take our time." I planted a light kiss on his lips and went to slide out of this frame when Jean cried, "Wait!" I'd never heard him shout before; it startled me.

"The floor here by the new installation," he explained, "it's got a motion-sensor alarm. I don't know if they turn it off at night like the others. It's probably safer to go around."

"Good call," I said. Now that Jean had reminded me, I remembered Jamie mentioning something about that. I walked until I was within the world of the painting just to the right, and I successfully dropped to the ground, outside the alarm's radius.

I turned back to him to say good night and he waved in response. I hustled over to my mop, but my hustle was more like a skip tonight. I was so happy; my legs couldn't contain themselves.

I felt a wave of guilt in that moment. How could I be this happy without Luna? This was the first night in months I hadn't been there to tuck her into bed, a ritual I'd fallen right back into the rhythm of. Could I ever be a good mother if I could find such happiness while I was pretending my kid didn't exist? Would my life ever feel complete if I always had to choose between the two of them?

I had just slopped my mop onto the ground when Linda reentered the room, the jump scare of her unexpected appearance nearly knocking me to the floor.

"My *god*, Linda, you scared the shit out of me!" I all but yelled. I remembered I'd taken off my mask in Jean's world and dug around in my jumpsuit pocket for it. Thankfully, it was there, and I looped its strings over my ears as quickly as I could.

"Sorry," Linda said, clearly not sorry. "I didn't hear any sounds coming from here; I thought you'd moved on."

I couldn't quite figure out her motives—was she there to inspect my work? Was she there to read the journal herself? I realized just how dirty the gallery must look to her detail-oriented eye.

I tried to cover for myself. "Slow start is all, getting back into it. I was looking at the art," I admitted, hoping that would atone for my rate of work tonight. I caught a glimpse of Jean out of the corner of my eye. He had taken a seat in the painting above the journal, trying to look like a natural part of the setting. "Just checking on all the familiar faces," I rambled on.

Linda nodded but gave me a disapproving glare. She took one last look at the journal before she told me she'd see me downstairs and left me alone. I turned to Jean and wiped an imaginary line of sweat from my brow, smiling to let him know we'd survived that close call, and finally got to work.

When the room was immaculate enough to pass muster with Linda, I blew Jean a kiss. He had stayed right where we'd parted and watched me work. He pretended to catch my kiss, pulling it into his heart. I forced myself to leave, which was only possible with the knowledge that I could come back tomorrow. But I also knew that tomorrow, it was time for me to come clean. My stomach turned at the thought. Once I told Jean, there'd be no going back.

35

JEAN

'd wandered back to the journal, wanting to make sure we'd gleaned all we could from today's page, when Odette re-entered. I didn't turn to look, but from the absence of her skirt swishing, I could tell she hadn't left immediately upon seeing me there.

"Hi," I said.

"Hi," she responded, slowly inching farther into the room. I turned back to look at her, rising up from where I was seated on the floor to find a chair. "Sorry about earlier. I didn't mean to make things awkward."

"You didn't," I said. "So, um, you're here for the journal?"

"Just wanted to see what all the fuss was about."

"Well, you should check it out. It's all yours. I'd best be getting home now, unless you need any help interpreting it?"

"I think I've got it from here."

"Right, right, well." I stood and backed out of the room,

leaving Odette a clear shot to the book. "Enjoy." The last thing I saw as I exited, turning back to check over my shoulder, was Odette pressing her way up against the edge of the frame, her signature graceful neck twisting so she could get a better look. She really was desperate for new reading material.

As the museum's powers that be had hoped, the presence of the journal ensured the constant attendance of visitors the next day. I even recognized some people who I had seen the day before, back to read what came next. Some came in small groups, tittering nervously among themselves as they waited their turn to approach the day's page. Others came alone, lingering silently until the small crowd had cleared away. They brought notebooks, scribbling down notes in their few moments of glory with the text, or snapping a photo on their cellphones. Susie came again, no tour group in tow this time.

I could tell from the second she walked in that night that Claire was frazzled. She was rushing and accidentally steered the mop into the doorframe, spilling her bucket of soapy water across the floor.

"Shit," she cursed as she threw a handful of rags on the puddle in a futile attempt to mop up the liquid. "Ugh, whatever, I'll deal with you later," she told the mop as she hurried over to me. I helped her in.

"Are you okay?" I asked.

"Yeah," she lied. "Just a little in my own head today is all."

"Do you want to talk first or go see the journal first?" I was eager to put her at ease and couldn't tell which she needed right now.

"I think—I guess talk?" she said. "I'm worried we're going to run out of time."

"It's okay," I reassured her as I took her hand in mine. "We don't have to get it all done tonight. The close call with Linda last night startled me as well." She chewed on the skin around her thumb. I could tell it was already raw from a day of worry.

"What about a compromise—why don't we talk on the way to the journal? And wherever we get to, we'll pause and pick it up again tomorrow?"

"Okay," Claire exhaled. "Okay."

And as we walked through fields, taverns, living rooms, and studios, she began to let me in.

"I'm not sure where to start. I don't know where this story even begins. I was so young when we met, only sixteen. And he was older, much older, in a different part of life, but I couldn't see that at the time. At first, it was just about him. I didn't realize I was falling for him until he made a move and it was clear the feelings were mutual. Well, maybe 'mutual' is the wrong word, because of the age difference. I'm doing a terrible job of explaining this . . ." she trailed off.

"It's okay," I assured her. "I'm understanding, so far."

"Things moved slowly and then all at once. For a year, we hovered around each other, but his presence kept anyone else from standing a chance at getting my attention. And then all of a sudden, we were together and . . . Well, there was no turning back. At first, he was so excited. He convinced me to come here, to the city, with him. He promised me that life I'd always dreamed of, a life of excitement and glamour, and I thought this is it, this is growing up. I was so young, I was seventeen, I asked my mom what to do. I'd been hiding him from her and she freaked out. She threw me out. Said I was going against everything she expected of me."

"She did what?" I interrupted. "She threw you out? For dating someone she didn't approve of?"

"It's more complicated than that," she said. "There's more to the story. My mom holds very tightly to her convictions. If you're wrong, in her mind, you are always going to be wrong."

"That's not fair," I said, mad on her behalf, but I could tell she didn't want to linger on that part of the story. "But we'll come back to that. What happened next?"

"I moved to the city with Jeremy. He promised me it would be beyond my wildest dreams. But it was never going to be like that. He knew that, but I didn't realize he was lying until we started to live it. I didn't know anyone here, so I just went to work and back to the apartment every day. He'd take the day shift at home and then as soon as I got back in the afternoon, he was off to 'work.' I never really understood what he did. And that's how he liked it. He wouldn't come back until the last possible moment. He stayed out until all hours of the night, never answering my calls, even during the day. It didn't take a rocket scientist to figure out what was going on, that he'd gotten bored of me and of the life I could offer him. I called him out on it—the next week, he proposed. I'm pretty sure he did it just to shut me up for a while. He never actually planned to marry me. It had the intended effect; I kept trying to make our life together work. Until one morning, he just didn't come back."

"At all?" I asked. I found it impossible to believe someone would choose to leave Claire.

"At first I thought he'd show up again after a few days, but weeks passed, and then months . . . And that was the end. Of the Jeremy chapter," she said. "I can see that now, but it took me years to wrap my mind around the fact that he was just gone. I kept wearing the ring until . . . well, until I met you."

We'd arrived at the painting above the journal. Claire seemed sad, these memories having stirred up terrible feelings within her.

"Thank you, Claire," I said, "for telling me all of that. It means so much to me that you would trust me."

"It's not all," she said. "There's so much more."

"It's okay," I said. I didn't want her to be sad for a moment longer tonight. "There's tomorrow and the next day and the next day. A page of the journal, a little more story."

"Okay." Claire gave in. "We can do it that way." I couldn't

tell if she was relieved or if she was anxious to keep dragging it out. She still wouldn't let me in all the way, wouldn't tell me what she really needed right now. But I had let her off the hook for the night, and she was taking me up on the opportunity. Claire crouched down to get a better look at the journal and read aloud.

"Today, I found myself in his studio unattended. He'd again invited me over to model but must have forgotten that he'd done so, because he was nowhere to be found at the agreed upon time. But the door was unlocked and I figured he'd left it so for me, so I let myself in. I waited for a bit, but the sun was setting and his arrival was clearly far from imminent. I stood up to explore. Sure, I was a bit nosy, but it was he who had broken our . . ."

" 'Appointment,' " I translated.

"I found myself drifting towards a canvas that was covered with a large cloth. I can't say what drew me to this one, but it was like something was silently calling me. I pulled back the sheet to reveal a finished salon scene, with a chatty group seated on the various pieces of furniture across the room. They felt so alive, I could almost hear what they were saying, if I just leaned in a little closer . . . Oh my god, I can't believe that's how it ends."

"I wonder if I know that painting," I said, trying to picture such an arrangement of subjects. "It feels familiar, but no image actually comes to mind."

"Jean," Claire said, her tone serious.

"What is it?" I asked, concerned about her sudden shift in mood.

"What do you think happens next?"

"What do you mean? We'll read the page tomorrow."

She cleared her throat. "Do you think she goes in? To the painting, I mean? That's how I'd always felt, before I figured out that I could—" She mimed climbing into my frame. "I wonder what will happen, if she follows that instinct. I have to read more. I have to know."

The impact of her words hit me. "You think maybe . . . no, that's impossible. You think she's like you?"

"I mean . . ." Claire fidgeted with a handful of her hair, twining it between her fingers. "There can't be many of us, if you or anyone else in here have never heard of it happening before. Y'all certainly have institutional knowledge. But maybe there are just a handful of us who have gone so far as to learn that it's even possible. It wouldn't make sense for me to be the only one . . . ever."

I thought about what she'd said, and realized I wasn't certain that there was *no one* in here who might know about something like this. It was possible some stones had been left unturned. I had been so wrapped up in our romance, I'd long ago left behind any investigation of the magic that allowed us to be together.

"That's a good point," I said.

"I guess we'll find out tomorrow," Claire mused. "I wish I could just slip down there and turn the page."

"If only you wouldn't send the museum into lockdown," I warned. "That couldn't possibly be worth finding out what happens next."

"We'll wait, then." Claire looped her hand through mine. Then she described to me an invisible network of communication that she called "social media," where people could spread photos and gossip from the phones they all carried in their pockets.

"Is it like how you said you could look the old version of me up?" I asked, unable to remember the word she'd used for the process.

"Yes, it all usually starts at Google, totally. But there are these different sites that Google links to, where these conversations can, well, spiral."

I struggled to picture the reality of this seemingly cosmic-level web of information, but Claire said it wasn't necessary to visualize it; even she found it unfathomable.

She was using it to do some research on the journal, and I was shocked to discover it was taking the internet, a term I'd learned from her, by storm. Yesterday's visitors had uploaded photos and abbreviated testimonials of the contents of that day's page, and curiosity about the identity of the writer grew exponentially. Claire said there were people thousands of miles away who had joined in on the conversation.

"It's absolutely wild. Maybe people still have more time on their hands than before, or everyone's obsessed with true crime and thinks they can solve the mystery themselves, but I've seen full social media accounts, TikTok videos, blogs even, spring up overnight dedicated to dissecting each painting in the museum, cataloging every woman featured, ruling out anyone who we know enough about to know that it's not her."

"Why does everyone care so much about it? And what's a blog?"

"Oh, a blog is like a personal website—I mean, a page online that any one person can make that everyone else can access on their technology if they want"—I didn't interrupt, but I was so lost—"but also probably no one else is reading it."

"Why not?"

"Because there is so much space and noise online, not everyone can have someone who cares about their work. It's hard to explain. Some people write, or post, just for the sake of doing it. It doesn't matter whether anyone else is looking. It's like their way of saying something out loud, even if they're in the room alone. It's beside the point."

"I'll take your word for it."

"As to why everyone cares so much? I don't know." Claire paused, contemplating the question I'd raised. "I think maybe there's been so much darkness in the world this year and this, like, tingles with magic." I threaded my fingers through hers.

"If only they could see you."

"They'd lose their freaking minds."

"Have you ever told anyone about this?"

"Kind of. I tell it like it's a bedtime story at home."

"To your grandmother?"

"Yes." Claire dug two of her teeth into her bottom lip. "Her and my—"

The alarm blared.

36

JEAN

We looked out through the frame in front of us to see that two figures dressed head to toe in black were standing there. One of them held the journal in their hands. The alarm had scared them—had they not expected it? They appeared frozen in place, just how we were supposed to be. In their moment of hesitation, I grabbed Claire's hand and dragged her behind the chair in the living room we were currently in, pulling her to crouch down next to me. Everyone left in the paintings in this gallery stopped in their tracks.

One of the thieves shouted at the other, but I couldn't make out what they said over the sound of the alarm. They gestured wildly, pointing toward the exit. The one holding the journal shouted back and they both took off running toward the door. Just before they could make a clean exit, they stepped in the puddle of water Claire had spilled when she'd arrived tonight, both falling to the ground next to her cart in a flail of limbs. With a lack of coordination that would have been comical had the moment not been catastrophic, they got to their feet and finally made it out.

Around us, the alarm continued to ring and we could hear the sound of locks thudding into place at all the exits. The figures in the paintings scattered, racing back to the frames they were supposed to be in. Claire stood up and shouted over the sound: "I have to go!"

"No!" I yelled as I grasped for her hand. She was safe here. I couldn't protect her out there. "You should stay here with me. You'll be safe and we'll be together. I love you!" I shouted as the alarm screamed in the gallery.

"I can't get stuck here, Jean, I'm sorry!" Claire leapt from the frame, landing beside the now empty journal stand. She ran off to her bucket and was making to leave when she stopped, staring down at the floor. All I could see below her was the puddle of rags, now a soggy mess from the thieves' fall. Claire bent down, like she was looking for something, but she straightened back up only to throw the pile of rags into her trash can.

I didn't understand what she was doing. I waved my arms and yelled, "Get out of here!," hoping she'd be able to read my lips. Then, on the floor below, we both heard sirens, police cars screeching up to the front door. Claire rushed away into a different gallery, dragging her cart behind her.

For a few seconds, it was just me and the alarm. I looked across to the plinth, empty of its former treasure. I could hardly believe my own eyes. I sat back on my heels, looking around, and made eye contact with Odette, standing in the doorway behind me, mouth agape at what had just happened. She too left in a hurry, crossing away from me and, presumably, back to her painting. We weren't going to be alone for long; it was time to get back in position. I sprinted to my living room.

The cavalry arrived at the same time that Marguerite and Pierre rushed into our frame, gasping for breath from their exertion. The room filled with men in uniforms—security guards and police officers shouting at the top of their lungs that no one was to leave the premises, trying to be heard over the perpetually blaring alarm. More than one person slid on what was left of Claire's puddle, skidding along the floor until they found something or someone else to steady themselves.

"What did they take?" one police officer screamed at a security guard. The guard scanned the room, not seeing anything missing from the walls. Finally, his eyes alighted on the empty stand for the journal.

"It's this new installation," the security guard yelled in response. The alarm finally cut off in the middle of his sentence, leaving his voice booming across the room. He looked around sheepishly and continued at a normal volume. "Some kind of journal or something."

"Let's go," the officer said, "we have to lock this place down."

Twenty minutes later, Christie, Henry, and Lisa hobbled into the gallery in various states of disarray. Christie was wearing a nightgown, pants haphazardly pulled on beneath it. When she saw the bare plinth, she howled a bloodcurdling scream.

"It's *gone*," she wept into Lisa's arms. "What happened?"

Lisa kept one arm curled around her shoulders as she turned to a security guard. "How did they get in?" she asked.

"Pretty sure they broke in through the service entrance," he answered. "We found a guard unconscious and a janitor bound and gagged on the first floor. No sign of any other alarms being triggered until after the journal's alarm went off. The southeast fire exit went off about forty seconds later, leading us to believe that is how the thieves exited."

"Has the FBI been alerted? What's the protocol for something like this? How do I not know this answer?" she peppered him with further questions. "Where's Jamie?"

"Yes, the FBI has been alerted. An agent from their Phila-delphia branch will be here soon, joined shortly by their col-leagues from the D.C. art theft department. And I'd imagine you don't know, ma'am, because we have never had so much as a break-in in the almost century of our existence as an in-stitution," he finished proudly.

Lisa glowered at him. "Until tonight," she corrected.

"Until tonight," he echoed.

"What happened?" Marguerite was crouched beside me on the ground, whispering into my ear. "Did you see the thieves? And where's Claire? Is she here, hiding?"

"She's gone," I whispered.

"Obviously no one leaves," said the security guard, "until the FBI has cleared them. And we'd prefer to keep this on a closed circuit, not telling anyone about the theft for the time being."

"It's already all over social media." Henry stepped forward, showing their small group the screen of his phone. They crowded together as he continued. "My daughter just sent me this thing on Twitter from @art_hei5t: 'Blind item: something irreplaceable went missing from a certain trending museum tonight. Any guesses on what it is and who's got it?' "

"How do they already know?" Christie asked.

"Some kid probably picked it up on a police scanner," the security guard said, glancing at the cops milling around the room. Crime scene tape was being wrapped around the jour-nal's stand and Claire's spill. A man with a large camera set off his flash multiple times as he captured the scene. The room fell into a productive hum as everyone quieted down to get to their jobs, Christie calming her cries to a gentle burble.

A man arrived in the midst of all this, wearing the pants, shirt, and tie of a suit, but in place of a traditional suit jacket was a navy athletic jacket with large yellow letters that spelled "FBI" on the back. It was the middle of the night, but he had sunglasses tucked in his shirt pocket.

"Who here has been in charge so far?" His voice boomed. The security guard who had filled the board members in earlier timidly raised his hand. "I'm going to need you to walk with me. And bring up everyone who was in the museum at the time of the theft, I understand they are all still here—janitors, guards, anyone else. I'm going to need to talk to them all, one by one."

The few security guards in the room scattered to the various exits, off in search of those remaining, as a team of people in FBI jackets that matched the lead agent's streamed into the room. He turned back to the chief security guard.

"Mark Smith, special agent for the art theft team."

"Stan Kaminski, former police chief; I've been head of this security team for five years now. Wow, you got here fast." Stan checked his watch; it couldn't have been more than an hour since the journal theft, right? Time was moving in an unusual way tonight.

"My team was in the area for another case. Ballpark it for me—what went wrong tonight?"

Officer Kaminski looked back over his shoulder at his four museum colleagues; Jamie had slipped in during the FBI's arrival. Mark read his cues and went over to address the group.

"Hi, everyone, Agent Smith," he introduced himself. "You can call me Mark." He offered his hand to shake. Henry clasped it as Christie readjusted her face covering. Mark asked, "What affiliation do you have to the museum?"

"I'm Henry Wallingham, this is Christie Hall"—Christie sniveled in acknowledgment of her name—"and Lisa Meyer." Lisa nodded. "We're on the board and are chairing the committee on this installation. And this"—Henry indicated the fourth member—"is Jamie Leigh; she's the president of the museum."

"Might I ask you all to make yourselves comfortable, perhaps in one of the offices or library spaces? I think it's going to be a while until we have anything to report," Mark said.

"A representative from the museum needs to be present," Christie snapped.

"Absolutely." Mark was nodding. "Jamie, you're welcome to stay." Jamie looked at the rest of the group with regret as Mark's people escorted them from the room.

"I'll come and update you soon," Jamie promised. Mark had moved back over to Officer Kaminski. Henry, Lisa, and Christie shuffled out slowly. Jamie rejoined the inner circle.

"So," Mark said to the head security guard. "You were saying?"

"Like Henry said, there's this new installation that was put in the day before the museum reopened to the public. It has really limited security—no glass, no nothing, just this little barrier with a warning sensor"—he kicked against the bar that kept the viewer away from the plinth—"and an alarm that activates if someone gets too close for comfort."

"Tell me about the book," Mark said to Jamie.

"It's a journal that a woman discovered in her grandmother's effects; the author is an unidentified model from the same era as many of the artists featured in this museum, as well as an artist in her own right."

"What's the reception been like?"

"Well, it's been terrific so far. The donor instructed us to turn one page each day until the entire journal has been revealed, and we've started doing exactly that. Patrons have already been returning to read the next page, Reddit threads have sprung up around the world, the art community is abuzz. There are theories about who the author is that span from the ancestors of French nobility to Matisse's own daughter. No one can get enough of this story."

Marguerite let out a single involuntary, "Ha," and I was sure the journal was not hers.

Mark turned his head to either shoulder, relieving cricks in his neck. "We're going to need to do some digging into those online boards. Typically, they do more harm than good in situations like these."

"What do you mean?" Jamie asked.

"Well, it's a multipart answer. Once we get to the investigation, they can get in our way—trying to solve the case on their own with whatever clues they can find. Sometimes they're off, but they turn the public against us. And sometimes—rarely, but sometimes—they're actually spot-on and they blow up a lead before we've gotten a chance to investigate it. It's also possible they've already been stirring the pot—creating so much intrigue around this installation that they fed the idea for this theft right into the criminals' hands."

"Ah, technology." Jamie sighed. "Friend and foe."

"Regardless, I'll have my team keep a close watch on any new activity, see if there's anything we should be paying attention to."

"Maybe the perpetrator is a member of one of those groups themselves," Officer Kaminski added.

"It's possible. Then we can get into the tricky territory of them trying to protect one of their own. No offense to this journal, but in just taking a glance around, it has to be one of the lowest-value objects in the room. On that wall alone there's a Modigliani, a Rousseau, at least half a dozen Matisses. You're sure nothing else was taken from the museum?"

"We'll have to do a closer inspection," Jamie said. "But it seems like they came here for one thing and they got it."

"I've seen some pretty enthusiastic fans in my many hours of service here," Officer Kaminski added. "Maybe someone just really wanted to have the journal for themselves."

One of the FBI agents entered the gallery, Claire right behind him. A few seconds later, Linda followed. He brought them over to the bench in front of us and gestured silently for them to sit. They did so, and he went over to address Mark.

37

CLAIRE

"Sir, I've got the janitorial staff for you," the FBI agent who had brought us up here announced.

The man who was seemingly in charge of this operation stared at us. "Just these two?" he asked.

"It's a small museum," Jamie answered.

"That one," the FBI agent said as he pointed at Linda, "does the ground floor and the other one"—he pointed at me—"does all this up here." Linda was clearly offended by being called "that one," and I didn't blame her. I tried to make eye contact with her, to establish some form of camaraderie, but she refused to look at me. I could tell she was shaken from the night's events.

Then again, so was I. I'd been acting weird even before the alarms went off. Always with the worst timing, Jeremy had called twice as I was on my way to work. I sent both calls to voicemail. Once I was parked, I deleted both of his messages without listening and fired off a quick text telling him if he wasn't going to show up for Luna when he promised, he wouldn't get a second chance. I told him to never call us again. I wasn't sure he was going to listen to that, but it had shut him up at least for the time being.

I looked down at the skin around my nails. It had reached a startling state of redness; I had shredded my cuticles, and I couldn't stop myself from picking them raw. I had to stop. I was going to make myself look guilty. And I wasn't guilty, at least not of what they might have thought. Unless they knew what I'd really done. They'd been up here for a really long time. Was it possible they already knew? Had they seen something on the camera footage? I scanned the room for the cameras I knew were located in the corners of the ceiling. I didn't think they could see where I had climbed out of the painting, but I couldn't be sure. The cameras must have caught me leaving the gallery afterward. I needed to come up with a good explanation, I thought as I chewed my nails again.

"Hi," the lead investigator said, "I'm Mark Smith. I work for the FBI in the art theft department."

Linda thrust her right hand at Mark. "I'm Linda, head of the janitorial staff." She shook his hand like she was closing a business deal.

"Claire," I said quietly, afraid to extend my hand for fear of him seeing my nails.

"I'm sure this has been an overwhelming, even scary, evening for both of you. I'm going to want to talk to each of you individually. Are you okay to wait around for a bit more?" He phrased it as a question, but I couldn't imagine we had a choice. Any attempt to leave right now would certainly not be welcome, though I had considered faking some emergency. But, of course, this was the emergency.

The flurry of commotion in the gallery was simmering down. The crime scene photographers were reviewing their shots and the plastic bags of evidence were sealed and stored in large black bins, their latches clicking into place. The teams shuffled off, heading back to what I assumed was some kind of office to review the facts of the case or the security camera footage. I recognized that everything I thought I knew about nights like these came from TV dramas. Already, I could tell it was much quieter, less frantic than Hollywood made it out to be. Soon, the room felt practically empty again, just us, Mark, Jamie, and a few others.

"Claire, I'd like to start with you. Linda, why don't you go back to the break room with Leon? You'll be more comfortable there." Leon led Linda from the gallery, Jamie and the others trailing behind them. I wondered if Mark thought we were alone, when I knew we were far from it in here. It made me nervous, knowing Jean would hear all of this. I was too afraid to look at him, worried Mark might be able to see something on my face that he would read as guilt.

"Do you mind if I record our conversation?" Mark asked as he pulled a small tape recorder from his pocket. Once again, it was a question that didn't really feel like a question. I nodded, wanting to seem accommodating. Hopefully, a few more hours would pass and I'd be out of there, free to go home, free to hug my little girl and never let her go. I had to get out of there, for Luna. "It's just for my own memory," he explained. "And I want to remind you that at any time, you can say stop and we'll stop, and start again when you have a lawyer or whatever you need."

"I don't have anything to hide," I said, hoping he couldn't hear the lie in my voice.

"Okay," Mark said. "What happened here tonight?"

"I don't fully know," I admitted. That was true. I'd witnessed as much as anyone could, and even I didn't know who those thieves were and what they wanted with the journal.

"Tell me anything you saw," he said. "Please."

"Well, I was cleaning the room as normal," I said. Thank

god I wasn't hooked up to some kind of lie detector. Did they even use those things in real life or was that just in the movies? I hoped I wouldn't have to find out. "And I heard some people coming, voices I didn't recognize. I just had this moment of, like, panic. I could just feel something was wrong. So I hid."

"Where did you hide?" he asked.

"I hid behind the closest thing I could find." I pointed to the journal plinth. I'd thought it over while we'd been waiting, what I would say in this moment. I thought this was the only thing that *might* be believable whenever they watched the security footage. Otherwise, how else would I explain where I'd popped up? But as soon as I'd said it, I realized it didn't make sense. Wouldn't I have set the alarm off? It was too late, I'd committed. Maybe it would be a blurry timeline, confusing enough for them to not know which one of us set off the alarm. I forged ahead.

"All of a sudden, I heard them on the other side of the stand, arguing. I heard them run out and I crept around. I could see the journal was gone and, I don't know why, my first instinct was to run after them. Like my brain couldn't believe what my eyes were staring at. But sure enough, the journal was gone."

"Did you ever see either of the thieves?"

"No." I shook my head, even though I had stared right at them through the frame with Jean. It didn't make any difference. I still had no clue who they were.

"What happened then?" he asked.

"The alarm was still ringing like crazy. I could hear them running out of the museum, and figured I had to go find Linda or Tony or one of the other guards, and that the police would be here soon."

"And you took your cleaning cart with you?"

"Honestly, it was habit. That's what I always do."

"What did you find when you got downstairs?"

I shuddered at the memory. "Linda was gagged and tied to

a bench. I guess she hadn't had time to hide. I helped her get free and then we ran to find Tony. And Tony was . . . he was unconscious next to the back entrance we all use. It was awful. I thought he was dead." I felt tears pricking at the corners of my eyes.

"He's going to be fine," Mark told me. "The thieves didn't do any permanent damage."

"They're good people," I said, "Linda and Tony and everyone who works here. They did right by us as soon as the lockdown ended."

"How long have you been working for the foundation?"

"Almost a year now," I told him. "Minus those four months we were closed."

"Did you get another job during that time?" he asked. I didn't see what that had to do with anything that happened here tonight.

"No," I said, "I was at home with my family."

"And who does that family consist of?"

"My grandmother. And my daughter, Luna. She's four."

"That's it?"

"Her father walked out on us."

I couldn't help it; I looked at Jean. All these months and all of a sudden the truth was out in the open, just like that. He was staring right at me, still as a statue, just as he was all day long. I studied him for any sign of a reaction, but he gave me nothing. Marguerite, on the other hand, let her jaw drop. It was so subtle and she caught herself almost immediately, but I saw it.

"He's not in the picture anymore," I repeated. I didn't want any implication that Jeremy was anywhere near this place.

Mark hummed. "Thank you, Claire," he said as he stood up and offered his hand to shake. This time, I took it. "I'm sure we'll have more questions."

"Well, you know where to find me, it appears."

"Yes," Mark confirmed. "We have your contact information. But if there's anything else we should know about reaching you, be sure to let us know. If you don't pick up when we call, things get more complicated on my end."

"I'll be there," I promised. For the first time, I was beginning to let myself believe I was going to get to go home. The FBI hadn't figured it all out. I held it together just a little bit longer. "Am I good to go home now?" I asked.

"I don't think they've lifted the hold on the museum yet, so I think you'll need to sit tight while we talk to Linda." So close and yet so far. "We're grateful for your patience," Mark said as he gestured to the doorway that led back to the museum. "I'll walk you back; I've got to go get your co-worker."

As much as I wanted to get out of there in one piece, I didn't want to leave Jean. A part of me considered running toward his frame, jumping in before anyone could stop me, and curling up in his arms.

Instead, I followed Mark silently out of the room. He traded me for Linda and left me in our locker room with Leon. A few minutes later, Leon's cellphone rang and he looked up at me.

"You can take it," I said. "I'm just going to change out of my uniform, if that's okay. Mark said we'd get to leave soon." Leon nodded and stepped out to take the call.

I jumped into action, grateful I'd brought an oversized sweatshirt to wear home that night. I reached into my trash can and grabbed the bundle of rags, pulling the journal out from the bundle I'd hidden it in and stuffing it into my waistband. It was risky, but I couldn't see any other way of getting it out of there.

When Leon reentered the room, I was dressed in my street clothes and emptying my trash can into the larger bin. Leon ignored me and went back to scrolling on his phone. Soon enough, Linda was returned to us, still looking incredibly shaken.

"Hey," I said, touching her arm. "You okay?" It was hard to

do this with masks on. I could only see her eyes. She didn't say anything, just pulled her arm away from me. Leon waited for her to get changed and then walked us through the caution tape to our cars. I nearly collapsed with fear as we walked out through the metal detectors, but, of course, the journal did not set anything off.

Soon enough, I was back in my car, heading home. I couldn't believe what I had done, but I had to find out how her story ended.

38

JEAN

Mark did not bring Linda up to our neck of the woods. That made sense, I guessed, that he would also question her in the place where she'd been tonight: the gallery where they'd held her captive. I hoped Linda was okay.

And Claire too. Was she completely panicking right now? I'd been sure they were going to lock her up immediately, that someone would have seen her emerging from the painting somehow. Sure, that wasn't the crime they were investigating, but it had to be some kind of rule breaking. I'd been so relieved when Mark said she'd be able to go home.

Home to her daughter. Claire had a daughter. That fact didn't bother me, of course it didn't. I bet she was an amazing mom. But why had she chosen to keep it from me for all this time? Why didn't she want me to know that side of herself? How much did I truly know about Claire?

The urgency of the evening seemed to lessen with each

minute that passed since the theft; each hour left it feeling a little more normal, familiar even. This was the state of our world now, until it wasn't anymore and we'd adjust to some new way of being. Was this my and Claire's new way of being? Would I adjust to that too? Would Claire come back tomorrow?

"This is what we'll be known for now." Marguerite exhaled a long, steady cloud of smoke. "When people ask, 'Which museum is that again?,' they'll say, 'The one with the theft.'"

"Unless they find it," said Pierre. "Then it's something entirely different. The whole value of this relatively mysterious object could change in just a few hours because of what happened tonight. You heard Mark, it was far from the most valuable thing in here, but if it's found, its value may have just grown exponentially."

"I don't know that we'll be seeing that journal again," Marguerite said, her voice laced with skepticism.

"Jean, you were there!" Pierre exclaimed. "You truly have no further information?"

"There were two figures, completely covered from head to toe except for their eyes. I know no more than you." I could tell how frustrated he was with me. I'd be frustrated with me too, if I could think of anything besides Claire.

"It's absolutely mind-blowing," Pierre said, "that we witnessed it and we still know no more than the investigation team. If only we knew more, we could help them. Claire could tell them! It's not too late. It's probably still in the city. It's maybe even still in the museum!" He was getting worked up and took a breath to steady himself. "What do you think they plan to do with it anyway?"

"Sell it," Marguerite said. "What else would they do?"

"Read it?" I guessed. "I wonder what happens now," I ruminated, dread pooling in my stomach. What if they shut the museum down again? As if on cue, Mark, Jamie, and the head of security strode into the room.

"So," Jamie asked, "what happens next?"

"Well, the short version is we try to get the journal back immediately. The longer an art crime goes unsolved, the more likely it is that the item won't be seen for a generation, when it's less risky to sell."

Jamie looked like she was going to be ill. Mark continued.

"We begin our investigation. We'll stay in town, continuing to monitor the museum, following up through our outside channels, putting together any leads we might have from the information we've gathered here tonight. We'll have people watching for the item to pop up, for sale or for ransom. We'll have our digital team dig into the online scene and see if they can find anything there. We'll probably need to talk to all the staff again, as well as any key players who weren't on-site tonight. And we'll go back over these security tapes until they start to make sense. We'll talk to Tony, figure out why he let them in. Where did Claire hide? There are weird corners cut off by the camera angles, typical in a building like this one that has spaces of all shapes and sizes. We'll cross-reference the footage with our database of known conspirators, see if we draw any familiar faces out."

"Familiar faces?" Officer Kaminski asked. "Is there a pool of usual suspects for something like this?"

"That's what the movies would have you believe," Mark said. "But, to be honest, no. It's rarely, if ever, some all-powerful art connoisseur pulling the strings. It's far more likely for it to be tied to a local crime ring. Our Philadelphia branch will handle that part of it, looking for possible connections. Because this piece has been in the news so much, it might have crossed someone's mind as an easy target. Alternatively, since they only took one thing, it's possible we have a rare personal collection case on our hands. It's hard to speculate. We'll see what we find."

"Should we open the museum as normal in the morning?"

"That's up to you and the board, I would imagine. From my experience, you're going to get a crowd who shows up specifically to see the absence of the thing. If you're okay with that, we can't tell you how to run your museum, so it's really up to you."

"I'd imagine we'll choose reopening; after four months of closure, I don't think we can afford to do it again."

"In that case, I'd double security for the next few days. I'm less worried about someone making it out of here with something than I am about someone *thinking* they can make it out of here with something. We see it all the time, one theft blazing a trail for other attempts."

Jamie nodded. "Good point. Officer Kaminski, can you handle that?"

"Absolutely, I'll do so as soon as we're done here. There will be no copycats, not on my watch."

"From your mouth to God's ears," Jamie muttered under her breath.

"Are there any other items here you think might be at risk? Anything you might want to better secure before letting the public roam the halls once more? Or anything the journal might be connected to?"

Jamie seemed to run the question over in her mind. "I don't think so. We've never had a problem like this before."

"We'll keep the whole museum safe," Officer Kaminski said, confusingly optimistic for a man who had been caught unaware by a theft of indeterminable value just hours earlier.

"All right, case is open. Let's get down to it. I'll be back tomorrow to continue what we need for the investigation on-site," Mark said, packing up his notebook and recorder in a leather messenger bag he'd abandoned at the foot of the bench earlier that night.

"I know you have to do what you have to do, but will you be wearing that jacket?" Jamie slowed Mark down from barreling to the exit, her eyes scanning the bright yellow letters on the jacket's back.

"You mean you don't want me traipsing around here while the guests are inside."

"You're welcome to be here, of course. I'm just sensitive to the possibility of causing a scene."

Mark looked ready to snap back, but he clearly liked Jamie. "I'll do my best to keep the public interactions to a minimum. And I'll try to blend in a bit more."

"Thank you," Jamie said. She and Stan turned to go; Mark didn't follow them.

"I'll be down there in a minute," Mark said. "I just want to take one more look around."

Alone now, he dropped his bag on the bench and took a full turn about the room, just as Claire had done when she first started visiting. He stopped in the center of the space and breathed in deeply. He opened his eyes, looking right at us, at all of us, frozen into stillness by shock and habit on the walls in front of him.

"What the hell happened here tonight, guys?" he asked. We all kept our mouths shut. He picked his bag back up and headed out of the room. Minutes passed and the automatic lights finally shut off, but the sun was peeking its way into the sky. The room was awash in the blue light of almost dawn.

39

JEAN

I would call what happened the following day mediated chaos. Night had crashed into morning, leaving little time for reflection before we heard the front doors unlock, swinging open into the summer air. The associates who usually floated through the gallery on their way to answer a patron's questions were replaced with two austere guards, who stood on either side of the doorway into our room. The first few patrons appeared, giddy and trepidatious to enter. Looking at the guards for permission and receiving nothing more than a grunt of acknowledgment, they scurried into the room and right up to the pedestal.

One man extracted a small pole from his coat pocket, extending it to a length of a few feet. He clipped his cellphone to one end and held on to it like it was an extension of his arm. He leaned forward and pressed something on the phone's screen. Instantaneously, his face brightened from concentrated to animated.

"Hi!" The sound of his voice burst like a balloon across the silent gallery. "As promised, I'm coming to you live from gallery nineteen, right in front of the plinth we know held the lost journal until mere hours ago." *The lost journal,* I thought—it already had an epithet. "Apart from a few other curious folks"—he seesawed his body left and right, presumably showing the other patrons who had cautiously backed away from the gaze of his front-facing camera—"I'm pretty sure I'm the first one in here this morning. Wow, what a momentous occasion." He closed his eyes and took a performative breath of air. One of the guards, watching with disbelief, muttered into the headpiece that connected to a radio strapped to his belt.

"So, what do we know? Well, I can't say I've learned much more than what I had for you all late last night—sometime around ten P.M. on Thursday, July 30, the lost journal was taken by two thieves who escaped into the night. The identity of the thieves is unknown, and the FBI has no leads as to their location. I'll be around all day, bringing you the news as soon as I know it. That's my solemn vow. In the meantime, I want you all to pop off in the comments! Tell me who you think did it. Drop *all* your theories in the chat, I don't care how wild they are! I—" He was cut off mid-breath by Jamie, looming right before him.

"I apologize for the interruption." Jamie's voice was layered with sweetness, a stark contrast to the intimidating nature of her presence. "You cannot do that here."

"Okey dokey," the broadcaster said into the camera, breaking eye contact with Jamie. "I'm getting the"—he drew a line across his neck as if he was slicing his own head off—"from the museum staff, so I guess you'll have to carry on without me for a bit! Talk to you all later and remember, I am nothing without you and your solitary sleuth ways!" As soon as the camera was off, so was he. "Seriously, dude?" he said. "You can't just let art be art?"

I saw the words *You think what you're doing is art?* flicker across Jamie's face before she decided not to engage further. "We have a strict no-livestreaming policy," she said.

"I know that's not true; I checked the website before I came and it didn't say anything about recording in the museum."

"Well, we reserve the right to make such decisions contingent on the circumstances, as I'm sure you understand," Jamie said with finality, her patience tested by this encounter. The sense of decorum she'd impressed upon Mark last night was slipping away.

"Mm-hmm," the broadcaster hummed. He looked around aimlessly. "Well, what do I do now?"

"Well," Jamie parroted, "you could patronize the museum." The broadcaster slunk away to a different corner of the room and reluctantly looked up at a painting, clearly not intending to engage with it at all. Jamie left, but not before stopping by the guards stationed at the opposite doorway and muttering something to them.

The next hour passed without incident, until another ambitious patron attempted to climb across the guardrail that encased the empty plinth. Of course the alarm began to blare, startling everyone in the room, including the unfortunate guest who was now on the other side of the bar. Security descended instantaneously, and the patron was whisked away. We could hear them crying over the sound of the alarm, "I wasn't trying to take anything, I swear. I was *looking* for it!"

Mark reappeared around lunchtime, having traded in his FBI outerwear for a more innocuous suit. He looked fancier than your average modern museumgoer, but not an obvious figure of authority. To be quite honest, he looked a bit like me—his style was anachronistic for the times.

He entered alone and said nothing. The amateur sleuth from earlier haunted the galleries all day, wandering out of sight only for a few moments before he reappeared, afraid he'd missed something. When the patron set off the alarm, I would have sworn the sleuth was filming it on his cellphone.

Mark's lurking was different, more confident. He leaned against one of the benches, silently observing. He checked neither his phone nor his watch.

"Oh my god!" Jamie exclaimed as she hustled into the gallery, out of breath. "There you are. Someone just thought to tell me that you were back."

Mark examined Jamie. "Have you gone home?"

Jamie hesitated before shaking her head. "No, I haven't had the chance yet."

"Go take a shower and a beat, Jamie. You don't need to be the one to guard the museum." Jamie's eyes stated a silent *If you want something done right, you have to do it yourself.*

Instead, she lowered her voice and crouched down closer to Mark. "Any updates?"

Mark spoke at a normal volume. "The investigation is proceeding as planned. Nothing further to share at this time."

"Okay," Jamie said, unconvinced. "Well, you'll let me know if that changes, of course."

Mark nodded. "Of course," he reassured her. Jamie was clearly wary of the agent's choice to spend the afternoon lingering in the gallery; no doubt she imagined his job would involve actively chasing down leads. Mark was apparently content to wait it out.

Mark worked tirelessly to settle every curiosity, sniffing in corners, pouring water on the ground to test the slipperiness, bouncing in and out of the alarm zones. He was testing their accuracy, experimenting with the camera angles, searching for what the cameras could not see.

I liked watching him work. He was much more physical than I'd expected someone in his position would be. He preferred to be up on his feet, to try things himself. I would have guessed that an investigative job involved more paperwork, more bureaucracy, and maybe it did, but this was Mark in his element. He frequently referred back to a technological tablet he carried with him; it was similar to the cellphones all the patrons carried but significantly larger, more like the size of a periodical.

I could tell he was trying to piece something together. He was wandering into the various corners of the room and looking back at the screen. I thought he might be somehow watching himself through the security cameras, testing how possible it would have been for Claire to hide as she claimed she did.

Mark had a second setting: quiet contemplation. When the patrons began to overwhelm the space, he would sit silently on one of the two benches, moving very little as the crowd of the gallery ebbed and flowed around him. Even when someone got too close to the stand that hitherto held the journal, and a guard would have to walk them backward, Mark was unperturbed, remaining seated, a silent sentry at his assigned post.

When Jamie returned around the end of the day, the gears in Mark's brain were spinning in full force. Jamie delivered a paper cup, presumably full of coffee, and Mark gratefully accepted. Jamie could tell Mark was in a good mood.

"Do you think you've learned something?" Jamie asked; she couldn't help herself.

"Maybe, maybe," Mark equivocated, unwilling to expose what might be an incorrect theory. "I don't have enough data to know yet, but I'm getting there. The strings are starting to unravel."

Jamie's skepticism was easy to read on her face. "Anything you need from me?"

"Yes, yes, actually. I need to speak with the staff members who were here last night—are they on tonight and could that be arranged?"

Jamie nodded. "Claire and Linda are on each night that we're open, Wednesday to Sunday, barring illness of course. And I'll have to check on the security staff, but I don't think it will be a problem. Do you want me to call them in now? I can see if they're available."

"Not necessary, I don't want to worry them," Mark said, though I guessed there was an ulterior motive to this choice, his not wanting to give anyone time to prepare. "If you could just let me know when they arrive, I'll be around."

"Should I send them up here?" Jamie asked.

"No, I'll come and find them when I'm ready. I have a few things to look up first."

"Okay," Jamie said. She appeared to weigh whether or not to say what was on her mind before asking, "Do you think one of them is involved?" She looked positively ill at the thought of it. I knew how she felt.

"It's hard to say. Of course, once I have any more certainty, I'll let you know."

"Right, because we wouldn't want someone to continue to work here if they might be . . ." Jamie didn't know how to finish her sentence.

"We'll get there," Mark said. Jamie reluctantly went on her way. The sun slid down and Mark was still there, having now experienced the day in its full cycle. A bell chimed to alert patrons that the museum would be closing in ten minutes, and the last crowds of the day dispersed. A guard escorted out those who lingered past their welcome.

"You can come back tomorrow," the guard said jovially. "We'll still be here." The stragglers rolled their eyes at his kindness, impatient that they were being asked to follow the rules. The guard tipped his hat at Mark on his way out.

Mark stretched out on the bench, allowing himself an unusual moment of repose. His back lay flat against the bench's expanse. Even from many meters away, I could see the tension in his posture keeping him from being able to truly relax. I wondered if there were rules around how much he worked or if he was in charge of his own destiny. He seemed like the kind of person who wouldn't allow himself to rest until it was done.

But would it ever be done? I'd been in this world long enough to know that the most famous thefts were those that were never solved. Art was tangible, movable, and therefore takable. For as long as there had been art, I imagined there must have been theft, some explicit, alarm-bell-ringing theft, and some more discreet—a changing of regimes, the so-called spoils of war, a theft nonetheless. I'd imagine more art crimes went unsolved than solved.

Mark's cellphone rang, and he fished it out of the pocket of his pants.

"Jamie, hi," he said. I could hear the muffled sound of Jamie's voice, but it was too quiet to make out any of her words. "Oh, no, that's not necessary. They can get started as usual. In fact, I have something to show you first. Meet me in the security office?" Another pause before Mark said, "Great, see you there in five." He hung up and rushed out of the room.

I had no expectations for what this night would bring. Would Claire be allowed to return? Would she even want to see me again? Would she get to if she did? Would Mark intercept her on her way upstairs?

40

CLAIRE

I pulled down the sun visor in my car and slid the door open to reveal the tiny mirror. Jesus, I looked as awful as I felt, my eyes blood-red and the shadows beneath them reaching new depths.

I gave my cheeks a pinch, an attempt to bring some color back to them, and slammed the mirror shut. There was no use trying. I had been up all night; I knew it wasn't going to get any better than this.

By the time I'd arrived at home after Mark and Leon had let us go, the sun was already creeping its way up in the sky, and I had to battle the early-shift workers for a parking spot in my neighborhood. I'd found one eventually and let myself into our apartment. Gracie was up, at the stove, making coffee. She'd kissed my cheek and sent me to the bedroom, not asking why I was home so much later than usual. She knew I'd tell her in time. And I would, but first I had to figure out what I'd gotten myself stuck in the middle of, and how I was going to get out of there.

I let myself into the bedroom as quietly as I could, but when I saw Luna snuggled up in her bed, safe and sound, I couldn't help but wrap her in my arms. I lay next to her and she stirred momentarily before falling back asleep. There was a time last night when I thought we weren't going to get this moment. I'd felt like the sirens were coming just for me.

Gracie came to get Luna not long after, and they began the chaotic yet-another-day-at-home dance, leaving me alone to get some rest. As soon as they snuck out of the bedroom, thinking I was asleep, I shot up in bed, pulling the journal from underneath my sweatshirt. The leather cover was still slightly damp from its fall into the puddle and somewhat warm from my body heat, but the pages inside were remarkably undisturbed. I began to read.

I read from the first page to the very last, hours slipping by as I lost myself in the author's world. I had to use my phone to look up the occasional French word, but I knew I understood the story it was telling me. I knew her like I knew myself. And I knew what I had to do.

Here I was, bleary-eyed, walking right back into the most dangerous place I could be. As I tucked the journal against my body once more, I repeated what I'd been telling myself all day. Even if they suspected me of being connected to the theft, there was no way they would expect I'd bring the journal back. No one would be looking for it on my way in and I wouldn't be taking it back out. I could do this.

I tried my best to act normal as I checked in through security. Tony wasn't back yet; a guard I didn't recognize was filling in at his post. I waved and showed my ID, dumping my bag on the table for his inspection as I walked through the scanner. He took longer than Tony had, opening every pocket, pulling out my tangle of headphones that had one of Luna's toys wrapped up in it. I smiled apologetically and began to put my belongings back together once he'd waved me on. I headed in, taking one step at a time closer to safety.

I changed into my jumpsuit delicately, making sure the journal stayed in place under the waistband of my leggings. I checked myself in the mirror and registered that I looked pretty normal for a day of work. It was time to get to it. My chest tightened when I thought about seeing Jean. In the distraction of the past few hours, I hadn't had as much time as my anxious brain wanted to relive the consequences of last night. What would Jean think of me today? Would he even want to see me? I knew he'd never approve of the danger I was putting myself in right now, and so I could never tell him what I was up to. He'd try to do it for me, to protect me, and he couldn't. It had to be me.

Regardless of all the complicating factors, I couldn't wait to see him. I needed to get up there and explain myself. I made a beeline for Jean's gallery, but I ran into Linda just outside the doorway to the staff room. I couldn't tell how long she'd been standing there, but I was sure she was wondering whether or not she should go inside. This place that had once felt like it belonged to her was now soiled. I got that.

When I was honest with myself, I felt guilty. Linda had been in real danger last night. I'm sure she thought she could have been killed. I had been as safe as could be from the thieves; they couldn't hurt me while I was in Jean's world. I was impressed Linda had shown up again.

"Hey," I said. "How are you? Were you able to get any sleep?"

She ignored my question. "Where's your cart?" she asked me. She was right. In my haste, I'd totally forgotten my supplies.

"Oh god," I said. "My brain is so all over the place today. I knew I was forgetting something." I could tell she didn't want to chat, so I grabbed what I needed and got out of her way.

When I got to Jean's gallery, I ran straight for him, not

bothering with any pretense that I would be cleaning tonight. I saw Marguerite squeeze his shoulder before leading Pierre off with her. They must have stuck around to make sure I was coming but were now fading away to give us some privacy. I was glad to know they'd be there for Jean when he needed them.

For a moment, we just held each other, neither of us wanting to break the silence. But I knew the responsibility of this moment belonged to me.

"Claire," Jean said at the same time I brought myself to say, "Jean." We laughed a half-hearted laugh before both trying to start again.

"I have to tell you something—" he began.

"No," I interrupted. "No, I've put this off for far too long. And I really, really want to tell you. I was going to tell you last night but I thought we'd have more time." I took a deep breath before launching into it. The clock was ticking and this conversation was an emergency.

"I got pregnant with Luna at sixteen. My mom threw me out when I told her I was going to have a baby. Jeremy had been trying to get me to move to the city, and I had no choice but to go with him. He said we could start a family together, that this would be the first chapter of the rest of our lives. He never meant it. But Luna is the best thing that's ever happened to me. She is smart and lively and curious and, god, I wish you could meet her. She would love it in here, you'd never be able to get rid of her." Jean smiled at that and I could see him picturing a mini me bouncing around the overgrown garden.

"I swear, her father is out of the picture. I never lied about that. Well, he's mostly gone. He reared his stupid head again during lockdown, and I didn't think I could turn him away because he still is Luna's dad, whether I want him there or not. But I haven't had feelings for him in a long, long time." Jean said nothing, just held my hand in his while the words continued to rush out of me.

"At first, I didn't tell you about her because everything about this world felt so different. The parts of my life that were so undeniably real just didn't seem to fit in here. I didn't know that this would last so long or that I'd fall so hard. And then, at some point, it became much more difficult to think about telling you the truth. I got to be a different version of myself when I was in here, someone who didn't have to spend every waking hour worrying about making the right doctor's appointments and managing screen time and stepping on toys everywhere I turned. It was selfish of me, I know that."

"It's okay," Jean promised me. "It's all okay. I love you whether you have a daughter or no kids or a family of five. I bet you're an amazing mother. I wish I could see it for myself." I kissed him then because it was the only thing I wanted to do. I was so relieved, I could have kissed him forever, forgetting about everything else I had to do tonight until we heard footsteps arriving just outside our gallery, and Jean pushed me away.

"Claire, you have to get out now," Jean said. "That's what I had to tell you; Mark is coming to talk to you again." I didn't want to leave Jean, not in this moment, but I heard the urgency in his tone and understood it. He got it now; this never was just about him and me. I jumped down as fast as I could, but I didn't make it out before Jamie came around the corner, watching me as I crossed through that watery border and landed with both feet on the floor.

41

JEAN

In a split second, everything changed. Moments after Jamie's entrance, Mark followed, right on her heels but too late to see where Claire had been. I expected Jamie to react, to scream or ring some kind of alarm, walking Claire away from the paintings as quickly as she could. But she said nothing.

"Ah, Claire," Mark said. "If you don't mind, I have a few more questions for you, a few things I'm trying to figure out from the video footage of last night's events. Please, feel free to have a seat." Mark gestured to the bench in the center of the room and Claire sat as instructed. She swallowed hard, nervously running her hand along the waistband of her jumpsuit.

"So," Mark continued, "you said last night that you hid when you heard voices you didn't recognize in the museum. How long were you hiding before the thieves set off the alarm?"

"I don't know," Claire said, "a few minutes? At least. It could have been longer."

"Right, right," Mark said as he paced in front of her. "But you see, I can't find you anywhere on the security footage for a while before the two suspects made it up here. Like, many, many minutes. You're not on any of the footage in this room or any of the other rooms in this wing for nearly an hour. And if you'd hidden behind the journal stand, as you said you had, shouldn't it be you and not the thieves who set off the alarm? It's very odd; it's like you'd vanished into thin air."

I could see on Claire's face that she was wary anything she might say right now could incriminate her, so she said nothing.

"And," Mark went on, "something weird happened with the cameras when you reappeared. Everything got a bit fuzzy for a moment and all of a sudden, you were there, right behind the journal stand. Of course, we can tell you weren't one of the two thieves as we have footage of them both running through the museum at the same time, heading for the exit. But it's very peculiar. I've never seen anything like it. Do you have any explanation for it?"

"Maybe there's something wrong with the footage," Claire posited. "Maybe it's damaged." There was nothing more to say, we could both see it in Jamie's face. She had figured out exactly where Claire had been, and Jamie knew Claire couldn't and wouldn't explain any further. Mark might chalk it all up to a suspicious blip in the footage, but Jamie would always know better.

"Maybe it is," Jamie said. "But, and I'm sorry to say it, Claire, we're going to need to ask you to clean out your locker."

"Am I under arrest?" Claire asked.

"No," Jamie and Mark answered in unison.

"No," Mark clarified.

"Unfortunately, you are a person of interest at this time, having been so close to the crime yourself," Jamie said. "While no official judgment is being issued right now, we cannot have you here, unattended, for security reasons." Jamie and Claire shared a look, one that conveyed that based on what Jamie had seen tonight, Claire would not be asked back to the museum. She clearly had her reasons for not wanting to say anything in front of Mark, but this decision would not be reversed.

I'm sure, when it all came down to it, the museum couldn't employ staff who felt such ownership of the art, which seemed somewhat wrong to me. *Isn't that exactly the point*, I thought, *of art in the first place?* An artist puts what they choose on a canvas or a piece of paper or a wall or whatever they're working with, and at some point, they finish and they let go and they give it up to the viewer. They've done their work to make what speaks to them, but all sense of interpretation and meaning is out of their hands. That belongs to someone else, to each person who comes in contact with the art and invests in it a piece of themselves. They get to own what the artwork means to them, and therefore, a part of what it means as a whole.

Take me, for instance. Sure, I'm myself, with my thoughts and my desires, but I have a negligible amount of agency compared to the hundreds of people a day who come and view me. I am what they think of me. And even more so, I have been changed, formed, and codified, for now at least, by what Claire has perceived of me for the past months. Soon, I'll fade into something new, brought on by a new wave of thought or some yet-to-be-elucidated piece of "research" about my family. As permanent as I am, forever etched onto this canvas, the meaning of my existence constantly feels transient.

"You'll need to stick around town, of course," Mark added. "I'll be in touch. Don't go anywhere else just yet, okay?"

Claire's smile was tinged with sadness. "Where would I go? My life is right here, in this city."

Then Jamie shocked us both by looking right into my eyes, as if she was seeing the entire situation for what it really was. She looked down at her phone, which had not rung, and turned to Mark. "It seems that Tony is trying to reach us, that he is feeling well enough to talk to us about last night. Claire, Mark and I need to step into my office for a moment. I trust we can meet you in the locker room to turn in your uniform, once you've had time to change?"

Jamie knew, she knew everything, and she was giving us a chance to say goodbye. It was a risk on Jamie's part—what if Claire tried to stay here forever? But, of course, Jamie knew Claire was a mother and would likely not choose that course.

"Of course," Claire confirmed, and Jamie steered a somewhat confused Mark from the room. Claire took one last look around before reaching up to grab my hand for the final time. My fingers reached for hers, and I helped her in as I always did.

"I think this is it," I said, holding her close to me. We didn't have enough time now for anything but the truth.

"For the first time," Claire said as she pressed her face against my chest, "I'm wondering if I should just stay. Say screw it and make this my life, here with you."

I pulled away from her just enough to look at her face. "You know you can't do that," I said. "As much as it breaks my heart to say it, you have to go. You have people out there who need you." I was parroting the words she'd told me so many months earlier, finally understanding the true scope of them. Claire wasn't mine to keep; she never had been.

"I really loved you," Claire said. "This was never just about the fairy tale for me. I see you, the person you actually are, despite all the things that should keep us apart. I know we keep calling it magic, but this was real. This part was always real to me, Jean."

"I know," I told her. "I loved you too. I will think about you forever." We shared a deep, sad kiss, one I knew would live in my memory for decades, maybe centuries.

"Will you come back and visit?" I asked. "As a museum

guest? When time has passed and all of this is behind us, when they've caught the thieves and the journal is back where it's meant to be? Will you come and see me?"

"I don't know," she admitted. "It sounds too hard right now, to see you but know I can't be with you. But I'll try. If time can heal . . . I'll try." And I knew that was all I could ask for. I kissed her again, one last time.

"Goodbye, Jean," she said. "Thank you for showing me how wonderful life is here."

"Goodbye, Claire." I held her hand as she lowered herself down and, with one last look at me, climbed back into her world.

42

CLAIRE

t took every ounce of control I had to keep walking out of gallery 19, but I knew if I didn't go now, I'd never be able to bring myself to leave. And I was running out of time. I had one more stop to make before the metaphorical hourglass Jamie had turned over for me ran out of sand.

As I ran, I realized Jamie must have let me go without sounding the alarm or reporting me for a reason. I had two guesses as to what that reason might be. The first was that she'd read the journal all the way through, as I had, and knew what its creator had been capable of. The second was that she recognized what I could do, because she could do it too.

I scampered down the stairs, looking around corners before I took them. I had never made my way over here through the gallery hallways, I'd only moved from painting to painting, and it was with a few wrong turns that I made my way to the painting I was looking for. Finally, I found her.

Odette was seated as usual, draping her elbow over the

back of the chair. She was reading from a small book in her lap, slowly turning the pages with a single hand. I cleared my throat and she looked up at me, cocking her head ever so slightly to the side.

"Would it be okay if I came in for a moment?" I asked. She nodded and extended her hand down to me, as Jean had done each night. I took it, her fingers so much thinner than his, but they were long and her grip was strong.

Moments later, I was on my feet next to her, looking around the blue-green studio she sat in each day. Odette waited as I took in my surroundings, a curious expression on her face.

"Hi," I said. "How's it going?"

"It's certainly been eventful, these past twenty-four hours. How are you?" she asked.

"Oh, you know," I answered with a nonanswer. "I've been better. I actually—" I didn't know how to explain what had just happened. Had I been fired? It didn't feel like it. "This is actually my last night here."

The look she gave me conveyed sympathy and curiosity all rolled into one. "I'm sorry to hear that," she said, but she didn't ask about what happened. I appreciated that. I didn't have the time to tell her. "What brings you here, Claire?"

"Have you known all along," I asked, "that it was yours?"

"Not until I saw it," she admitted, instantly knowing I was talking about the journal. "From the way they described it, it could have been anyone. There were so many of us women at the turn of the century who had a passion or a talent for art but who faded into the recesses of history because we didn't have a rich husband or a supportive father who would help us pave the way. But as soon as they dropped it off, I recognized it. It was the last diary I kept before I went from that world to this one. I was in the middle of it when Modigliani painted my portrait here. I honestly don't know how it ends." She chuckled with disbelief at the situation. "I guess I, like everyone else, will never know."

"But you can do what I can do," I pressed. She looked at me curiously, trying to suss out how much I knew. Finally, she gave in.

"I can, yes. Or I could. It unfortunately didn't translate over to this version of me. I can't walk out of the paintings the way I could walk into them."

"Are there others like us?"

"You're the only other person I've seen do it. At some point in the last century, I'd convinced myself it was all just a dream. But when you showed up here, I realized it had been real. I remembered what that first time felt like, how magical and scary it was. There must be others, other people who are watching closely enough, others who dream big enough to have the guts to try."

"Sometimes," I said, "I've wondered if maybe everyone can. They just haven't thought of it."

"It's possible. Can you imagine the trouble that would cause for a museum? A mass movement of people leaping into the paintings?"

"It would be chaos! Surely not everyone would have good intentions. There would be no way to keep this world safe. I'm sure that's what everyone else like us has realized too."

"Right," Odette agreed, "that to share the secret is not worth the risk."

Speaking of risks, I turned my back to Odette and released a few buttons of my jumpsuit, wiggling the journal free from where it was tucked within my uniform. "I thought you should get to see how it ends," I explained as I held it out to her.

She took it in complete silence, pulling it closer to her and running a hand over its leather exterior.

"How did you . . ." Her question drifted off into nothing. It didn't matter. What mattered was that for the first time in more than a century, the journal and its author had been reunited. "Thank you, Claire. Jean was so lucky to know you. We all were."

"I was jealous of you," I admitted. "And intimidated. You and Jean were together once, right? You two have so much in common. You speak the same languages. You come from the same world."

Odette waved my words away like she was clearing the air of smoke. "That was another lifetime. Sure, we came from the same world, but that world doesn't even exist anymore. When we found each other here, it was different than it is for you two. We were companions, kindred, lonely spirits looking for a connection before we drifted our separate ways. It wasn't like what you had, the fire that pulled you towards each other. Jean loved me, but he was never in love with me in that madly, deeply all-consuming way he loves you."

I could feel that she was telling the truth. There were all kinds of love, the love I felt for Gracie, for Luna, for art and the way it invited me to dream. I'd never find a love like this one again, but that didn't mean there wouldn't be more love out there for me. I wished the same for Jean too.

"Take care of him for me, will you?" I said as I sat on the frame, swinging my legs to dangle over its edge.

"I will," Odette promised as she clutched the journal to her. "Be well, Claire."

I had just changed back into my street clothes as Jamie and Mark knocked on the door, checking to see if I was ready. I folded my jumpsuit and handed it back to Jamie, knowing it was unlikely the museum would need that size again. I considered asking if I could keep it, but worried she'd get suspicious about my intentions.

Soon enough, I was back through security and safely out in the parking lot. I turned to look up at the building one more time. It had once been so intimidating to me but had so quickly come to feel like it was mine. I wondered how long it would take to get over that love too.

43

JEAN

I could have followed Claire through the museum, trailing along behind her as she made her way to the exit. Instead, I stayed where I was. I thought I needed time to lick my wounds. I expected my heart to crack open wider than it had before. But I felt numb. The door had closed. There was no longer a question of whether I would ever see Claire again. I wouldn't.

I felt a part of me get locked up, the key taken out of the lock and slipped down into an unknown cavity. I would no longer need to edit those memories, that chapter of my life. It was written. I could look at it whenever I wanted, but there were no more changes to be made.

I stood up and my legs did not collapse under me. I chose to wander, heading in the opposite direction of where I thought my cohort would have gathered. I meandered through landscapes until I found the shore, walking down the boardwalk. I sat in the sand, facing the water, my back to the drama of the months past. I looked out at the ocean, the pier to my left jutting out into the water, its colorful flags flapping in the breeze. The wind was so strong, it might have been too cold to be out here were it not for the brilliant sun beating down. I folded my jacket and my vest and laid them gently next to me, cuffing my sleeves so I could lean back against my forearms and feel the sand dig into my skin.

Life out there was ever-changing. Dangers lurked every day, in emerging diseases, in being in the wrong place at the wrong time, in what could not be controlled. There were so many unknowns.

In here, life was permanent. We knew what to expect. Outside the varieties of our own character, everything stayed the same. And while there were thousands of paintings to explore and people to see, it was finite. At some point, we may have done it all, have tapped out.

I stood up and walked back to the boardwalk, looping around to stroll down the pier. I had never actually been here before and was impressed by how much there was to explore. Peering in through the windows of a bright blue building, I could see arcade games, prizes, cotton candy machines, the trappings of a summer on the New Jersey shore in the 1940s. I wondered at myself that I even knew what those trappings ought to be, having never visited such a place in my former lifetime. I knew so much about such an arbitrary assortment of things, the places and circumstances I had access to within this museum alone.

I made my way to the end of the pier and stepped up onto the bottom rung of the wrought iron railing. I leaned my stomach against the top of the barrier and stared out into the rolling ocean in front of me. The Atlantic, I was pretty sure. I thought of my home, more than three thousand miles across this expanse. My former home.

I turned away from the water, looking back into the museum from quite a distance. It all seemed so small. This, the waves crashing against the shore, seemingly stretching on forever in either direction, this felt like what was real.

I could see the sun beginning its arc across the gallery floor and knew my time to return to my post was approaching. A seagull landed on the railing just a few meters down from me—I had impressed him with my stoicism well enough for him to sit and trust me, reassuming his assigned seat for the day ahead. I tipped an invisible hat to him, and he gave me an ever so gentle wink.

44

JEAN

The next night, Mark swore up and down to Jamie that he would continue his search for the thieves who took the journal, but that he was there to let her know he wouldn't be in the museum as often, returning maybe the week following. "This is how it normally goes," he said to Jamie. They were back in our gallery; in an unexpected turn of events, it was Jamie now in the janitorial uniform. "Cases don't get neatly closed right before another conveniently opens. I wish it was like that, then maybe I could schedule a vacation or something too." Mark laughed. "I'm sorry, it's a little distracting to talk to you while you're doing that."

Jamie dunked the mop back into the soapy bucket. "We haven't yet found a replacement for Claire. I'm just pinch-hitting right now."

"It'll be hard," Mark said, "I'm sure, to rebuild that trust."

"Yeah," Jamie admitted, "maybe a bit of this is also a desire for pure control."

"Whatever works for you," Mark replied. "As they say all too frequently nowadays, these are certainly unprecedented times."

"So, what happens now?" Jamie asked.

"We go back to the bureau office and we run down any leads we have. We looked into Claire and didn't turn up much, besides some suspicious activity around her ex, but nothing concrete. We'll keep our eye on her but I have a gut feeling she wasn't involved. Something about it just doesn't seem right to me; she seemed to love it here too much. But what do I know. There is that often referenced stat that eighty percent of these heists are possible because they've got someone on the inside."

"Claire doesn't seem like the one to me either," Jamie agreed.

"While we're chasing down other leads, it's possible you might hear from the thieves yourself, that they might contact the museum to demand ransom. I can't figure out why the journal was all they took if they were already inside the museum, but maybe they'd hoped the museum would go to great lengths to get it back. It's also possible these thieves are like a lot of other art criminals—that they're what we call 'one and done,' and we'll never hear from them again. But we'll try our best to chase down every angle."

"Well, despite the circumstances, it's been a pleasure to work with you." Jamie offered her hand and peeled down her face covering, just for a moment. Mark did the same.

"Likewise. I'll be in touch." After a brief shake, Mark recovered his face and headed out of the room. Jamie looked around for company, confirmed there was none, and slipped her mask into her pocket. Then, it was back to work.

My sister and brother determined the drama was over for the time being, and that Jamie was not watching them. They stood up to go about their nightly activities. Across the gallery, I watched all my peers do the same. Soon, it was just me and Jamie.

As I watched her clean, I was reminded of Claire in her earliest days of employment—not a shred of sense about what she was doing but a lot of enthusiasm. I could tell how much she cared for this place; her efforts were attentive, though a bit chaotic.

Seeing Jamie in this uniform, I was reminded of the collector. Decades ago, when he was still alive, he too would camouflage in a borrowed uniform to slip between the crowds unnoticed. He said he loved to hear what unfiltered things people would dare to say if they didn't know who exactly could hear them. But I think he also did it because he loved to care for the museum, to wipe away the grime of the visitors, to keep us safe.

45

JEAN

Despite my feeling that it was impossible, time continued to move on. The museum filled and emptied of visitors each day. The summer heat faded to a more comfortable fall chill. Over the usual din of the gallery occupied with patrons, Susie's distinct bellow graced our ears from the hallway.

"Now, for all my book lovers out there, I want you to keep your eyes peeled—you might notice a recurring theme in this artist's work. There are at least five pieces currently on display in this here museum that feature some little introvert with their nose in a book."

She strutted into the gallery, a vision in color. Her predictably bizarre outfits were no match for today's ensemble. A bright yellow tunic was layered over a pair of stockings that were clearly meant to be reproductions of someone's art, Picasso's perhaps, but stretched as they were across human legs, were unrecognizable.

"Here is our first nerd of the day," she said, pointing directly at me. I could hear Marguerite and Pierre chortling with silent laughter as they struggled to keep their composure. "I'm only joshing with you all, calling him a nerd. That reading stuff has never been my cup of tea, but I know it works for some people. Anyway, he's the only one I'm going to give away. The rest you'll have to spot, and a postcard from the gift shop on me for anyone who can find them all."

The group she had this afternoon all shared something in their appearance, a family tour of some kind. They were excited to be there, laughing loudly at Susie's jokes, tittering among themselves in between her comments. A few sullen teenagers dotted the edges of the group, staring at their phones, twirling their hair, only glancing up every so often to glare at Susie, as if they were insulted by her presence.

Susie gave a version of her harebrained explanation of my family before tearing off into the gallery to my left. About two hours later, she returned with the same group. They were not as shiny as they had been when they started. Susie's voice had started to grate on them; only one of them still seemed happy to be there, a young woman, seemingly in her twenties or thirties. She excitedly twisted the diamond ring she wore on the ring finger of her left hand. With her right hand, she clutched the hand of the man I deduced was her fiancé. He looked like the kind of good-natured chap who "didn't really get museums" but had said yes to this excursion because of what it meant to her. The magic of that sacrifice had worn off, and he was now looking at the exit like he hadn't had a breath of fresh air in days.

"Sorry," the young woman said, "I know our time is up. I just had one more question. I was wondering if you knew anything about the journal? The one that disappeared?"

Susie's expression never faltered. In her perpetually affable tone, she chirped, "Hundreds, thousands of priceless works of art hang on these walls and that's what you want to talk about?" The snark of her words contradicted the smile on her face.

"Oh, I just meant, since we're here now, I guess. I'm obsessed with the case; I've been following it religiously on Twitter. I even joined one of the 'real people' detective Facebook groups. I never say anything, I just like to see the theories. I was just wondering if you had any inside scoop. It's the reason I wanted to come here, why I dragged them all in on family reunion weekend."

"You're planning to report back on the case? Dig something up?" Susie's tone remained light, but I could tell she was annoyed by this line of questioning.

"Not *even*," the woman gushed. "I could never, I'm not brave enough for that. I just wanted to come here, see it for myself. I think it's so cool that they left the empty plinth up."

I looked over in its direction, unsure if that was an unconscious choice or if it had been left intact as part of the crime scene. I guessed the latter and also thought that they'd decided to leave it up once they'd realized it was still a focal point.

"Unfortunately for us both, there's no news. Not a single development in weeks and I'll tell you, there's certainly been a lot less investigative personnel in the museum as of late. I think it's possible that's a sign that the world may never know." The young woman looked dejected. "This is what happens in this world. Most of the art you've seen in the world, the things displayed in the big museums, well, it's all been stolen or looted. The older the art, the higher the chance. It's awe-inspiring, sure enough, to see it and experience it, but the way it's hung on the walls in these institutions obscures its true provenance. I'm not saying you can't enjoy it; I'm just saying don't forget how it all got here."

Susie took a deep breath before she continued. "And a journal, something so small, it could easily be passed from pocket to pocket. We may never know where that thing is. That's the charge of the museum, after all, of all museums: to make the art as accessible to people as possible while still keeping it safe. It's a fine line to walk.

"This is yet another story of a woman in art who will never get the recognition or resources she may have deserved. For centuries, men did their best to keep women on the sidelines of this world. Women weren't even allowed to study the nude in real life until the end of the nineteenth century. Did she face that same discrimination? Did she prevail? She is now as she was before, lost to history."

The young woman's fiancé stood up from the bench, easily sliding his fingers back through hers, a gesture I was sure he took for granted. "Honey, our reservation is in an hour and you promised your parents they could swing by the Airbnb first."

"You're right." She squeezed his hand with gratitude. "Well," she said to Susie, "thanks anyway. You're a great tour guide. And I'm still holding out hope for a break in the case."

"I'm sure you are," Susie said through a stony grin. "I hope you have a wonderful rest of your weekend."

The associates began their pass through the gallery, letting the other visitors know the museum would be closing in fifteen minutes, ignoring Susie in their sweep. When the room was nearly empty, the last associate checked in with Susie, but she waved him off. He helped a patron in a wheelchair find the elevator as he left her with a "good evening."

Susie stood to face me, her left arm wrapped across her torso, her right elbow resting atop it so her fingers could flitter along her pursed lips. She took me in, blowing smoke from an imaginary cigarette, before moving on to Marguerite. Involuntarily, her fingers went to her own neck, tracing along the spot where Marguerite's black ribbon lay. There was something just a bit reminiscent of Claire's early days at the museum in the way she was quietly imitating us, but we didn't invite her in. She turned around and walked out, leaving us alone.

46

JEAN

When I finally found her, Odette was sitting in the grass, her skirts ballooned out around her, the journal nestled open in the tulle. Slowly, she leafed through the pages, soaking in each one. She lifted it to her nose and took a deep inhale, lying back on the gentle hill and clutching it to her chest.

"You know," I said, "there are a lot of people looking for that thing." I myself was shocked to see it again, and in Odette's hands at that. Suddenly, it all made sense.

"Oh, really?" she said, unbothered. "Let them keep looking. Who would have known so many people would care so much about a silly little diary I kept in my twenties?"

I lowered myself next to her, staring out at the horizon. "Did you recognize from the start that it was yours?"

"I paid little attention to all of the hubbub before it was delivered to the museum; it didn't occur to me that I could have risen through the ranks to 'anonymous author.' But as soon as I read that first page . . . I never knew what happened to it, of course. I kept it just before I became this." She gestured to her painted self. "I'd only filled in about half of it in that part of my life. Who knew I would have traveled all this way, had a family, that people would have wanted to pass this part of me down." Her tone was wistful, the magic of the moment was infectious. "It's so strange—it makes you wonder who else might have passed through these rooms, who we never even knew to look out for. They all seem so anonymous out there." She closed the journal and sat up, setting it to one side and turning to look at me. "I know she's gone; I'm so sorry, Jean."

"It's okay, it wasn't meant to be forever. That's not the way of her world." If I was honest with myself, the cracks had started to show even before the final wall went up between us. We had been living the impossible. As Claire's world became clearer to me, I understood how unsustainable our love story was.

Odette gave me a friendly pat on the back, tapping gently between my shoulders before folding her hands in her lap. "What are you going to do now?"

"Whatever I did before? Keep drifting along in this weird way of existence? I don't know what else there is."

Odette was quiet for a moment, but then she said, "I have an idea of something you can do."

"Oh?" I wasn't sure what was coming next, or if I was ready for it. I might have convinced myself I was okay, but I was still grieving the end of this era. "And what's that?"

"I think you should write this all down."

"What?" I laughed through my lack of comprehension. "But I'm not a writer."

"How do you know that? You have no idea what you be-came. You're not a writer *yet*. Come on, I bet there's some paper and a pen somewhere around here that you could borrow. You can write it all down, while it's still fresh, and then you'll give me something to read when I'm done with my walk down memory lane." She patted the journal. "I can add it to my rotation."

"What if I'm no good?" I rubbed the back of my neck. I'd never tried anything like that, I didn't know if I could hack it.

"Jean, I've read every book in this place and most of them are really bad. And even then, I enjoyed reading them. I won't care if it's not very good. I'll love it anyway. And if you hate it, we don't have to tell anyone else. It can be just for us. Like this is just between us, right?" She squeezed the diary to her chest.

"Of course it is. That's yours, it belongs to you."

"You've been a real friend, kid, over the last century."

"You too, Odette." Her confidence in me was contagious; I felt my mind changing. "I'll give it a go, our project, as long as you'll be honest with me if it's complete bollocks. Anything will be more interesting than reading the same pages of that blasted book over and over again." I got to my feet, and she reached one arm up to me. I pulled her up to stand, and she fluffed her skirts back into place.

"Well, I guess this is where we part. You'll come and find me soon?" she asked.

"I will." I turned to go, before something struck me. It had been so natural to see her with it, I hadn't questioned it when I first happened upon her. "Hey, how did you end up with that?"

"Claire gave it to me."

I nearly choked on my own tongue. "She . . . what?"

"In the madness of the alarm, those two thieves got all tangled up. Claire grabbed it when she left with her cart that day. She snuck it out of the museum and back in the next night. She sought me out before she left. It was incredibly brave and I am in her debt."

"How did she know? How on earth did she know it was

yours?" I was shocked. There was something I'd missed all along.

"I guess she's a close reader. She saw a part of herself in me too. She saved it all. Because of her, I get to read to the end of my own story." She looked at me with kindness in her eyes. "We were lucky to know her, weren't we?"

"We really were," I said. I could feel a tear hot in the corner of my eye.

"Will we ever see her again?" Odette mused. "At least I'll be looking now. After all, you never know who's out there."

"Or what's in here," I said. "Certainly no one will ever find that journal now. It's vanished from their world. I wonder how long they'll look for it?"

"Or if they'll ever catch the thieves who attempted to take it with them?" she pondered. "Unlikely, since they never even possessed what everyone thinks they stole."

With that, she tucked it safely in her pocket and left. I realized we were on the very bluff where I'd taken Claire many months ago. I sent a wish out toward the ocean, hoping that wherever she was now, she'd feel it somehow.

FIVE YEARS LATER

"So," Marguerite said. "I read your little project."

I was surprised. It had been about half a decade since I'd first started trying to put my story down on paper. Odette had been, as promised, a gracious first reader. She never mocked me, even when I'm sure I deserved it. About halfway through my first draft, she gently asked if I was interested in her feedback. I practically begged her for her thoughts and, as anyone could have guessed, they made it better.

It took me about a year to get it all down. By then, our peers had started whispering about us; we spent every night together, after all. In an effort to dispel false rumors, I accidentally told them all the truth. We weren't in a relationship; Odette was just helping me with my book.

A mistake on my part, I'll admit. I had no idea how starved everyone around us also was for any new kind of entertainment. I was presented, a few weeks later, with a sheet of names with the order in which they'd signed up to reserve time to read my pages. I thanked them for their enthusiasm, but politely declined sharing what I'd written. No one understood, of course.

But when the writing was done, I felt my mind changing. This story wasn't just mine. It was ours. This place belonged to us, no matter what any documents of ownership may say, and so did the events that had occurred here. I wanted to share it, I was surprised to find after a bit of self-examination. And I thought I'd done a pretty good job of getting it all down. A part of me wanted to see if they agreed.

On it had gone, to have a life of its own in the hands of others. I offered to copy it over, make a second version that could circulate in tandem, but I could never find someone in the chain who was willing to wait to read it once their turn had arrived.

I'd lost track of where it was in the building, allowing it to go on its own way. Which is why I was shocked to know it had made its way to Marguerite. She had exhibited visible disinterest at first, embarrassed by the attention I was drawing to myself and by relation, to her. After giving me the silent treatment for quite some time, she began to thaw as the praise dissipated. Apparently, she'd fully melted.

"I was bored; it was time for a change," she answered my unasked question.

"What did you think?" I asked.

"It was good. I liked it. I came off quite wise, didn't I? A little aloof, but . . ."

"But that's how you like to be."

"Yes, well, I'm glad you wrote it down." We were settling into our usual seats, the sun rising in the sky for yet another day. I opened a fresh notebook in my lap, a pen surreptitiously tucked up my sleeve. I was working on something else as covertly as I could.

"Thank you," I said. Pierre had slipped back into the room and sprang up onto the piano bench next to Marguerite.

"Good morning," he said.

"Good morning," we chorused as we heard the front doors open on the floor below.

Hours passed and I drifted away into the day, my mind chewing on ideas for my current work in progress. I had lost track of the time until a young girl stopped directly in front of me. Her dark hair was plaited, and she looked incredibly familiar. I could hardly believe my own eyes.

"Is this the one, Mom?" she called over her shoulder. As if everything was moving in slow motion, Claire appeared like a dream in the doorway. She looked at me first, her eyes meeting mine in greeting, before taking in the rest of the room.

Little had changed in the gallery since she was last here. Yes, people no longer wore coverings over their faces and walked comfortably within six feet of one another again. But I was in exactly the same place where she'd left me, as were the benches she had once dusted. Even the empty plinth hadn't moved an inch.

Claire had changed. She looked stronger, sturdier on her feet. Her dark hair fell down her back, bangs covering her forehead. They flattered her, as did the little crinkles next to her eyes as she smiled at me. She walked up next to her daughter, who was already the same height as her, though she couldn't have been more than ten years old. Together they stood exactly at my eye level.

"That's him, right?" her daughter asked again. "The guy you told me about?"

"Yes," she said. "That's him."

At the sound of her voice, everything inside me crackled. In putting her down on paper, I'd inadvertently disentangled us, just a bit. Now she was back, wrapping herself up in my story again.

"He's cute," Luna said, drawing out the u sound into multiple syllables. Claire bumped her with her hip, laughing as she did so.

"I know," she said shyly. "He really is. He's too young for me, though." Claire caught the look on her daughter's face and quickly warned, "And way too old for you."

"He looks so real. Like I could just reach right through and touch him." Luna let out a big sigh. "I wish you still worked here," she said. "This place rocks."

"That was a different chapter of my life. You wouldn't like it if I was working nights again; we wouldn't get to watch TV together anymore."

"Yeah, good point. But can we at least come back sometime soon?"

Claire replied, "We definitely can," while looking straight into my eyes. Her daughter had her by the hand now and was pulling her into the next room. Claire repositioned their hands so their fingers wound together and walked out in step with her.

In and out, people continued in pairs, groups, by themselves, as if nothing notable had happened here today, their world so close to ours, running parallel but never touching.

Acknowledgments

I am profoundly grateful to my editor, Hilary Teeman, who guided me to craft a version of this novel that brought Jean and Claire's love story to light. Thank you, Hilary, for your creative and kind feedback; I am so proud of what we have made. Thank you to the entire team at Ballantine Books for helping *The Art of Vanishing* find its way into readers' hands: Kara Welsh, Karen Fink, Angie Campusano, Kathleen Quinlan, Emma Thomasch, Kim Hovey, Debbie Glasserman, Elena Giavaldi, Loren Noveck, Jane Sankner, Annette Szlachta-McGinn, Elsa Richardson-Bach, and Caroline Weishuhn.

Ariele Fredman, I will never forget the way my heart raced when I opened your email and saw the selfie of you and Millie in front of the painting; I knew then we were going to do this thing together. I am so thankful to have had you as an advisor and friend every step of the way. Thank you to my entire UTA team: Addison Duffy, Olivia Fanaro, Meredith Miller,

Laurie-Maude Chenard, and Paloma Ortega. I am so lucky to work with you all.

Thank you to my parents, Gentry and Roger Hoit, and my brother, Jackson Hoit, for encouraging me to walk confidently in the direction of my dreams. Thank you to my grandparents Grancy and Groger, who hosted me for "Camp Wheelgate Farm" every summer and taught art history lessons in their living room. Grancy, I am proud to say I get my creativity from you.

I am so grateful for the friendships that this chapter of my life has brought me. Thank you to Kyle Alderdice, who created a place to share writing and community when I needed it most. Thank you to Becca Freeman, Laura Hankin, Genevieve Wheeler, Alli Hoff Kosik, and Victoria McGinley for the internet company during those long writing stretches. Thank you to Annie Turnbull for being the first reader of the first draft of this story; your notes gave me the tools to keep going. Thank you to Mary Pauline Lowry for reading my query letter and consistently checking in on me. Thank you to every friend, in person and on the internet, every co-worker, and every follower who has cheered me along on this journey. Thank you to every bookseller and librarian who has recommended *The Art of Vanishing* and to every reader who has picked up a copy.

Thank you to Cleo the cat, who spent so many hours with me and this manuscript that she should probably be credited as a co-author.

Finally, thank you to my husband, Dylan, who is even more excited that you are reading this book than I am. Dylan, thank you for your patience as I crafted this world and for your commitment to making nearly every conversation with anyone—friend, family, or stranger—an excuse to brag about my work. I am so lucky to be loved by you and I can't wait to write the next book so you can read that one too.

ABOUT THE AUTHOR

Morgan Pager is the director of marketing and social media at Atria Books and the content creator behind @nycbookgirl. A graduate of Duke University, Morgan lives on the Upper West Side with her husband and their cat. *The Art of Vanishing* is her first novel.

morganpager.com
Instagram: @nycbookgirl
TikTok: @nycbookgirl

ABOUT THE TYPE

This book was set in Walbaum, a typeface designed in 1810 by German punch cutter J. E. (Justus Erich) Walbaum (1768–1839). Walbaum's type is more French than German in appearance. Like Bodoni, it is a classical typeface, yet its openness and slight irregularities give it a human, romantic quality.